No Snow in December

Also by Maria Lewitt:

COME SPRING
An autobiographical novel
JUST CALL ME BOB (for children)
GRANDMOTHER'S YARN (for children)

Extracts from this book were published in
The Melbourne Chronicle, Outrider and *Overland*

AUSTRALIA COUNCIL Published with the assistance of
The Literature Board of the Australia Council

No Snow in December

an autobiographical novel

by

Maria Lewitt

HEINEMANN
MELBOURNE

First published in 1985 by
WILLIAM HEINEMANN AUSTRALIA
(A division of Heinemann Publishers Australia Pty Ltd)
85 Abinger Street, Richmond, Victoria, 3121.

Typeset in Hong Kong by
Setrite Typesetters
Printed in Australia by
Macarthur Press Limited

National Library of Australia
Cataloguing-in-Publication data:

Lewitt, Maria, 1924-   .
  No snow in December.

ISBN 0 85859 421 8.

I. Title.

A823′.3

To the people of Australia,
including my husband,
my Australian children,
my even more thoroughly Australian
   grandchildren,
and my family in Europe.

My thanks go:

To Julian for his patience, goodness and support.

To Mary Harber for putting my articles and tenses in their rightful places.

To Karin for assisting me with the final draft.

The bulk of 'No Snow in December' was written in the seclusion of Monash University, thanks to Radha Rasmussen and Dr Gil Best who offered and arranged the room for me.

If the clouds be full of rain, they empty themselves upon the earth; and if the tree fall toward the south, or toward the north, in the place where the tree falleth, there it shall be.

ECCLESIASTES 11:3

ONE

Our luggage hung in the air. We heard a whistle blow. The suitcases and the trunk swayed for a while, then came to a stop. They looked like parcels in a string bag, but they were all we possessed.

'The crane must have broken down,' said Julek and his voice was puzzled.

'How would I know? You are the English expert, you tell me.' I was holding Jozio's overheated little hand; my own was also hot and moist.

'I'll go and investigate. Don't you dare to wander around ... Stay where you are.' Julek pushed his way through the crowd.

'I want to go with daddy.' Jozio tried to free his hand from mine.

'You can't. We have to wait till daddy comes back. You heard what he said, so that's that.'

Jozio nodded his head.

We were standing on a long platform between the ship and the huge shed. Our five weeks' journey was over. What had been our home for that time looked quite huge and solid. The waters of Sydney Harbour swished against its belly. The sky was morning blue but the sun was already hot.

'Are we home? I want to go home.' Jozio stomped

from leg to leg. He couldn't see much from the pedestal of his three-year-old frame, only the mass of bodies of all the other migrants waiting for their luggage to be put ashore. There was an urgent eagerness in all the faces. One more obstacle, customs to clear, and then A New Life.

I lifted Jozio up, he was also entitled to see the Australian sky. He cuddled up to me and pointed. 'A bird, look. A bird.'

'Oh yes, I can see', which was a lie because I couldn't and didn't even bother to look properly. 'How d'you feel?'

'Fine, mum ... bird ... look, look.'

'Yes.'

Australia at last. Our luggage still hanging. Customs to go through, but I didn't care. We had already smuggled in our forbidden cargo. I hugged Jozio and smiled.

'Look, chimney', he said.

'Yes.'

We had left Poland in 1947 and stayed for one whole year in Paris, all of 1948. We had arrived in winter, but it wasn't really winter as we had known it in Poland. There was no snow on the Parisian streets and people seldom used overcoats.

I had always wanted to go to Paris; my father, who had studied there, had called it 'the enlightened city'. Julek's brother Simon lived there with his French wife. Paris meant Liberty, Equality, Fraternity. Paris meant the Louvre. Throughout my childhood, I had formed a mental picture of the city and nursed it within me all through the war. The stairs of the Sorbonne were worn down by the hurried steps of an endless procession of students. Pasteur had walked there, Maria Curie-Sklodowska, Emile Zola. Paris and its cafés. Toulouse-Lautrec and Gauguin, Degas

2

and Manet, Vincent van Gogh and Renoir. The city of Diderot and Voltaire. Parisians, the people who had dared to argue that kings rule by the grace of their subjects, not by the grace of God.

When we reached Paris I was beyond myself. The harmony, the grace of the city, was overwhelming. Simon and Genevieve kept on apologising: that Paris wasn't what it used to be in prewar days, as if it was their own responsibility that the boulevards were badly lit or that food was still rationed and scarce.

We dragged Jozio through every known gallery and fell in love with Rodin. We dragged Jozio through the Latin Quarter, just to mingle with the crowd. But to the Sorbonne, I went on my own. The steps were worn down, as my father had described. I climbed them cautiously, as if with piety, thinking of all the people, great and lesser, who had walked the same route before.

And then spring arrived. It came with the fanfare of new foliage and cascades of flowers in public gardens and squares. Jozio, armed with a long stick, was pushing a toy boat in the pond of the Luxembourg Gardens, together with scores of French children. He loved it more than walking through the Louvre. We watched him and his boat sailing and from time to time allowed our excitement to escape in a timid 'Oh, là, Là'. We used to go home tired but happy, through the streets where, at every corner, the women were selling fresh flowers. And if they were not selling, they knitted, clicking their long needles, as their predecessors must have done while watching the heads of the French aristocrats roll during the Revolution. I loved the crowd, the open cafés, the feel of the place.

My friendship and understanding for Simon and Genevieve grew. I considered buying Julek a real French beret; but then Jozio became sick, so I never did. It was something to do with his lungs. He was feverish.

The doctor yelled at me because Jozio was crying when he was examined and X-rayed. The foreign sounds and surroundings must have frightened him. So I whispered to him not to worry. And then one of the doctors yelled that I shouldn't pamper the child. 'It would have been better, Madame, if you had looked after your child properly and prevented the disease.'

Jozio cried even more and my eyes filled with tears. Simon said something sharp to the doctor, but I didn't even try to make an effort to understand what was said.

'Ah *bon*, — oh well', the doctor concluded and announced in his cold, impersonal, medical way that Jozio's glands were greatly enlarged, he must have 'a complete rest', for several months, at least. 'You'd better do it,' he added. Les Australiens don't want migrants with mental, venereal, or lung problems... Neither do we.'

We left the surgery and eventually Jozio quietened down. One good point was that we had already left all the necessary papers with the Australian Embassy when Jozio's lungs were still acceptable.

Simon rented a small place at the Bois-le-Roi, near the impressive palace of Fontainebleau, with an enormous black forest. From the outside, it looked inviting; the huge trees swayed at the top, rustled, the ground soft. We went to the forest once and were driven away by swarms of patriotic mosquitos guarding their dominion from the intrusion of foreigners. After all, the grounds were once graced by the Emperor Napoleon himself.

The house was gloomy and consisted of a room and a kitchen. The door led to the garden, a wide path separated the lawns. At the back there were a number

4

of fruit trees, but we were not allowed to go there. Not that it mattered; we were content to have a bit of grass in front of our door. It was important for Jozio's progress to stay in the country, far from polluted Paris. And we nursed Jozio to health. For months and months he wasn't allowed to walk. How could one tell a two-year-old that he mustn't run, or play, must only be carried to and from bed, pram, and deckchair?

One could.

We hid his shoes and put them on only when we went for his periodical X-ray. On our return home we tried to take the shoes off and then Jozio cried. 'Don't take them away. Mummyyy, Daddyyy.'

But we took them off anyway.

We spent all our time with Jozio, read to him, played all the 'sitting' games, took his temperature three times a day and fed him. He was a little boy, pale and skinny, but always so good. And then gradually his skin lost its pale glow, the temperature stabilised and he was eating better. Then it was even harder to keep him still and one day when we left him outside for a little while, he stepped down from his deckchair, picked up a few pebbles, took a few steps, looked around frightened like a criminal checking in case somebody saw him, and then he climbed back into his chair, and let the pebbles fall to the ground. We watched him through the window and I cried and couldn't stop, and Julek put his arm around me and I was sure he cried too.

Towards the end of that year, the doctor told us how lucky we were, that Jozio had made a remarkable recovery, and he allowed us to go. 'The Australian sunshine will do him a lot of good. *Bon voyage.*' He even shook our hands.

I can't recall the doctor at all. I visited him often enough, spoke to him, looked at him, most likely stared at his surgery wall. I must have done. He must have had a face. The walls must have been covered with his diplomas, perhaps a picture or two. But I remember only that medical, metallic voice of his, nothing else.

It was sad to say goodbye to Simon and Genevieve, but we had to go. The voyage went all right, except for a few days of cyclonic weather when almost everybody went down with seasickness.

The night before we entered Sydney Harbour people talked and made plans. One man declared that one could make a fortune by pulling out the platinum threads from British banknotes. Another announced that the medical authorities were to take new X-rays because too many people entered Australia suffering from T. B. 'I heard it from reliable sources,' he added. Julek looked at me and we left the gathering and went back to our cabin. Jozio was asleep. I was frightened we would be deported, once our 'crime' was discovered. The French doctor had assured us that Jozio was well, though in the same breath had urged us to take good care of our child. Plenty of fresh air, plenty of good food. 'Otherwise the trouble could recur.'

But on the following day the Australian medical clearance went without a hitch. The people in charge didn't take new X-rays. They just examined our outstretched hands, looked through our hair, that was all. What they looked for wasn't clear, perhaps some skin disease or lice; we simply were not told and didn't know. They gave us some papers; Julek filled them in quickly. How lucky for us that he had studied in England and therefore knew English well. While other migrants struggled with the forms, ours were returned and Julek offered his assistance to anyone who needed it. The forms were like so many others; name, destination, occupation, what languages were known. Obviously prospects of work would be

6

greater for those who knew several languages. And then the fellow who was going to make a fortune by pulling out platinum from British banknotes told us that the languages had nothing to do with a job. The Australian authorities couldn't care less how many languages a migrant knew; they just wanted to play safe. In case they wanted to get rid of someone, they would give an unwanted migrant a dictation test in a foreign language; if he was unable to pass it, then according to some old legislation, he would simply be deported. We were speechless. But when we handed our papers in, the officer smiled at us and even mussed Jozio's hair. It took a long time till my heart beat normally again.

So there we were, only a narrow strip separating us from the Australia of Our Future, the Australia of Our Dreams.

Julek returned and Jozio ran to him. My son looked all flushed; I wondered whether the trip hadn't been too much for him.

'Guess what happened to the crane?', Julek was smiling. 'Apparently the workers have time off, a quarter of an hour for a cup of tea, to smoke a cigarette, or whatever ... How about that? It's called "smoko".'

'Are you sure?'

'That's what I was told ... The crane ... It starts moving again. Look!'

'Look', repeated Jozio.

Our luggage was coming down. I grabbed Jozio's hand, while Julek took care of our worldly possessions. The door to the customs hall opened, we walked through and then were advised to wait our turn. People were everywhere. The hall was stuffy and full of noises. I don't know, because wherever I looked everyone seemed quiet, as if lost in thoughts, anticipating what The Future might bring, or perhaps plain frightened of customs. Jozio wanted to go to the toilet, so Julek went with him; but not before he urged me once more not to move, to stay put, because I might get lost. I felt stupid, child-like and sat on our trunk and didn't dare to go anywhere.

I wondered what Australia would be like. We were to settle in Melbourne, where Julek's mother's cousins were supposed to welcome us. To make my life more interesting, they had to be two maiden sisters, ancient, older than my mother. They had landed in Australia just before the outbreak of the war. They had sent us a landing permit, a form of visa, and had written us letters. Not exactly. The letters were addressed to Julek only. They never sent any regards to me or to Jozio. One could have argued that the sisters didn't know me, we had never been officially introduced. 'Dear Julek', they wrote, as if Jozio and I didn't exist.

How I would find them I wasn't sure. They ran a poultry farm, which was a peculiar occupation for well-educated European ladies. We were to live with them. That bit didn't bother me much. Since the war we had shared accommodation with many people and, except for the year in France, had never lived on our own. So one more sharing experience wouldn't make much difference. Though this time, the situation was slightly more complicated. We were to invade the peaceful existence of two old maids. I had my doubts.

I had left my family in Poland. All of us had survived the war together. Our separation was to be temporary; I couldn't imagine life without my mother, sister, aunt, uncle, and my funny, skinny cousin Marek. We would send them papers, as soon as possible. With Simon and Genevieve the situation was different; they were settled in Paris and wouldn't dream of leaving France.

Back in Poland, we had a few friends. There was no one in Australia. I hoped Julek would introduce me to his gracious Australian cousins. I felt very lonely. The only fellow passengers we liked were to settle in Sydney.

'Move over, join the queue,' someone urged me. I dragged our luggage across the floor and though the distance was negligible, I panicked. What if Julek didn't find me? He had told me not to move. Alone, without a husband, without a child, without English ... I held onto Jozio's teddy bear and wondered why I had ever considered migration.

The customs officers were working behind long benches. They were dressed in uniforms. I didn't trust uniforms, not after my war experiences. They talked in English and it reminded me of when I was a little girl and my sister Tania and I tried to imitate English. I think it was after seeing some American movie. We stuffed our mouths with hot potato, rolled it around and tried to speak at the same time; we produced some unrecognisable sounds — that was how English seemed to us. We giggled till we sprayed the table with mashed potato and then we were stopped by our very stern governess, 'or else'.

The customs officers spoke so quickly, I couldn't distinguish one single word. Not surprising, as I hardly knew any.

I spotted Julek and Jozio and waved frantically to them. They reached me just in time for Julek to place our baggage on the inspection bench. He opened the suitcase and the trunk. The officer looked at us, said something, smiled. Julek smiled too, saying a few words and then, he told me it was all over. He slammed our luggage shut. It seemed incredible. They didn't look at the contents, they didn't rummage through our belongings. When we had left Poland, every item had been taken out, touched, shaken. In a sharp, hostile voice, the customs officer hammered at us that a lot of prospective migrants never left Poland, all because of their own stupidity — their luggage proved to contain foreign currency, art objects relevant to the Polish heritage, so obviously they never left Poland but were sent to prison instead. The customs officer appealed to us to disclose what we intended to smuggle out, make it easier for ourselves because he would find it anyway and the consequences would be grave. And when he didn't find anything objectionable I was subjected to a personal inspection. It wasn't pleasant, but because I had nothing to hide, it didn't worry me too much. The only things I smuggled out were my memories, and yet another one was added to an already long list of bitter ones.

The French behaved better; they just conducted a normal search. Simon was with us. And then the customs officer discovered six blocks of chocolate given to Jozio by my mother. His eyebrows arched. 'Six,' he wondered. Simon asked him to help himself to one and take it home for his child. 'You look as if you were a father,' Simon said, at which our customs officer announced that he was indeed. As a matter of fact he was blessed with two offspring. 'They're lovely kids, well behaved. But you know how it is in Paris, Monsieur. Shortage of food, milk. My children have seldom eaten chocolate. A rarity nowadays.' So Simon gave the man two blocks and we all agreed that it was very noble of our customs officer not to have six children.

But entry into Australia all went so quickly.

We were free to go. Julek led the procession, followed by Jozio, then by me. We went through the door and found ourselves in another hall. We were not sure what to do next, neither were the other people. So we clustered all together, talking about our experiences in the customs hall. There were a few

10

strangers moving about. From time to time they would approach our group and single out a family or a person. They were volunteers, a welcoming committee. Whenever someone left, we went through the motion of exchanging addresses, saying goodbye and ardently expressing the hope that we would meet again. 'In the near future.'

'What language do you speak? Where are you from?' a well-dressed man asked Julek.

'We come from Poland.'

'Splendid. I represent the Jewish Welfare Society,' the man said in passable Polish. 'Must have you on my list. What's your name?'

He scanned the list and stopped at our name. 'Here you are. Two adults and one child. Good, I'll take you with me.'

We had been selected, and said farewell to our fellow passengers.

'You're going to Melbourne? Yes, yes . . . I can see. Your tickets have already been arranged. Your luggage will be taken care of. Your train . . . Let me see . . . Yes, the train's not due till late in the evening. You have plenty of time to kill. I will take you around Sydney and then to lunch.'

He was older than us, efficient and brisk.

'I came from Poland too. My whole family did. Before the war, that is.'

Lucky you, I thought.

TWO

It was difficult to part from the people who had been
our companions for the five long weeks, so I kept on
looking back, while our welfare man urged us to
follow him. There was something about the man
which made me think that he considered himself very
important; perhaps he was. Some people greeted him,
and Jozio asked again if we were going home.

The sun was piercing-white; I couldn't see a thing.
Jozio turned his head away from the blasting light.
The man was somewhere in front of us. 'Are you
coming? This way.'

I was boiling in my 'new-look' coat. Simon had
bought it for me on the day of our departure. We had
nearly missed the train because of the coat. The traffic
was heavy, the streets overcrowded, it was only two
weeks before Christmas. Simon said that one could
feel the return to normality, and about time too. The
war had ended two-and-a-half years ago and he was
happy to see the bright window displays. 'Not as
imaginative as in prewar days, but improving nevertheless.' Suddenly he insisted I couldn't leave Paris
without one decent piece of clothing. When we left
Poland, women's clothes were worn rather short.
When we arrived in France, the couturiers of Paris

had just launched the new long look. So I cut my few dresses in half and inserted pieces of matching material, thus making myself less conspicuous. I was happy with what I had, but Simon and especially Genevieve weren't, and insisted that I was to choose something to wear as a farewell gift from them. I kept on postponing the purchase till the last day and in the end Simon bought me a raincoat.

'At long last you look smart, but you made us worry', said Genevieve. 'What took you so long? Trains don't wait. Thank God nothing happened; we didn't know what to think.' She hugged me and hugged me before we boarded the train for Trieste, where we were to meet the ship which was to take us to Australia.

I wore the coat a lot on our journey but it was far too heavy for an Australian summer.

'You look half-cooked,' observed my observant husband, as though I didn't feel it myself.

'What would you suggest?'

'Take the dumb coat off.'

I took it off and it weighed heavily on my arm.

The man was always a few steps ahead of us, turning his head back, urging us to hurry; he threw open the door of a huge car. I followed Jozio into the back seat, Julek found himself next to the man. The engine started, the car jerked, reversed, jerked again and went forward as if driven by a maniac. Streets, houses, shops, people flashed before our eyes. It was a change from the endless horizon and the sea, sometimes calm and blue, sometimes grey and angry. The road turned and wound, the traffic was heavy and people rushed. Gloved women in stockings and hats, men in suits and ties, and all in hats. (They must be hot.) The car stuffy; I pulled the window down, the hot air hit me, but I didn't mind. It was fresh air.

I remembered a picnic, three of my school friends and I just before the war. We went by car, a convertible. The wind and sun, the trees and the whole country-side were all around us. We sang and chatted; we were intoxicated with a new experience. Not many people had cars in prewar Poland; but our friend Eve did. She used to come to school by chauffeur-driven limousine, which caused a sensation among the other girls, who used to walk. She invited us to her place and we went, curious to see how she lived. We didn't want to admit it, of course, even to ourselves. Eve lived in a huge house, while we lived in flats. The butler ushered us into a hall, asked our names, then left us standing there in order to advise 'the young Miss' of our arrival. We were thirteen years old then. The hall was overpowering, with a staircase going up and the ceiling somewhere high, high up. One of us said 'Now we have to wait for the young Miss to descend from her parlour', and we all laughed, an uneasy laughter because servants were everywhere, the furniture was beautiful but strange, and all the walls were covered by pictures which seemed to us to be out of place in a private house. Eve tried to make us feel at ease but, again, the afternoon tea was brought in by servants, the table setting was unfam-iliar, the whole atmosphere was foreign. And afterwards Eve became the topic of our discussions. We branded her a snob and decided to teach her a lesson. I invited her to my place. I begged our one servant, Kazia, to follow my instructions and in the end she agreed, but not before she pronounced me crazy.

When Eve rang the bell at our flat's door, she wasn't let in; Kazia opened the door, asked Eve who she was to announce to her 'young Miss' — and slammed the door in Eve's face. I had Irma and two other friends with me and we giggled and were very proud of ourselves; we had taught Eve a lesson. We waited for a minute or two before we let her in. She had tears in her eyes, but pretended that all was as it should be. She had guts.

So we discussed her again and again and decided to 'give her a chance'; we felt very noble. We all enjoyed what she had offered us — picnics, unheard-of food and cakes — and pretended we didn't. But in the end we became good friends, not because of her wealth but because of her strong character. She stopped using the car for school and whenever we visited her, she was waiting for us outside.

After that last picnic, there were no more. The war started, we were scattered all over Poland and when the war ended I was the only one who had survived. Eve's wealth hadn't helped her.

Why I always have to go back to the war years I can't explain. There I was, being driven through the streets of Sydney, Jozio fast asleep, Julek chatting with our man. We were on the brink of a New Life. I felt warm, not only because of the Australian sun but also because of that uncontrollable mind of mine.

Sydney rushed past the car. The suburban houses, the sea, and suddenly we found ourselves in the city. It was terribly hot. People hurried. The shops tantalised and our man talked.

'Look to the left; the biggest department store in the Southern Hemisphere.'

He took us to some rooms where a group of women served us cups of hot tea and sandwiches. Jozio slept on my shoulder and when he woke up, asked if we were at home. One woman and then another came up to me. They wanted to know what our plans were and how it was in Poland during the war. I didn't know what to reply, so I told them that somehow we had survived. And before I could add anything else, the tall, dry one with the long, manicured nails asked about our financial position.

'We haven't got much', I said.

The one with kinder eyes looked at Jozio with pity. 'You realise, of course, that both of you must go to work in order to reach an acceptable standard of living. The child will be in your way.' I listened to them and wasn't sure what they meant though they spoke in Polish. Both of them were well dressed and I was sorry it was too hot to wear my beautiful Parisian coat. For the first time I felt uncomfortable in my extended dress.

'Would you consider offering your child for adoption? How old are you?'

'Twenty-four.'

'You are young, there is plenty of time to have more children.'

'What are you talking about?' I pressed Jozio's hand and felt his body small and frail, full of trust and love, resting against me. 'No, never,' I thought I must have screamed, but obviously I hadn't because Jozio was quite unconcerned and Julek didn't even look in our direction.

'All right. There is no harm in asking. I still maintain that the child would have a much better chance with a well-established family.' Her eyes were never still. If she wasn't more careful, they would roll out of their sockets. 'I am more mature, I know life better than you,' she addressed me though her eyes were somewhere else. 'Think about it. If you change your mind, let me know. I have a lovely family in mind. Here is my name, address.' She extended her hand to me, but I withheld mine.

'Thank you for looking after us. I never expected so much consideration on arrival.'

'Don't mention it. We were migrants ourselves, so we know how it feels.'

Julek came, holding the train tickets, and it was

time for us to go. I wasn't sorry.

Back in the car, the man never stopped talking. 'I want to show you more of Sydney. The Harbour Bridge, not only the biggest span in the Southern Hemisphere but also in the whole world. Like it?'

'Oh, yes.'

'Oh yes, is that all you have to say?'

'I feel tired. Sorry.'

'You are too young to be tired. When I was your age, I was working like ten men. We went through rough times, the Depression. You heard of the Depression? You are lucky to arrive in Australia when there is plenty of work. You can't imagine how dreadful the situation was during the war. I was in the army myself, but my family really suffered because of all kinds of shortages.' He talked and he talked and I tried not to listen. Poor Jozio was in a state of bewilderment, hardly moving, hardly saying a word. We were driving along the bay. I had never seen any other town as beautiful as this before. The sun covered the water with a glittering, silver veil. I made a mental promise to Jozio; one day we would all go to the beach and build the biggest sandcastle in the Southern Hemisphere.

I was glad when we were eventually driven to the station. We thanked the man and went inside the train. Welfare had secured a sleeping compartment for us. 'Till Albury,' we were informed. 'The border between New South Wales and Victoria. You will have to change trains then, because of the different rail gauges.'

I wasn't absolutely sure what the man meant. We had travelled from Poland to France, crossing the Czechoslovakian, Austrian, German and French borders and had never changed trains. The rail gauges were uniform throughout Europe; what the reason was for having different gauges between the Australian States we were not sure.

THREE

'I'm sick and tired of trains,' complained Jozio. 'Not again.'

'I know, darling. I know. It won't be long now. Go to sleep now and when you wake up, we'll change trains. Then before lunch, we'll be in Melbourne. Say "Melbourne", our new home town.'

'Melbourne, our new . . . You promise?'

'Yes, I promise.'

Before Jozio went to sleep, Julek told him a story about all the things we would do in Melbourne. Like going to the beach, buying toys and a house, drinking as much milk as Jozio would wish, having a dog and, who could tell, maybe even a car. It was the craziest fairytale I had ever heard.

Jozio fell asleep. Julek and I climbed up to the top bunk. It was quite comfortable. After all, we had slept on floors, in cellars, on a single army stretcher. We were very excited and slept only a little. The train rattled, it was dark outside, even the stations we passed through were dark and deserted, quite unlike European stations, where even in the middle of the night the platform is alive with vendors offering hot drinks and food.

Early in the morning, we were awakened by the

train attendant, who brought us cups of strong tea, dry biscuits, and advice to get ready to change trains in half an hour. Julek said something in English and shortly after, the attendant presented Jozio with a tall glass of milk. The tea was too strong for Jozio, even for us. We were used to ersatz tea since the beginning of the war. Tea was still a rarity in Europe.

It was still grey outside, then suddenly the sun rose very quickly, the trees stood against the light as if cut out from black paper. It was beautiful.

The train stopped, we changed trains and found ourselves in a compartment together with four other travellers; for the first time face to face with Australians. And I thought how lucky Jozio and I were to have Julek, who could communicate in this most alien of languages. It was a strange twist of fate that Julek had studied in England. It would help us to settle better and more quickly in Australia. And then I thought that even if he had not known any English, we were still lucky to have him.

We watched the train attendant standing on the platform, holding a green flag in one hand and a whistle in the other. Then, he waved the flag, puffed his cheeks and whistled. The train started to move. We began the last leg of our journey, through the state of Victoria.

We shared the compartment with two couples, who were either chatting in undertones, or looking through some magazines and newspapers, exchanging smiles, watching the scenery. One woman was powdering her nose. They all behaved in exactly the same way as any other travellers throughout the entire world, but perhaps more discreet. They didn't stare at us, but I was sure they knew what we looked like. We kept our voices low; even Jozio was talking in a whisper, that funny whisper of a child, either impossible to hear, or almost loud. I caught a smile on the face of one of the other travellers and was pleased.

I wanted so much to make a good impression on them. So, while that game of concealed smiles and observations went on, the Victorian countryside rushed past the windows. The scenery was as remote from the European as we were from the place of our birth. Flat stretches of sun-scorched land, huge and foreign, gum trees, trunks and branches bare, exposed to the blinding sun, only the outside branches in leaf. The burnt-out gums were as if shattered from within, with twisted, splintery branches. Some darkened the scenery, others highlighted it. Charcoal and silver, they would have been ideal as a backdrop to some sombre, mysterious theatre production.

The train clattered; two of the passengers dozed off. The scenery hardly changed. Except in the vicinity of stations, there were no people, no houses, not even animals to be seen. Just the never-ending, yellowish-brown flat land being continuously bombarded by the sun. The sky was enamel-blue with hardly a cloud around. Only the sound of the train was the same as in Europe.

I shut my eyes and thought of the Polish countryside: villages, pine forests, rivers, cities, people, poplar trees, goats, cows, children shielding their eyes from the sun and waving to the passing train, dogs, fields spiked with sheaves, birds, flower-filled country gardens and rows of cottages, birches, as graceful as young brides, horse-drawn carts ... Endless images rolled through my mind, but when I opened my eyes, the Australian reality chased them away. It was a vast, overpowering country; but foreign and I felt sad.

'I want to get out,' declared Jozio. 'I've had enough of trains.' We hushed him and once more assured him that our travels would soon be over. Restless, twisting in his seat all the time, he was very bored. Julek dug into our overnight bag and pulled out Jozio's teddy bear, a couple of books. For a while everything seemed all right. Jozio cuddled his teddy bear and listened to the story. And then he started all over again.

'I've had enough of trains.' Julek started on another story. Jozio listened reluctantly and started to yell at the top of his voice. We bribed him with a chocolate, we threatened him, we tried to soothe him both with lollies and words, we begged him to stop. There was no way; if he didn't yell, he cried; if he didn't sob, his nose dripped. I felt humiliated, useless, helpless. I wanted to make a good impression on the Australians. They must have hated us, together with all the other migrants who set foot on their soil.

If they did, they gave no indication how they felt. They didn't seem to notice us, and specially our screaming successor, at all. They were either reading or watching the scenery they must have known by heart anyway.

In France, in a situation like this, we would have been advised what action should be taken to help our 'poor little cabbage' regain his composure. In Poland, someone would have remarked that behaviour like this was typical of Jewish bastards. In Australia, nothing. Just the rhythmical, rapid rattle of the train and the not so very rhythmical but equally continuous yell unmistakeably escaping from the sweet little rosy lips of Julek's son. 'From *your* son,' corrected my son's father and the veins on his neck stood out. By then Jozio had slipped to the floor, kicking his feet and nobody had even batted an eyelid. I felt warmly towards Australia and all its people. I was even ready to forgive her repetitive scenery.

We let Jozio stay where he was. It must have been

the wisest decision we had ever taken; Jozio carried on, then fell asleep at our feet. The train sped towards our destination while Julek and I relaxed till the train chugged into suburbia, chuffed, and came to a stop. No more trains, I thought and picked Jozio up. The other travellers smiled at us when they left the train. Julek went off to find his twenty-times-removed cousins. Jozio opened his eyes — clear, large and innocent.

'Where are we?' he asked in a voice which would have put all the angels to shame. I could have killed him.

Julek returned. 'They're waiting for us. Let's go.' He picked up the bag and was already on his way out. 'Jozio all right?... For God's sake, take that stupid coat off; it's terribly hot outside.'

We followed Julek into the hot, sticky air. I could hardly breathe. Other people were rushing past as if unconcerned with the heat, so there had to be some hope for us. Perhaps we, too, would learn how to breathe in this inferno one day.

Julek pointed out two middle-aged women. My cousins. Neither of them rushed up to greet us, as any normal people would do. I had to remind myself that neither Jozio nor I were introduced. The gap between us was closing in, my body felt sticky and Jozio's face was covered with tiny droplets. We walked towards where our two statues of liberty were standing. The train hissed once or twice, as though it wasn't hot enough, and sent up some steam. I was tempted to drop my coat and leave it behind, but then I remembered Simon and how glad he had been that I had something nice to wear; I almost saw his good face and knew that the coat and I were stuck with each other. Jozio was chatting, and people around us produced rapid, foreign sounds. The language, the heat, the pending introduction to my new family, consisting of two old maids, worried and perplexed me.

Julek introduced us in the most idiotic, formal way. Ania and Freda. We shook hands. They were of average build and height. Their faces were caked with powder. They looked very much alike and smiled in the same way, though it was Ania who bent down and gave Jozio a kiss.

'She gave me a wet kiss', Jozio kept on wiping his cheek. 'Mummy, you hear me? She gave me . . .'

'I heard you. You're hot, that's all. I heard you.' I hoped Ania hadn't. She pretended she hadn't, but by the way she looked at me, I knew she had. I was more than sure she was blaming me.

Both ladies were neatly dressed and their hair was plastered down by 'invisible' nets which could have been detected from as far away as Europe. Ania grabbed Jozio's hand but, trust my son, he wiggled away and stuck his hand into mine and wouldn't let it go. All this in sweltering conditions.

'You like hot weather?', asked Ania.

'Not much, I'm afraid.'

'Nothing to fear. The nights are cool in Melbourne', she said. 'So there is always a chance of a good night's rest, which you obviously need, as does your son.'

'Yes, we are rather tired, as you must understand', Julek came to the rescue.

'Yes, we'd better start moving', said Ania. 'Freda, get a taxi.' Freda did as she was told. She marched away in a rather un-ladylike manner, with us trailing behind.

'How was Sydney?', asked Ania.

'Hot.'

'Sydney is hot day and night. Weeks and weeks of heatwave. Melbourne is different. It's hot until the change, when the temperature drops by twenty degrees in a matter of a few minutes.' Ania offered information as if she were a paid employee of the Tourist Ministry.

'Mummy, carry me ... My legs hurt.'

I pushed my coat into Julek's hands, for which he thanked me with his usual charm. And then he joined in with Ania and allowed me to carry his son.

It was stuffy in the taxi, but Ania wouldn't let us keep the windows down because this very morning she had had her hair done.

'My hair was done too,' added Freda. 'We could keep the window down though.'

'No,' said Ania.

The taxi went through industrial areas spiked with electricity poles. In Europe, even in Poland, the electricity poles were absent from cities, and were used only in the country areas. I looked around me and didn't like it. Freda kept on repeating that Melbourne was a beautiful city and that the suburb we were passing through wasn't representative. 'Not as beautiful as Europe,' said Ania.

'Ania, really,' said Freda. 'You'll frighten them away, it's really beautiful here.'

'Beautiful but hot, though this year summer is hotter than usual,' Ania had the last word, and then she recalled the heatwave in 1939 and 'Black Friday'. I didn't understand what she was talking about and when she tried to explain bushfires and the temperature reaching 40° centigrade, I had just had enough. Jozio's head seemed hot, he hardly spoke. I worried. We must find a doctor as quickly as possible. What with all that heat, deadly spiders, bushfires, snakes, a shortage of water, of which Ania gracefully informed us between one traffic light and another. A doctor was a must. On the way to Australia, a man had told us of a chest specialist. 'One of the best. Worked in a sanatorium near Warsaw.' The man had given us the doctor's address. Apparently he couldn't practise officially because foreign qualifications were not recognised in Australia. 'But he is a good doctor, trustworthy and experienced,' our companion had assured us. At least we wouldn't be afraid of denunciation, because the doctor himself was involved in practising illegally.

The taxi left the industrial part of Melbourne. We were passing through rows and rows of small houses resting comfortably on small plots of lands. Gardens!

'Palm tree. Over there. Look, Jozio, a palm tree! We'll have to take a photo and send it back to Europe. To your grandmother. To uncle Simon, to everyone. They won't believe it! A palm tree growing in a garden!'

'We chopped ours down. It was such a nuisance. All palm trees are.' What Ania said really bothered me or rather not so much what she said but the way she said it. A despot, I wondered?

'It looks exotic to us. My sister once grew a palm. From a date stone. In a pot. It didn't look too healthy. But still, a palm.'

'In a week's time, you won't even notice it', replied Ania.

The poultry farm was hidden behind a huge hedge. The house was weatherboard with a green roof. The windows were all shut and the blinds drawn. There was hardly any clucking of chickens to be heard.

'You will have to excuse me. I have to make sure that the water hasn't evaporated. I must also feed the birds.' Making this announcement, farmer Freda opened the front door, walked through the whole length of the house and after a minute or two we heard the door slam.

'Don't slam the door,' called Ania. 'She always does it. I only hope she changed into overalls,' she sighed and then took us through the house. Off the hall, there were two rooms. The one to the left was to be ours. It was a large room with an iron double bed, a wardrobe and a small table. The walls were clean. I wanted to open the window, but Ania told me that I musn't; so I didn't, though the smell of fresh paint was oppressive.

'You should be comfortable here. All you need is a bed for Jozio. You will have to buy one. Meanwhile he can sleep on a settee in the dining room. We had it recovered just recently.'

'We'd rather have him with us, in the same room, if you don't mind. The new environment, you understand?'

'As you wish. I'll have to find a piece of plastic to line the settee; Freda would hate it to be ruined.'

'No problem. Jozio is completely trained. He hasn't had any accidents for ages.'

Across from our room there was a lounge room.

'We use it only when we have visitors', announced Ania. The furniture stood there in semi-darkness and collected dust. I couldn't help thinking of my parents' home, where every room was bright and used by us all. But our new landladies were not my parents and they had every right to live their own lives in whatever way they wished. They were kind enough to let us come and live with them. I knew it all, I did appreciate it all, but somehow I couldn't dismiss the growing feeling of uneasiness.

Ania led us through a stupid-looking, skinny arch. 'What you have seen is the new part of the house, built on some twenty years ago, by its previous owner.'

The corridor was narrow and dark.

'This is the original part.'

There were doors to the right and to the left. 'Our bedrooms,' pointed Ania, and then she opened the door at the end of the corridor. 'The living room.' It was pretty big, with one narrow window and a fireplace with a protruding iron grille. On both sides of the mantelpiece there were two built-in cupboards. The table was long and seemed unsteady. The chairs didn't look much. Next to the window stood a cane chair that looked as though it was never used. A settee rested against the windowsill. There was no way to tell much about the new cover, because the whole surface was covered by an old blanket.

'Sit down, sit down. Make yourselves at home,' mooed Ania. 'It'll be your home for some time to come.'

Jozio held on to me and Julek smiled as if he was perplexed.

The kitchen was also built on; it was tiny. A narrow table, 'specially custom-made', filled in the space between the door and the stove. The sink was covered by rubber mats.

'Was it also custom-made?', I asked.

Julek kicked my leg, which made me feel even hotter. Jozio was boiling too. He hadn't been very amused when we had dragged him through the art galleries of Paris, and now our poor child was subjected to a conducted tour of a house which belonged to people he hardly knew.

'It's all very fascinating, Ania,' I said, 'but I'm sorry, we would like to wash, unpack . . . Would you mind!'

'As you wish. I thought you would be interested in the house. It is what we have achieved in the last ten years. If our poor parents only knew how we live, they would have died over again. Their daughters — poultry farmers. Freda hardly knew how to pour her own cup of tea, she knows eight languages. But no one wanted a philosophy scholar when we arrived in Australia, so we bought this farm. No one believed we could run it properly.'

'It's tremendous,' said Julek with admiration.

'Not bad for two spoiled European ladies, eh?'

'It's really tremendous!'

'The bathroom,' Ania carried on. 'We have just installed a new gas heater. We used to have a chip heater before.'

What a revelation, I thought. I wanted to be left alone with my family, but before we were allowed to go to our room we had to go through an introduction to the laundry and to listen to Ania's plans to replace the wooden trough for a cement one, and the fuel copper for a gas one. 'Hopefully in the not-too-distant future,' concluded Ania. Or almost concluded, because the toilet was outside, right next to a shed which was used to sort and pack the eggs. So our minds absorbed yet another piece of vital information. The farm had six hundred birds. 'Not bad for two women, is it?'

'I want to see a chicken,' demanded Jozio.

We had promised him, he certainly deserved it. He had behaved in an exemplary way, better than I had. So we dragged our feet and followed Ania over the path constructed from two rows of bricks to a long, low shed. The birds hardly moved. They seemed half dead. Ania explained that the birds were affected by the heat and that sometimes they must even be watered to prevent losses. I fully sympathised with them. The stench of manure was strong though, even if the birds were not.

'Phew', Jozio pinched his nostrils shut.

'You can go now, if you wish,' said Ania. 'I have to help Freda. We eat in an hour's time.' Ania left us. 'Freda, Freda, where are you?'

A whole hour to ourselves! We went inside. The air was heavy but much cooler than outside.

'What d'you think?' I wanted Julek to tell me his feelings.

'What d'you mean, what do I think?'

'Of our position, of staying here, of Ania.'

'Have you heard of a better place?'

'No.'

'Keep that in mind. "Is it custom-made?" You're really ... I don't know ... Couldn't you find anything else to say?'

'Like what?'

'Like what tremendous women Ania and Freda are. Could you imagine your mother or aunt running a farm?'

'We did more difficult things during the war.'

'It's not war now, is it? Ania's not a fool. She must have noticed your childish stupidity.'

'Don't reprimand me in front of my son,' I said in Russian. By then Jozio must have known that whenever we quarrelled, we used a foreign language.

FOUR

We stayed at the farm eight long months. Naturally, Jozio wet the freshly recovered couch on the very first night we spent under our cousins' roof.

'You said he is trained.' Ania wasn't pleased.

'Sorry', I said.

'Sorry won't take the stain away.'

Ania was right. I felt rotten and only brightened up after the arrival of my mother's letter. 'All is well at home,' she wrote. 'The spring is exceptionally warm this year.' I read and then was sad.

Ania didn't display much warmth towards me. She and I couldn't see eye to eye. Even when I wanted to please her, I hardly succeeded. What worried me was the fact that it was all so petty. I had never suspected that I would ever allow myself to care and fret about stupid, irrelevant things like who should clean which part of the house, or who should prepare the meal, or who should wash the dishes. Not after months of living in cellars during the war. It didn't make sense.

But I truly admired the sisters. They were terrific. The farm was run efficiently, they worked hard. Ania was a born dictator, an organiser; Freda was the work-force. They looked so much alike. Both were tall, two exclamation marks turned upside down.

Both always wore gumboots when working and moved with ease and a certain grace which belonged to the end of the nineteenth century. Both had thick hair, which I suspected they tinted. They really loved Jozio and were glad to have two men around the house. Julek helped them quite a lot, even after he started work at the textile factory. We shared all the food expenses with our hostesses, but didn't pay any rent. 'Put the money aside for your own house; we don't need your rent,' said Freda and winked. Ania wasn't amused.

It was time for me to make our relationship work.

We got in touch with the Polish doctor. To reach his place in Elwood, we had to change buses and trains four times, and then we had to walk for about fifteen, twenty minutes. There was no other way; we had to know how Jozio was.

We showed the doctor Jozio's X-rays. He looked at them, then placed Jozio on his X-ray machine. There was no need to make plates, he informed us. He was blessed with an exceptional visual memory, so 'just to have a look' would be sufficient. His memory, not only visual, but also in general, was so good that he remembered all his patients. If not their faces, their lungs for sure.

He was telling us all this while shadowing the outline of Jozio's lungs on a piece of paper.

'Jozio is far from cured,' he declared. 'I want to see him next month. As a matter of fact, once a month. Meanwhile feed him well and restrict his activities. He could do with a lot of rest.' My heart, and I was sure Julek's too, sank.

'Jozio's temperature has stabilised, he hasn't got any. It's a good sign, isn't it?' I almost begged him.

'Lack of temperature is a good sign, but it doesn't necessarily mean that your child is healthy.'

We were given another sentence. Back to the old routine. Only this time it would be even more difficult. Jozio enjoyed helping Freda, climbing trees, his newly discovered freedom.

On the way home, we were silent. Jozio fell asleep. I was reproaching myself for allowing him to run about freely, before we had consulted the doctor. What right did we have to subject our child to a strenuous sea crossing lasting almost five weeks? The French doctor had allowed us to go, he had assured us that Jozio was well enough to go and now, after a few months in Australia, his health had deteriorated because of neglect, or the sea voyage, or the change of routine, or climate, or everything put together. I felt very sad and lonely, and just couldn't imagine that it would be possible to force Jozio into immobility — to take away his shoes — once again.

We arrived home disheartened. I placed Jozio on a deckchair, in the shade. Julek stayed with him. I went to the kichen to help Ania with the preparations for tea. And then Ania announced that two pieces of chocolate were missing from the block in her cupboard, I kept peeling potatoes and didn't attach much weight to what she said. I kept to myself.

'I wonder who took the chocolate? Maybe Jozio?'

'Ania, really! He's too small to reach your cupboard, but even if he were the right size, he wouldn't have taken your precious chocolate. He has his very own whenever he wants to have any.'

'The fact remains that the chocolate is missing. It couldn't have disappeared on its own.'

'No, it couldn't have, I agree. But tell me, how d'you know? Are you in a habit of counting how many pieces of chocolate you have?'

'You are insulting!'

'It's you who abuse me. How could you honestly suggest that any of us had stolen two pieces of chocolate? Please tell me. I don't understand.'

Ania stormed out of the kitchen and left me to my thoughts and potatoes.

Freda, though a strong suspect, moved throughout the chocolate crisis as if she wished to be invisible. She never dared to stand up to Ania's constant bullying. Freda worked hard, did everything Ania wanted her to do and progressively became more and more like a slightly underfed chicken herself. She was an intelligent woman, more alert than Ania. How she tolerated the situation we couldn't understand. She had studied philosophy and had done her doctorate, all before the First World War. She had travelled throughout Europe by bike, which was quite unheard of for a young woman at the beginning of the twentieth century. What Ania had done with her life we were not sure. She was a good cook and loved painting. There were three canvases, all unfinished, stuck away in her room. 'One day, I'll go back to them,' she told us many times. Perhaps she even had a creative talent, though her forte was to command and rule over others. Freda's existence was organised by her sister. She worked and moved as in a treadmill. She ate, fed chickens, collected eggs — like a robot. She listened to the radio. She never ate a piece of fruit without leaving half for Ania. She was a fussy eater, as fastidious as Ania was sloppy. She kept to herself most of the time, rolled her own cigarettes, and seldom took part in general conversation. She would come out of her shell only when Ania was not at home. Then she had plenty to say, and knew how to say it. Why she had never married was well-kept secret. I supposed she was a war victim too, they both were, though they had arrived in Australia before the war. Poultry farming wasn't what they had been trained for.

The farm itself was very primitive and the so-called

equipment really belonged in a museum. Freda cut the grass with a sickle and then chopped it on a hand-operated cutter, as blunt as her sickle. She mixed the mash in a wooden, splintery trough, and performed acrobatics wheeling the wheelbarrow along the brick path. 'You wouldn't believe it, but my figure used to be good', she told me once without much regret.

Ania was in charge of collecting the eggs and sometimes helped to fill the water. She also looked after the house.

We helped them with the eggs. In the evening, we would all gather to wash and pack them. They were always dirty. There was a hand-operated machine, but Ania wouldn't allow us to use it. She must have derived some satisfaction from seeing our hands covered with chicken shit. If there were two ways of doing anything, Ania would always choose the harder one, especially while supervising others to perform the task. 'You wouldn't believe it, but Freda was quite attractive once,' she told us. 'Look at her now. That's migration for you.'

But that wasn't my main worry. Ania was Ania, and she wasn't all bad either.

FIVE

Julek was working and because we didn't pay any rent, we managed to save money from week to week, hoping that one day we would have enough to buy a place of our own. So everything should have been all right. It was, except for that constant nagging worry about Jozio. He was bright enough and happy, he was eating well, but our doctor wasn't satisfied with his progress.

We visited the doctor every month. Once or twice he concluded that 'the child seems better', but in the same breath he warned that 'the road to health is a long one'.

And then I missed a period. I wasn't very concerned and even thought how nice it would be to have another child. Jozio was over three and except for Ania and Freda we had no one in Australia. It would be great to present Jozio with a sister or a brother, so he would have someone else to love and be loved by besides his parents. Julek received the news calmly, we even started making plans and decided to ask our doctor where I should go and who I should approach to look after me during the pregnancy.

The doctor made us wait; we had learned to know

that practice of his. Whenever we had an appointment, we were never admitted to the surgery until the next patient arrived. He often kept us waiting a long time.

First the doctor examined Jozio. He X-rayed him and compared the results with his previous notes. 'Not bad', he pronounced, 'but still a lot to be desired, though much better.' Julek thanked him and left the surgery, taking Jozio along. I sat facing the doctor alone, feeling the threatening presence of the X-ray machine. I was a very shy twenty-four and couldn't bring myself to spell out my case.

'Yes,' said the doctor. 'Could I be of any assistance? If you want something, please say so. I have further appointments, as you know.'

And then, when I was sitting there facing him, without looking at him, he said: 'You must be pregnant.' I nodded and all the blood left my body and rushed to my face; it was burning, while my hands were icy cold.

'You have got yourself into a fine mess.'

I wanted to protest that a pregnancy is not a mess, but my throat was still tight and I couldn't produce a sound.

'I will help you. Don't worry. I will give you the name of a person who will take care of you problem.'

'What d'you mean?'

'You haven't been foolish enough to want another child; it wasn't planned, or was it?'

'Not really.'

'To have another child in your position would be totally irresponsible. Your son is still sick. You have to put all your emotions aside and use logic instead. If you choose to have another child, you will automatically neglect Jozio and, by God, he is in need of all the attention and care he can get. Another fact is that the baby could easily catch T.B. There is only one way out of this mess, abortion. You can consider yourself lucky that you came to me. I know of a person who does abortions; he is fully qualified and well equipped to perform a small operation like that.'

I sat there, not knowing what to say or what to do. The doctor scribbled something on a piece of paper and before I realised what had happened, he was shaking my hand, leading me to the door.

'Nothing to worry about, I promise you,' he said and gave me a note. 'Let me know as soon as possible so I will make the necessary arrangements for you.'

'How much time do I have?'

'Not much. A couple of weeks. Not more than a month.'

I was out of the surgery before I knew it.

Julek rushed to me. 'What did he have to say?'

'Nothing I didn't know. He gave me an address. Asked me to let him know within a month.'

The note the doctor had given me was all crumpled; I handed it to Julek and picked Jozio up high in the air. 'My precious boy,' I said. Jozio giggled. I turned to Julek. 'We'll discuss the whole matter later, O.K.?'

'O.K. with me. Fine.'

We had our discussion once Jozio went to sleep. Julek said that the decision depended on me. He couldn't possibly tell me to proceed with the pregnancy or to insist on abortion. He urged me to have a good night's rest. 'In the morning, you'll see, the future will look less bleak.'

He was perhaps right, but I couldn't sleep on a decision like this. I wasn't in conflict because of my religious feelings, so that part didn't bother me much. I had to think of Jozio, what was best for him. We had to bring him back to health. He really looked better, his face had filled out, he was laughing a lot, his temperature was normal, he was eating well. I had no right to risk a relapse in his condition. The doctor must be right. I would have to follow his advice. I dozed off, to waken to my dilemma while Julek and Jozio slept peacefully. The only logical choice left to me was obvious, but it took me almost the whole night till I allowed myself to spell out clearly to myself; till I accepted the fact that I was going to have an abortion. Once I reached the decision, I wanted to go ahead with the operation as soon as possible, perhaps I was frightened that I might change my mind.

I was trying to divert my attention from the problem, but all day long I caught myself thinking about it. If only Jozio were healthy, how happy I would be with my pregnancy. If only my mother were with me, or Julek's sister, everything would be different. There was not even enough time left to consult either of them. For a return letter, I would have to wait for a month. Time was running out and I couldn't stand the situation as it was for much longer. At night I would lie awake, and if I slept, I dreamt disturbing dreams.

The day I had the appointment with the abortionist was cold and gloomy; it was drizzling and windy. Julek kept me company. A young, smiling girl ushered us into a surgery which looked normal, as did the doctor. Julek did all the talking and translated all that was said. The doctor, an Australian, wanted to know when and where we came from, where we lived, how much money we had and what was Julek's job. And the reason for an abortion. He listened with some interest and instructed me to come at ten the following morning, with a plain envelope containing thirty pounds which was to be left with the receptionist. He mentioned that the normal fee was around the eighty-pound mark. While we thanked him, he reminded me to come on an empty stomach.

'Nothing to worry about. You'll be able to collect your wife by lunchtime.' He shook hands with Julek and hardly looked at me.

So, on the following day, Julek took another day off work and delivered me at the surgery. He told me not to worry. The doctor told me not to worry. Why did they keep on telling me not to worry if there was nothing to worry about?

'See you soon. Everything will be well. Don't worry.'

'See you.'

The nurse said something which I didn't understand, so she herself picked up the envelope I was clutching in my hand. She looked inside and then placed it in a drawer. I was wondering what was going to happen to me. The nurse smiled and took my arm. She was talking to me, so I followed her. I was calm and wished to have it all done with as quickly as possible. I wondered whether it would hurt and how Ania and Freda were managing with Jozio and whether Julek had gone home.

The nurse took me to a small cubicle and gave me a white gown.

'Put it on,' she said and left me behind the drawn curtain. I undressed and suddenly thought that I hadn't even checked whether I was pregnant. I had assumed I was, but no doctor had ever examined me, no test had been done. I was changing into the gown, ready for the operation. It was too late to stop it; the doctor was waiting for me, he had already received his money. I couldn't even communicate with him. I envied Freda's chickens and thought that if a Polish bird would land in Australia, it wouldn't have any difficulty in communicating with its Australian counterpart. And then I wished my fears were true. Let him keep our thirty pounds, let him operate and let him find that I wasn't pregnant at all. The nurse must have been waiting for me — as soon as I put the gown on, she returned to claim me. She took me by my hand and led me to the operating theatre; I thought she gave me a reassuring squeeze. She helped me on to the table. The doctor, only his eyes visible from above the mask, was ready for me. He took my pulse. He said things I couldn't understand, but his voice was kind.

'I pregnant?' I pointed at myself and my heart beat in anticipation. The doctor looked at me in disbelief.

'You are pregnant, aren't you?'

'I'm not sure.'

'You have been examined by your doctor?'

'No.'

The doctor took the mask off. He looked at the nurse, at me, at the ceiling, at his watch; he walked across the room, came back to the table, consulted the nurse.

'You listen to me,' he said very slowly. 'I — examine — you. You, understand?'

'I understand.'

'O.K. Ready?'

'O.K.'

The nurse gave the doctor a pair of rubber gloves and pulled my knees up. I shut my eyes and tensed up. The examination was brisk and painful. The nurse straightened my legs. I opened my eyes. The doctor was standing next to me removing his rubber gloves.

'Yes. You are pregnant. Sure. Now we operate.' And then I cried, very slowly and very quietly. The doctor had his back to me, I heard the tap running, so he must have been scrubbing his hands, getting ready. The nurse was busy with the lower part of my body and I cried and cried. It would have been better if the doctor had not examined me. I could have pretended I

40

wasn't pregnant. Now I knew for sure that I was. I felt so lonely, so small. The nurse glanced at me. She patted my head. 'You are all right. All right. You understand? Don't cry. All is well.'

The doctor reappeared within the circle of my vision. He held a syringe; the nurse placed a rubber band above my wrist and I felt a prick. I felt distant and indifferent. Nothing mattered.

When I woke up, I was back in the cubicle and the nurse was bending over me.

'You — all — right. You, fine ... Drink — tea. Make — you — feel — better. Drink.'

I drank my tea.

'Now you go home. Your husband is waiting for you. Ready?' My abdomen felt bruised. I tried to get up and was surprised that I could. My mouth was all dry, I drank more tea. It was all over, done, and had to be forgotten. Jozio was waiting for me; it was the first time he had spent a day away from me. One day he would be strong and healthy. We had been right to choose Australia. It had plenty to offer. Plenty of food, plenty of fresh air. Julek was working and his wages were more than sufficient to meet all our needs. I'd learn English yet. And one day, if everything went our way, we'd have another child. And meanwhile I wouldn't think of my abortion any more.

The nurse helped me to get dressed and to reach Julek, then both of them took me to the waiting taxi.

'You look after her,' the nurse said to Julek and I pressed her hand as a thank-you gesture.

The taxi drove off. Julek put his arm around me.

'Was it very painful? Are you all right?'

'I'm fine. A bit wobbly. But fine. How's Jozio?'

Great, really great. He helped Freda feed the chooks. He asked for you once or twice. I told him that you won't be able to lift him up. D'you think you'll be well enough to look after him tomorrow? I'd better go back to work. Two days off, you understand.'

'Sure.'

'I told Ania and Freda you had a curette; they promised to help you. Try to make friends with them; they really mean well . . . Are you sore?'

'No.'

'Are you cross with me?'

'How could I be? Tell me more about Jozio.'

'I've already told you. He's fine. He had a good day. I put him to sleep before I left. I covered him well — it's really cold . . . Are you cold?'

'No . . . How much was the taxi?'

'Not to worry. Not much. The main thing is you're all right.'

'Yes.'

The traffic was heavy and I felt a strange sensation in my stomach. The lower part of my belly hurt. Not all the time, only when the taxi came to a sudden stop.

I went to bed as soon as we arrived home.

Jozio climbed on my bed. 'Your tummy hurts. Daddy told me, I know.'

'Only a bit. How was your day? Did you have a nice nap?'

'You were not there when I woke up. Daddy said I'd see you when I woke up.'

'Sorry, darling. We were late. But I'm here now. I'm very sleepy. Tomorrow, tomorrow I'll play with you. Not today. Run along, help Freda. She told me what a good helper you are.'

'All right . . . You promise, tomorrow?'

'I promise.'

Julek led Jozio out. I shut my heavy lids tight and placed my palms on my belly. It hurt. I was glad to be left alone. I pulled the blanket up to my face. It was dull outside, it must have been very cold. I shouldn't have sent Jozio outside, not in that kind of weather. He should have been inside, warming himself next to the fireplace. I didn't really care and that hurt me more than my belly.

The Australian Dream was turning sour. The promise of a better future had gone astray. The first job. Julek put an advertisement in the paper. 'Textile engineer, trained in England, seeks employment.' The response was overwhelming; ten, eleven letters requesting Julek to arrange an interview. We were so happy — and then our hopes dwindled. Everywhere Julek went he was met with courtesy, his degree was appreciated — and then he was told that it would be very difficult to give him a position in accordance with his qualifications. 'Sorry. We would like to employ you, but you must appreciate that the Australian workers won't tolerate a foreigner stepping into a managerial position. Our mistake, we have to admit, we just assumed you were British.'

It was a blow. We hadn't expected that kind of treatment. Julek's English was fluent; his English degree should have been like a pass to a good job.

It was I who was bitter, who wasn't ready to accept the situation; Julek approached the problem in a more resigned and rather realistic way. Without elaborating much further, he took a job with a migrant who had a few textile machines to assemble.

What he thought himself was difficult to guess. He must have been disillusioned, but he never showed it. He worked very hard, while his bosses — because he was blessed with two — stood over him, sighing all the time and urging him to work faster. They were anxious to start, in order to show the whole of Australia how to run a textile plant properly. I kept

43

pointing out to Julek how unfair it was, what a waste of human potential for Australia.

'It doesn't worry me. The main thing is my weekly pay. After all, we're migrants, we can't expect the same treatment as the native-born. Stop dwelling on it. It doesn't worry me.'

No matter how often Julek explained his attitude, I didn't believe him. He must have been disappointed, he must have.

My belly felt empty, my thoughts were jumpy. I thought of my family so far away and wished our situation would change for the better so that we would be able to bring them over to Australia. We had to have a decent dwelling before they could come. We were lucky the sisters had offered to let us stay with them as long as we wished. We were lucky we didn't have to pay rent. 'Put the rent money in the bank, save it for your own house.' So thanks to Ania and Freda, perhaps one day we would have a place of our own. I wasn't really fair towards them, I should have tried harder. They were good to us, it must have been quite an upheaval in their lives to have a strange young couple with a three-year-old child living with them. If only it weren't so cold. Ania insisted that it was healthier to sleep in an unheated room, but somehow she never convinced me. Even during the war we had tried our best to keep ourselves warm. It had been easier to accept hunger when one wasn't shivering all the time. It was ironic that my old chilblains should reappear and torment me again, in Australia, in the land of plenty.

Ania stood at the door.
  'How do you feel?'
  'Very well, thank you.'
  'Really?'

'Really.'

'I heard that after a curette, one is sore ... Where does it hurt?'

'It doesn't really hurt.' I wanted Ania to go away. I wanted to drift in my thoughts again.

'I heard it does.'

I closed my eyes.

'For how long do you have to stay in bed?'

'I'll be up tomorrow. I could even be up today, had I wanted to.'

'I heard one should rest after that operation. I can take care of Jozio, no need for you to overdo it. An operation is an operation one should remember.'

'Thank you, Ania. I do appreciate your offer, but there's no need. I'll be fine. I'm fine.' How I wished she would stop her inquisition and leave me!

'No harm in making a suggestion.' I didn't bother to reply and kept my eyes closed.

'Are you asleep?'

I felt her approach my bed and lean over me. The stench of chickens hit me — Ania must have watched me closely. I lay very still, having only one wish; to be left alone.

I heard Ania's cautious steps leaving the room.

'If it depended on me, I would keep Irena in bed for another day or two. I can look after Jozio. She fell asleep on me, it's a sign of exhaustion if you ask me.'

'Thank you for your concern, Ania, we'll see. If need be, I'll take another day off.' Julek was speaking quietly, but Ania's voice was booming.

'You already spent enough money as it is. I can look after Jozio. Every day off work is a loss.'

'I'm well aware of that.'

They carried on and on, till I pulled the cover over my head. I had to admit Ania had shown a lot of consideration, so why did she irritate me? I wasn't sure. I still heard their muffled voices — and then I didn't hear anything. I must have dozed and when I came to my senses again I heard them chatting incessantly. I was wet all over, hot and cold at the same time. I wasn't sure what time it was, my belly hurt, my head felt funny.

'Julek,' I called.

'Julek,' I called again and again, but he didn't come. He had deserted me, hadn't even checked how I was. For all he knew or cared, I could have died. I could have bled to death. My mother would have stayed with me had she lived in Australia. My poor mother. I could see her crying after learning that I had died as the result of an abortion. And Jozio, what would happen to him! My poor, orphaned child. Ania, Freda, would they take care of him? Julek would remarry, that was certain. At the very prospect, I started to cry. I knew it was ridiculous, but I couldn't stop. All the incidents of women who had died after abortions crowded in on me in my self-pity. I craved for my mother and the touch of her motherly hand. I didn't want to be used as a statistic by some loud-mouthed anti-abortion fanatic. My abdomen hurt. I wasn't myself and felt so very lonely. I lost control over my thoughts, they just kept on coming in a procession of gloom, in visions. Jozio, a poor orphan, all in rags. Ania pulling him by the hand. Julek smiling at a woman, smiling the smile which should have been reserved entirely for me. I cried and cried and called Julek till my mind became blank. And then I slept for hours, till midday of the following day, as Julek informed me. He was next to me when I opened my eyes.

'Why aren't you at work?' Another day off!'

'Never mind. I wanted to be with you.' And he looked at me with all the warmth to which I hold a special licence.

Towards evening Freda came to see how I was.

'Ania is preparing the meal', she said, while the whole room absorbed the chicken aroma. 'Take it easy. I know how you feel. I had an abortion once,' she turned her head away from me. 'Jozio is fun. We both love him ... Ania never knew. About the abortion. you understand?'

'Tell me more about yourself?'

'There is nothing to tell. It was a long time ago. Not worth remembering ... Take care. It's good to have you here.' Freda bent down and stroked my hair.

SIX

I didn't die. My convalescence was a quick one; it had to be, because Jozio wasn't well. His nose was running. A cold, a plain cold, I kept on reassuring myself. And then he started to cough, his temperature went up and I was frightened. I blamed myself, Australia, Ania, Julek, the poultry farm, the unheated house, dampness. I rang our doctor and begged him to visit Jozio. He flatly refused. He couldn't possibly come over; all that long way, which would take him hours even by car. He couldn't afford to neglect his other patients who undoubtedly would crowd his surgery while he was with Jozio. He was obliged to look after all his patients and to be ready to see them whenever they were in need of his professional assistance.

'Doctor, my child is very sick. He needs you, He's your patient too. I don't know where to turn. Please tell me what am I to do ... Perhaps I should call a local doctor? Surely he wouldn't denounce us?'

'I wouldn't be too sure. To call a local doctor would be risky. You had better come over to my place. I will see your child outside the queue.'

'How could I possibly bring him over in weather like this? He's running a high temperature; it takes us almost two hours to reach your place.'

'Why don't you take a taxi?'

What was the point of all this conversation? The telephone booth was dirty, and the painted surface covered with scraped-out names and telephone numbers.

It rained outside.

'Hello, hello?' said the doctor. 'Are you there? Hello!' I hung up the receiver. I wasn't even angry with our ex-doctor.

The wind was blowing hard, its viciousness wrinkled the water in the puddles and made the trees almost screech. The rain, the wind lashed at me and I remembered how during the war I had cried in the rain and had been glad there was no need to apologise or explain the reason for my emotional outburst to anyone. But on that day, I didn't cry. I simply didn't know what to do; I only knew that our recommended doctor was a bastard. I kept on repeating to myself that Jozio would be all right. Little children didn't die because of a cough. There were no gas chambers in Australia, the ones in Europe had been turned into museums. So I need not worry. No one was going to kill my child. There must be some solution, we'd find a way.

The mud ridges in the road looked like an old man's wrinkled forehead. The air was noisy. Nature and its hundred strings.

Jozio called to me from our room when I reached home. He was even more feverish than before, or perhaps it seemed to me that he was because my hands and face were half frozen.

'My throat hurts.' He coughed.

'Never mind. I'll get you something to drink. Tea and honey ... Gargle, that's what you should do, you should gargle your throat.'

'It hurts when I swallow.'

'You'll be fine.'

I tucked him in. The room was cold, almost as cold as outside. The wind kept on smashing the raindrops against the window.

'I want to speak to you.' Ania reappeared from nowhere, her hair plastered under the invisible net.

'Please do.'

'Not here,' she said, making faces, implying she wouldn't do it in front of Jozio, as if he were an idiot, incapable of understanding all her stupid signals.

'Stay with me, Mummy.'

'Ania wants to tell me something. It won't take long.'

'Promise?'

'I'll be back with you in a minute.'

'I don't want to be alone. My head hurts.'

'I have to go for a moment. I'll be back very, very soon.'

I followed Ania into the living room. It had the reputation of being the warmest room in the house and though the fire was out, Ania peeled off one of her cardigans immediately.

'Something has to be done,' she said.

I didn't bother to ask her what she meant.

'Before you came here, Julek informed us that Jozio had recovered from his lung infection.'

'That's what out French doctor told us.'

'And now he is sick again.'

'I wish he were healthy.'

'T.B. is contagious.'

'Yes. But hopefully it's only a cold.'

'Who knows ... I worry for Freda's sake. She is very susceptible to any disease ... You know what I want to say?'

'No. You don't make yourself very clear.'

Ever since I had left the phone booth, or rather since the doctor had refused to come to see Jozio, I had felt as if I were an observer, seeing myself and our situation from some distance. At the same time there was that constant, pestering realisation of being alone. If only my mother were somewhere close by, or any other member of our family, we wouldn't have to depend on Ania and her hospitality, there would be some other place for us to go.

'I wish you would pay attention to what I am trying to say. It's not easy.'

'Sorry.'

'When we agreed to you staying with us, we were convinced Jozio was cured. Now with him being sick again the situation has become impossible. No matter how distressed I am, you will have to look for other accommodation.'

'All right,' I heard myself saying. 'Is that all you wanted to tell me? Jozio is waiting for me. I have to go back to him.'

'I want you to keep all his dishes separately. As a precaution, for Freda's sake.'

'Of course. I'll see to it.'

My legs carried me to our room. Jozio was asleep; his breathing was heavy. I sat down. Soon Julek would arrive home from work. He'd be exhausted. I'd have to tell him that Jozio's doctor wouldn't come, that Ania wanted us all out, that I didn't feel like myself, that something had snapped in me and that nothing was important any more. I piled another blanket over Jozio and sat down trembling and waiting.

Julek fixed it all up. Without him, I would have gone to pieces. He listened to my never-ending tirade of all the misfortunes which had fallen upon us. He must have been upset, though he never interrupted me. He sat next to me and kept on clearing his throat, which was a familiar sign of his being perturbed.

'Don't get over excited; we had better not wake Jozio up,' he almost whispered. 'Our doctor is not the only doctor in Australia. I'll find another one who will be happy to look after Jozio. Relax, it's not the end of the world. I'll go to the chemist and make enquiries. Stop worrying. Have something to drink, something hot. I won't be long.'

The doctor arrived even before Julek had a chance to return from his SOS mission. Our new medico was very tall and addressed me in the most beautiful Polish. He said something like: 'Your husband has explained your situation. Don't worry. I settled in Australia just before the war, went through my medical studies all over again. We are practically neighbours. You'll have to come and meet my wife and children. But first, let me see your boy.'

He followed me to Jozio and before even examining him, our new doctor and my son exchanged views on teddy bears in general and dry throats in particular.

'Breathe deeply. Cough. Once more ... Once more.'

I felt at ease when I handed Jozio's X-rays, one by one, to this most wonderful doctor. Just then Julek arrived. I wasn't frightened any more; with a husband like mine, with a son who was capable of behaving in such an exemplary way, with a doctor who looked at the X-rays with such calm concentration, who didn't even say 'hmmm' or 'I see' our future looked promising. I sat on Jozio's bed and while I stroked his hand, Julek mussed up all his hair.

'Stop it, Dad.'

The doctor kept on examining and comparing the X-rays. I wanted to know, to guess, what he was thinking, but it was impossible; his face had adopted that famous professional sphinxy expression.

'The X-rays are fine', he said and handed them back to me. 'There's nothing wrong with your son; he is completely cured.'

'I know, the X-rays were taken in Paris, but since we came to Australia, the picture has changed.'

'And where is the more recent X-ray? I would like to see it.'

'Our doctor didn't believe in taking plates, he just used to report to us what he saw.'

'It's fine. Give me his name and I'll get in touch with him. From what I can see, the child is all right.'

Julek looked at me and I knew we were not going to disclose the doctor's name. Why not, I wasn't sure; he didn't deserve our loyalty.

'I'm sorry, but I'd rather not; his name was given to us in confidence.' Julek stood up.

'It would be of help to hear what caused the relapse, you know?'

'We decided not to contact him again.'

The new doctor gave us an understanding look. 'Oh, well . . . In that case, I would suggest to you to come and see me once Jozio's temperature drops to normal. I personally think your child has the flu, nothing to do with his lungs. He has as much right to catch a cold as any other child. But just to reassure myself, I would like to X-ray him. I have the proper equipment in my surgery. We'll make a plate for future reference.' He fished out some tablets from his old-fashioned bag, leaving enough to keep us going till the next day, 'to spare you the trouble of finding a chemist on duty.'

He shook hands with us.

'If you have any doubts, don't hesitate to get in touch with me. You have my phone number, don't you?' Julek waved a piece of rumpled paper and uttered a very shaky 'Yes'.

'Splendid,' said the doctor. 'See you soon, Jozio.'

We took him to the door; we thanked him. The cold air rushed in and I couldn't stop thinking of the crinkled shred of paper and how Julek must have crushed it in his palm while he waited for the doctor to respond to his plea. I pushed my body against the door, to make it easier to shut it.

'Are you all right?' Julek's voice was back to its steady pitch.

'Mhh.'

I wanted to say something else but didn't manage, and then we heard Ania approaching.

'What did he have to say?'

'Who?' I said, and looked at her and was glad to see the annoyance spread across her face.

'The doctor, of course. Who else visited you tonight?'

'He said it's the flu. Jozio has the same right to catch flu as any other child.'

'I wonder if he is a good doctor. I heard he is very young.'

'He studied medicine twice, once in Poland, the second time in Australia. He must know it by heart.'

'Who told you?'

'He told me, over the phone, when I rang him,' said Julek.

'I'd better go to Jozio,' and he went, leaving me to Ania.

'What else did he tell you?' Pure syrup was oozing from her, which I was determined to resist because of the hurt she had inflicted on me.

'I'm to see him, that is, he wants to see Jozio in a few days' time.'

'What for?'

'To make sure all's well.'

'He thinks something is wrong?'

Julek reappeared and urged us to keep our voices

down because Jozio was asleep. 'Go to the dining room.'

We all sat at the table and Julek told Ania that the doctor didn't think there was anything the matter with Jozio. 'On the contrary, our doctor thinks he's fine.'

'If he is really healthy, what I mean, if it's not T.B., you can still stay with us as long as you wish.'

'You didn't . . .' started Freda and then she sat passively, as usual, not even trying to participate in the conversation. We ate in a chilling atmosphere. I left for our room as soon as I had finished with the dishes.

The visit to our new doctor brought me a lot of joy and a lot of bitterness. The X-ray disclosed that Jozio's lungs were healed. The only way of turning my thoughts from the abortion was to keep on repeating that Jozio was well. And it didn't always work, either.

We were invited to a birthday party. Jozio was sparkling with pride; he had already met the birthday boy. His name was John and he lived next door. Ania advised us to start calling Jozio 'Joe'. Perhaps she was right. To Australians, the name was obviously difficult to pronounce. We tried it on a few people who used to buy 'the fresh farm eggs' from the farm. The result was a hair-raising, ear-grating disaster.

I explained to Jozio why we would call him Joe. He looked puzzled, but after having all the reasons listed, accepted the situation.

It was difficult to change one's own child's name and I kept on calling him Jozio when we were alone, when I bathed him, when I combed his hair, when I cuddled him.

But on the day of John's birthday party, Jozio was

Joe. We went together and Joe delivered the present which we had admired and bought that very day, a Dinky car. We said 'Happy Birthday' (which we had practiced for the whole morning, under the guidance of Ania). Apart from this, I didn't say much, except for 'thank you' when a cup of very strong tea was handed to me, and 'ta, ta', when Jozio — sorry, Joe — loaded with balloon, party hat, lollies and whistle, left the party.

In the evening, Joe summarised his first social outing to his father. He re-created how Alan and John and Jim had played either cowboys and Indians, or policemen and robbers, he wasn't sure which. The core of the matter was that one had to shout 'bang, bang' and 'Oooowwww', depending on whether one was shooting or being shot.

I listened to Joe and Julian, the two men in my life, who not so long before had borne names which had sounded warm and beautiful to me. I had to learn how to associate all my feelings with their new, foreign-sounding names.

SEVEN

Dear Uncle,

The money you sent us proved to be sufficient for a deposit on a house. Julek's boss has promised him a private loan of £100, and we have managed to secure another £100 as a second mortgage. I can't tell you how grateful we are. It would have been so much easier just to embrace you, so consider yourself embraced over and over again.

But wait till you hear about our house. First, I want to tell you that there is an English saying, 'My house is my castle'. This is exactly what our house is going to be. Plus, our refuge, our security, our dream come true. It is a two-bedroom brick veneer, an Australian invention. I won't bother you with technical details because I know that my explanation wouldn't satisfy your expert interest in the field. And besides, Julek would do it so much better. To tell you the truth, I don't really care what the construction of our 'castle' is. It's set in a garden which Julek calls 'the jungle' and which, I have no doubt, will blossom into a Garden of Eden where Jozio will play and fill his lungs with pure Australian air.

The houses in the street are similar to ours,

except that the others already have established gardens and some even have trees of the right size for little boys to play in. There are children in every house, about the same age as Jozio. There are dogs; one day Jozio will have one of his own. There are curtains in the windows. One day in the future, our house will have curtains too. The road is unmade, which doesn't worry us; it provides Jozio with all those lovely potholes. It's muddy only when it rains, anyway.

The other day something incredible happened to us. Jozio and I go past our house at least once a day. Just to check on it; it's more reassuring than pinching oneself.

A bread cart went by. You have to know that one doesn't queue for bread in Australia, one has it delivered to one's home. I think that the horses know their route better than the drivers; it's fascinating to watch these noble animals move from one house to another while the driver makes his delivery. They usually allow themselves a nibble at the grass which flourishes in our street in great profusion, before they move on to the house of the next call.

I don't think I have told you how I feel about Australian animals or rather animals in general. I really envy them. I wish I could understand the people around me in the same way as I understand them. And they understand me; the other day the dog from next door ran to me, licked my hands all over and wagged its tail. I often think that if a Polish cat or a chicken had arrived in Australia, they wouldn't have any difficulty in communicating with native-born animals. It's not the first time I wish I were an animal; I remember how during the war I wanted us all to change into dogs, or cats, so no German would question our Jewish background. Birds — birds would have been ideal. The sky is open to them, no passport, no visa needed. They move from country to country, free as . . . as birds. When I look at them in the garden, or high up in a tree, I often wonder if they have ever been to Europe, to Poland. I know most of the birds I see here; one which was new to me is the kookaburra, the native of this land who literally laughs at the whole world. I can imagine what a fright it must have given to the first settlers here! Can you? The strange land, not an unsewered house on an unmade road, but an unknown, huge continent, with dense, foreign vegetation. A few white men. Their first night in the bush. They must have shivered the whole night through; the nights are mostly cold here. They must have searched the sky for familiar constellations — there were none. They must have listened for familiar sounds, but the Australian trees rustle differently from European ones. They are harsher. There is little softness in them, a rather more primeval, basic sound. They must have waited for the morning to come, frightened, not knowing what wild animal might get them. At this stage in time no one knew much of Australia. It was still unknown what wild animals lived there. (As far as the Australian fauna is concerned, the only danger to humans comes from various snakes, spiders, land and sea insects).

But the early settlers didn't know what the immigrants of the 1940s know. The night fell quickly on them; there was not that slowly fading illuminating light that they had been accustomed in Europe. One moment it was light, and then suddenly pitch-dark. The strange sounds surrounded them, magnified by cold, fear of the unknown, perhaps hunger. Some must have dozed, dreaming some distorted dreams of England and their loved *ones as we dream of ours.*

They must have been awakened by birds. It would still have been dark, with a suggestion of morning to come. The birds would have sung, chirped and warbled, making sure no one was going to escape their reveille. And then all would have become quiet again, not a sound. The men must have waited for more, shivering in the morning bleakness. And then it would have come. The laughter, loud, penetrating laughter, gaining in volume, fading away, stopping abruptly. Reaching them from different directions. First it would have been one voice, then others would have joined in. Laughing, laughing. God almighty, who? A madman, a beast? The devil personified?

Once I tried to dissociate myself from my knowledge about the birds. I think that the sound might have been rather terrifying for someone uninitiated. Only when you know of the bird performing, sort of gargling its throat, only then do you think it's wonderful.

What I actually wanted to do, Uncle, was to try to draw a picture of Australia as I see it. These are just fragments, disjointed, as my whole orientation is.

The last time Jozio and I went for a walk, we came across a mountain of bread. Just on the side of the road. It must have been dropped by the bread cart and left unclaimed.

'Look, all this bread!' exclaimed Jozio. I looked. I wanted to take a few loaves home, but because nobody else did, I didn't dare. A mountain of bread going to waste. Even dogs didn't bother to scavenge it. There was only one canine glutton who nibbled at one loaf, then lifted his hind leg, left his mark, and wandered on. Passers-by didn't take much notice of the bread. Can you visualise what *would have happened to a heap of bread had it been dropped in Poland during the war years, or even now? That's Australia for you.*

Goodbye, Uncle. Sorry for rambling so much. Thank you for the loan, it will change our life completely, it will speed up our emancipation.

I'm glad you liked the photos we sent you. I knew the palm would appeal to you all. I spotted it on the very first day in Melbourne. As far as Ania and Freda are concerned, you are absolutely right. I do understand what it has meant to them to share their house with us; it has been nothing short of a revolution in their peaceful existence. I know I shouldn't have been so bitchy. Perhaps I crave for a place of our own too much? I will try to keep my temper under control. I really do appreciate what they have done for us.

My love to you all and please write even more often if that is possible.

Irena

We moved into our house early in September, just in time to welcome friends of ours to Australia. Franka had been a school teacher who I loved because of her understanding of my pretty complicated character. She and Leon had organised underground classes in the Warsaw Ghetto and while they had attended to their pupils, their one-and-a half-year-old son Ludwik had played patiently and silently in a corner of their dark and stuffy room. Miraculously, they had survived the war and when we learned of their intended migration to Australia, we were only too eager to share our house with them.

Our bank manager, who gave us a supplementary loan, was less eager. 'It won't work. Two women, one kitchen, it can't work.' He demanded the installation of an additional gas ring, 'in case the ladies start

throwing pots at each other. Comply with my request
— otherwise I will be forced to cancel the loan.'

We did as we were told. There was no point in
explaining, there was no way to make the manager
see that Franka and I differed from the normal, pot-
throwing Australian or Polish ladies. That we had
experienced living conditions he would never suspect
existed. That since the war, except for a short time in
France, we had always shared places with others, and
they hadn't always been people of our choice. To be
free and to have the whole house to share between the
two families seemed like a long-forgotten dream come
true.

How we loved our house! A Polish poet once said:
'My mother country is like health and only those who
lose it can know how to appreciate it.' That was how I
felt about a place of our own. I walked through the
house full of unspoken emotions, full of images of my
parental home, full of plans for the future. It seemed
unreal to me. Our walls, our floor, a permanent spot
for Joe's bed. Shelves on which to store the suitcases
never to be dragged across the world again. We'll
welcome our family here one day, I thought. The
happy thoughts, the contentment!

Julek bought a second-hand table for thirty shillings. It was a beautiful table, covered with the most
superb green lino. Why anyone would want to sell it
was beyond my comprehension. It wobbled only
slightly and one coat of paint would make it look like
new. As if that weren't enough, a delivery van
arrived. Three brand-new mattresses: one for us, one
for Franka and Leon, and one for Ludwik. Our
mattresses were enormous, four foot six; I tried ours
out even before the delivery man left our place. Joe
started to bounce on it. 'You'd better stop it. It's a
new mattress, to last us a lifetime,' I said. I was not

having my property damaged, not even by Joe. He was badly in need of a bit of discipline.

'What shall I do?' he asked, and suddenly I saw myself as a child. I was surrounded by the familiar walls of my parents' room. My hair was all over my face and my body was going high up and coming back down to the softness of my mother's bed. That feeling of forbidden joy seemed so real to me that I called back my 'undisciplined' son.

'You can bounce a bit more; but be gentle, won't you, Joe?'

'Yeah.' And he jumped up and down to his heart's content.

Meanwhile the carrier brought six wooden chairs. They were exquisite and cost twenty-five shillings each. It was extravagance on our part, but we needed somewhere to sit. I tried them all out. My stockings caught on one of them. I had only had them for a month or so. I exploded using every single swearword I knew in Polish, Russian and French. Obviously Australian furniture left a lot to be desired, but it wasn't the end of the world; one could sand the chairs to perfection, anyway.

Till Julek came home from work I kept myself busy cleaning the stove and the bathroom and the toilet and the ice chest Ania had lent us. Joe had gone outside and I could hear him chatting to the kids next door. How they communicated would always be a mystery to me. Once Julek arrived, I took him on a conducted tour of our castle.

We couldn't settle down till late. Joe slept in a room of his own for the first time in his life. Our room was next to his. The mattress was superb and we wondered whether a bed was really such a must. What was wrong with sleeping on the floor, especially if one was blessed with a mattress?

During the night I woke up. I walked through our

house, touching the walls; and then I went outside. It was chilly, but the sky was very clear. I looked at the stars and felt sad that my mother couldn't look at them with me. Our roads had separated, the sky above us was different, even day and night were at different times. The polar star which I had watched so many times as a child was beyond my vision, everything that I had known and that was part of me was far away. My family, those few precious friends who had survived the war, all of them were out of my reach. I stood under the foreign sky and searched for the Southern Cross, but I couldn't place it. Julek would have to learn where it was, because otherwise he wouldn't be able to show it to Joe as my father had shown the Northern Sky to me, in a far, far away land. I looked and shuddered and then Julek appeared and told me off.

'You must be out of your mind,' he said. 'What are you doing?'

'Watching the sky.'

'What for?'

'There's not even one star I know.'

'You'd better go to bed.'

'Not even one.'

'I'm going inside, coming?'

'Not even the Great Bear Constellation.'

'What's got into you?'

'Leave me alone.'

'I'm going in.'

'Joe will never know what the Great Bear and the Little Bear look like. The Polar Star.'

'Can't you leave this discussion till tomorrow? I have to go to work. Franka and Leon are coming. We'll have plenty to do. I thought you were happy. A new house, the first house of our own.'

'I'm happy, but I'm a bit sad.' Julek took me by my hand; we went inside. He rubbed my icy-cold legs and

then I went to sleep. I dreamt one of my war nightmares and got up happy to face the new reality, even
if under a foreign sky.

EIGHT

Franka and Leon arrived! We lived together for three years and never threw anything at each other, not even cooking pots. In Poland, Franka had been a secondary school teacher. Leon, a chemical engineer, as well as an economist, had occupied a high-ranking position prior to his arrival in Australia. Neither of them could have even hoped to find work in their field. Leon took the first job available, that of a factory hand.

Joe spent a lot of time with neighbourhood children, who, after discovering our backyard with its old, abandoned chicken shed, claimed it as their own territory. The garden was far from established. The only thing we cared about was to keep the grass at an acceptable level. Apart from this, I planted a few vegetables next to the fence. Joe inspected them every morning and when the time came, he gathered a few pods of green peas, or radishes, a carrot. I watched, unable to speak, it all seemed unreal to me. My child, my garden, freshness, an almost idyllic setting. Whatever the future might hold, this moment belonged to me.

Ludwik, who was renamed Louis, started at a local State school. His teacher came to see Franka and Leon because he was concerned about Louis. The boy was eleven and bright, but unfortunately his English was poor.

'I have two sons,' the teacher announced. 'I could send them both to spend some time with Louis. It should be beneficial and hopefully, will speed up the process of learning the language for your lad.'

The teacher's sons arrived at our place the following Saturday.

'And what is your name?' asked Leon in very stilted English.

'Adrian,' answered the boy.

'Adrian?' repeated Leon.

'No. My name's Adrian.'

'Oh, Adrian!'

'No. Adrian.' The boy was stamping in one spot, like a horse with its legs tied up.

'Hold on a moment, I have to say it properly. Now I know. Adrian.'

'Nope. A-d-r-i-a-n.'

'A-d-r-i-a-n?'

'No.'

'Dad, we want to go outside,' Louis was getting impatient.

'All right, then. Go, but you haven't introduced me to your other friend.'

'His name's Bill.'

'Hello, Bill. Now you can go and play.'

'Thank you, sir,' said Adrian, 'but my brother's name isn't Bill, it's Bill.'

We sat around the table, Franka, Leon, Julian and I. Once the boys left, we didn't know whether we should laugh or cry. Except for Julian, none of us had heard any difference between Leon's and the boy's pronounciation. Obviously there was one, but we couldn't detect it. We were bewildered. We discussed

67

the matter and reached the conclusion that something had to be done about it.

'We must learn the language,' said Leon. 'Especially our ladies. Because of my work I am in contact with Australians, which should prove more beneficial than a thousand lessons. But you two are cooped up at home; we'll have to think about it.'

We left it at that and spent the entire afternoon practising how to pronounce 'Adrian' and 'Bill'. Julian was our arbitrator and a very severe one too.

It was different for Louis and Joe; their command of English improved daily. Leon was progressing well too. He was a determined and a stubborn man. He would write down every word he didn't know which he came across during his working hours, or while reading the newspaper. In the evening he would sit at the table, armed with a dictionary and never take any part in the conversation till he had memorised them all. All Julian had to do was to cement his knowledge of English, which he continued to do with great success. Franka and I were bogged down, which meant that our Polish was flourishing and our English non-existent. We only learned, parrot-fashion, how to prepare the weekly shopping list for Mr Mac, the owner of the local general store. Ania initiated us into the mysteries of the proper terminology for cuts of meat, which enabled us to shop at the local butcher's. His name was also Mr Mac. Fruit and vegetables didn't cause any problem. Twice a week, a truck pulled up in front of our place — a fruit shop on wheels. The fruiterer, an Italian, was an easygoing and easy-to-communicate-with fellow. 'Give me this,' was our usual approach. 'Si, Signorina.' We lacked for nothing.

We had a doctor if needed. Milk and bread were delivered daily. Our house, because of the limited amount of furniture, was easy to clean.

Franka and I chatted all day long. I spent some hours tidying the front garden. Spring was in full swing. When it didn't rain or blow a gale, the weather was pleasant and most Sunday afternoons, we spent in a nearby park, which had a lake, a playground, and a large area was covered with Australian native trees and shrubs. But if the temperature reached twenty-five degrees, we complained and remembered with nostalgia the gentleness of a Polish spring.

Ania and Freda visited once a week. We usually called on them on a weekly basis, mainly to buy eggs, the so-called 'crackeds', and to hear what had taken place during the previous week. Because our visits took place during the weekend, we felt guilty for not working. Ania and Freda made sure we did: 'Chickens have to be taken care of during weekends too ... You are holidaying again, aren't you?'

Julian and Leon felt utterly ashamed till Monday when they resumed their work.

Once Julian finished assembling the textile machines, his bosses came to the conclusion that they didn't really need his services any more. They were quite capable of managing production themselves, thank you.

On the following day Julek together with Leon started on yet another career, this time in a joinery. All they had to do was to feed raw pieces of wood into a trimming machine. According to our men, the timber weighed half a pound in the morning, became progressively heavier, and towards the end of a working day, increased in weight to at least a ton.

Franka, the boys and I used to meet them at the bus stop. Leon dragged his feet, so did Julian; they looked like convicts returning from forced labour, but they still managed a smile; and gradually they got used to handling timber. If for nothing else, we were grateful for the Australian wages which allowed us to live decently, and even allowed Louis to continue with the violin lessons he had started in Poland, though it did drain his parents' finances considerably.

In the evenings, once the children had gone to sleep, the rest of us would gather around our very own lino-covered table. Franka was the one who was convinced that something had to be done.

'I would like us to have a house of our own one day. At present we spend nearly all Leon's wages. Unless I start earning, we'll never manage to put money away. The same applies to you.'

Of course Franka was right.

Julek suggested that perhaps we should form a partnership.

'Without capital?' questioned Leon.

I had a bright idea. Toy production. The ones available in Australia were of poor quality and lacking in imagination.

'Let's be serious about it. Without capital?' Leon was at it again. 'Without know-how?'

'Just a thought. It would be nice. Something creative ... Weaving, perhaps. I could start making wall hangings. Full of colours. Something like the Polish kilims.'

Neither Julian, nor Leon, nor Franka showed much enthusiasm. I don't even think they listened properly to my brilliant ideas.

'If you want to earn additional money, you must go to work,' concluded Leon. 'There's no other way.'

'I will stay at home as long as Joe needs me,' I protested.

'I might look for a job,' said Franka, and then she told us how it was during the war in the Warsaw Ghetto, when they were fleeing from deportation, hiding in deserted houses without any food and how Louis, aged five, had regretted he was not an ostrich because ostriches could fill their bellies with anything, even stones.

'Stop with all those horror stories. What's the point, another sleepless night?' Leon was really angry. 'We should look to the future.'

'But that's exactly what I am doing. What I want to say is how much I'm looking forward to building a new life where Louis' violin lessons won't be a problem. I have never worked with my hands. If you can do it, so can I, but I can't stop thinking of the past. And no one is going to stop me from remembering.'

When I went to bed, I couldn't settle down. I pretended I was asleep. I thought how lucky we were to see Joe growing in our new home, far away from problems and the horrible past. We had also gone through some pretty traumatic experiences during the war, but what we had experienced was nothing in comparison to what Franka and Leon knew. To fear not only for yourself but also for your child, who because of some insane law, had been condemned to death, was more than anyone could endure.

Outside the window it was dark. The Australian night reigned over this vast land. It was time to rest, to dream. Julek was peacefully asleep, breathing evenly, slowly. I couldn't sleep. *And no one is going to stop me from remembering.*

I knew nothing would come of my toy or kilim production.

If I was impractical, I couldn't help it. This was the way I was. I wasn't prepared to go to work if Joe were to suffer. I myself had been brought up by a number of governesses. During my whole childhood, there had been only a few days when our mother had looked after my sister and me. This had been when one of our governesses had left suddenly. A few unforgettable days when mother had spent the whole day with us. I could remember her soft touch; none of our governesses had washed me the way my mother had.

I couldn't remember when I had made the vow never to place my children, if I were to have any, in the care of paid surrogates, but that vow had been made and I still stood by it. All I wanted was harmony, and the pursuit of money had nothing to do with that. I wanted Joe to have time to listen to the stillness of the night in peace and with trust. I felt warm. I snuggled up to Julian. He mumbled something and continued with his sleep. I went to Joe's room. The air was fragrant with contentment and rest. I looked at my child's face and promised never to desert him, money or no money.

Ania introduced us to an English teacher who agreed to give us lessons. He worked in a local primary school. Franka's hopes and mine rose high. Our teacher was very tall and very English-orientated. Photos of Churchill and the King adorned the walls of his study. It became obvious to us that he knew very little about the Continent. He was even surprised that the Polish alphabet was the same as the English. After this discovery, he became very enthusiastic and presented us with two copies of 'John and Betty' books. He instructed us to follow the spelling list, starting with Grade 1. My mind rejected the similar-sounding words like mat, bat, sat, rat, and so on.

Once our teacher learned that Shakespeare was taught in Polish secondary schools, he became very excited, introduced us to his wife and decided to include Shakespeare in our lessons. His disappointment must have been great. Somehow, Shakespearian dialogue in the original English was impossible for us to follow. We had to admit that our vocabulary grew from lesson to lesson; we progressed from three- to

four-, sometimes even to five-letter words, nevertheless we never responded to *A Midsummer
Night's Dream*. We showed neither understanding
nor enthusiasm for it. I think that our teacher never
recovered from that experience. Perhaps he even
thought we were making fun of him. He trusted me
when I told him I was selected for the role of Puck in
our school production. He just couldn't understand
that the Polish version was different from the
original, and even if we were familiar with one, it
didn't automatically mean that we were capable of
understanding, even of reading, the other plays which
he wanted us to do together with his wife and
daughter.

We parted as good, though quite distant, friends.
There was no point in continuing with our lessons.

The next teacher, whom we met once again through
Ania, proved to be more than we had hoped for. He
was a young student of Economics and Russian at the
Melbourne University. He knew Russian better than I
did and to my surprise his pronunciation was almost
faultless. He assessed Franka's and my knowledge of
English as nil and advised us to start from the
beginning.

I feared he would introduce the three-letter words
again. I resigned myself and was ready to accept the
situation, because I had to admit I didn't know all the
words anyway. But our new teacher surprised us with
a textbook, *English for Foreign Students*. Harry came
to us once a week. He was a good teacher, intelligent,
quick and full of enthusiasm. His remuneration was
four shillings per lesson. He had a wife and a young
child. We made good progress — especially Louis,
who by the end of the school year was promoted to
Central school.

I enjoyed the lessons enormously. Our teacher was

the first Australian with whom we were able to communicate on an equal footing. He was eager to hear our experiences and in exchange offered us his own. We were sorry for ourselves, but glad for him, when he received a scholarship to do his postgraduate studies at the London School of Economics.

That was the end of my 'formal' learning of English, but by this time I was already able to read, usually the books I had read previously in Polish. Apart from this, Joe's mates were bringing more and more English to our place. Initially they were shocked and bewildered that a grown-up person didn't understand what they were talking about. 'Didn't your mother teach you how to speak?'

We were their first contact with foreigners, a contact for which they had not been prepared. I had to convince them that I could speak and, to prove my point, I selected difficult-sounding Polish, Russian, French, even Latin words.

When they tried to repeat them, their pronunciation was as bad as mine was in English. They were impressed, and we became good friends. Even Adrian got used to the way I pronounced his name. I even taught the children how to sing an old Russian song. But with their parents, contact was limited to 'hellos' when we met.

NINE

Gradually the circle of people we knew expanded, mainly through Ania's and Freda's 'fresh-farm-eggs' connections. We were introduced to a family who had settled nearby. Their name was Lloyd, the Anglicised version of their real surname, though it was difficult to see the derivation. They had emigrated from Poland and lived in a fully furnished house on a made road. They manufactured ladies' garments, mainly dresses. They descended on our peaceful household one spring evening, inspected the house and were not impressed.

Mrs Lloyd was huge. Her buttocks swayed while she moved around and she was never still. One of her eyes looked to the left, the other to the right. I never knew which one to look at, though it didn't really matter because she shifted them about as if they were equipped with zoom lenses. Mr Lloyd was also huge, taller than his wife, but somehow he seemed smaller.

'You should save some money and buy yourself a fridge. An ice chest is no good.' It was the first piece of advice Mrs Lloyd offered me. It wasn't the last.

'I see you hung pictures ... Who needs pictures? You don't know, but in Australia they are out of fashion. No one hangs pictures. You know what they put on their walls? Mirrors! Everybody has mirrors. And they are right. A room looks three times bigger and you can look at yourself too.'

'Yes, I know what a mirror is for,' I said, which I shouldn't have, because our compatriots might be the answer to our work problems.

Mrs Lloyd eyed me with her left eye or perhaps with her right one, I wasn't sure.

'You have a sewing machine?'

'No, I haven't.'

'You go and buy one. You have a sewing machine, I give you dresses to sew. You earn big money. You know how to make dresses?'

'I'm afraid I don't ... But I would love to learn. I always dreamed of sewing dresses.'

Franka looked at me with her two eyes as she used to look at me when I was a schoolgirl and slightly out of hand.

'Irena was always very good with her hands. I remember that her handicraft teacher was always very happy with her.'

'You know her from Poland? I thought you were just renting half a place from them,' said Mrs Lloyd.

'I used to be a teacher. Irena was my pupil.'

'No good. A teacher is no good for sewing,' Mrs Lloyd made a pronouncement. 'But you know what I'll do? I'll try you out anyway. I have a good heart — it's my weakness. My husband, Harry, always says: "Emma, you have a heart of gold, nobody has a heart like yours". If you don't believe me, you can ask him.' And before we had a chance to reassure Mrs Lloyd that we believed her, she called out, 'Isn't it true, Harry?'

'Is what true?' responded Mr Lloyd. He was in another room, where undoubtedly he was advising Julian what to do with our house.

'You know! What you always say about my heart.'

'You have a good heart, like pure gold.' Mr Lloyd called out, and Franka burst out laughing. Luckily, Leon happened to walk into the kitchen and channelled the conversation into safe waters.

'How long have you been living in Australia, Mrs Lloyd?'

'Almost two years. My family sent us permits straight after the war.'

'You were lucky,' said Franka.

'We were lucky? They are lucky! They were lonely before, now they have us; they have our son. You can't imagine what a boy he is . . . Your cousin told me you have a son too. How old?' Franka said, 'twelve'; I said, 'almost five.'

'My John's only three. He's twice as big as your Joe, your cousin told me. But it doesn't matter. You can bring him to my John's birthday party, next Saturday. John turns four.'

'I thought he's only three.'

'You don't know. In Australia you are three till you turn four,' explained our know-all friend. 'Harry,' she called out as if he weren't in the next room, or as if she wanted to wake Joe and Louis up.

'Would you mind, Mrs Lloyd, keeping your voice down. The boys are asleep.'

'If a child is asleep, he sleeps — don't worry. We have to go, anyway. We're working people. If we don't work, nobody gives us money.'

'You want to go — we'll go,' said Mr Lloyd, whose huge frame filled the whole doorway; but once he stood next to his wife, he shrank to become only the second-most-impressive figure in our midst.

'I'll tell you something, confidentially,' Mrs Lloyd looked at us all. 'I'll help you. I can't help it. I'll show you how to sew. You buy a high-speed machine. You work for a few hours and earn big money. You can cook and wash, you can clean and look after your son, and in your spare time you sew dresses and make money.'

'I haven't got the sewing machine; how much is it?', I asked.

'Not much,' smiled Mr Lloyd. 'For a new one you pay a hundred pounds. You can get a second-hand one for fifty plus.'

'Hm,' reflected Julian.

'You shouldn't think about it twice. The machine works for you. No machine, no money.'

'I do understand, but we haven't got that kind of money,' said Julian and I hated to see him embarrassed.

'Maybe you have something to sell? Gold, a watch, a bracelet, a ring?'

'I have a camera.'

'I won't let you sell your camera,' I said, because I knew how much Julian loved photography and how much it meant to him.

'What's a camera?' Mrs Lloyd offered her unsolicited opinion. 'You can't sew dresses with a camera; you can make money with a machine. So first you sell your camera and buy a machine and the machine will buy you a new camera. A better one ... Anyway, what kind of camera is it, how much is it worth?'

'I haven't priced it, I don't know. In Poland it was quite expensive.'

'Poland is one thing, Australia is another thing.'

'I'll make enquiries and let you know.'

'You do it quick — time is money,' Mr Lloyd summed up the whole situation ever so nicely.

I wished they would go. They were moving towards the door when Mrs Lloyd stopped and said: 'You know what, Harry ... I want to help them. You know me.'

'I know you,' said Mr Lloyd and looked at the ceiling — next best thing to the sky.

'You know what I'll do for you? ... I'll give you dresses for finishing. You come to me tomorrow and I'll teach you. I'm a teacher too, don't worry ... You have to pick up the dresses from my place; our car can't take unmade roads ... I pay well, more than anyone. Harry says I pay too much. Don't you, Harry?' 'Yes, Emma.'

When the Lloyds left, the house resounded with reflections on what had been said and Julian was reminded of a fellow who went to a zoo and for the first time in his life came face to face with a giraffe. He looked at the animal for a while and then, shaking his head, said: 'It's impossible. I still can't believe that such an animal can exist.'

Mrs Lloyd was as good as her word. On the following day she demonstrated to Franka and me the art of finishing dresses; but not before she had taken us on a conducted tour of her house, which she called her 'castle', after adopting and totally endorsing the old English proverb and, she quoted: 'what better castle can you have than your own home'. So there was something Mrs Lloyd and I had in common. I, too, was impressed with the British concept of home-as-castle and even mentioned it in my correspondence with my family.

Mrs Lloyd gave Franka and me twenty dresses and instructed us to return them on the following evening.

'It shouldn't take you any longer than three hours,' were her parting words.

I dreamed of finishing dresses the whole night through. How to hold the needle, how to fold the material, how to secure loose bits. There was nothing to it. All it needed was a few well-executed stitches.

Morning came only too soon. Julian and Leon, dressed in grey overalls, left home for work. Louis followed soon after.

79

'See you later, alligator,' he called to Joe; to which Joe never failed to answer, 'In a while, crocodile.'

While Franka cleaned the kitchen, I took Joe aside.

'Joe,' I said, 'we have to reorganise our life.'

He looked at me with a certain dose of suspicion. 'What d'you mean?'

'I'm starting to work.'

'I know. When I want to play with you, you always say you can't because you're working. And then you speak to Franka.'

'That's not fair, Joe. I play with you a lot ... But now I'll have less time to play with you. You see, Mrs Lloyd gave me some work to do. You remember Mrs Lloyd?'

'The one with the loud voice. I know.'

'That's quite irrelevant. The relevant thing is that you will have to help me.'

'What's relevant?'

'Important, you understand? Your daddy goes to work and you don't see him till the evening. I don't want to do that. To go to work, I mean, so I'll work at home. But you must not interrupt me too often.'

'How often?'

'Joe, you are not listening. I have to work. To help daddy to earn more money.'

'Why?'

'Because you can't buy things without money.'

'What things?'

'Oh, for goodness sake. I don't know ... A fridge, a bicycle, furniture, a matchbox car ... Would you like that?'

'Mm.'

'So now you know. You can play with Chris and Susie and the others ... And when I finish my work there will be plenty of time to play and read and sing ... Agreed?'

Joe didn't even answer, but ran outside. I heard him

telling his mates over the fence that his mother had started to work so she would be able to buy him a bicycle and plenty of matchbox cars.

Meanwhile Franka had transformed our kitchen table into a workbench and piled the dresses up high. We picked one dress each and smiled.

'D'you think we'll be able to do it?'

'We have passed more difficult exams in our lives.' We set to work in silence. Needle, thread, scissors, unfinished dresses. Everything was too big, or too small, or too impossible to handle. Franka's finger was bleeding, but she said it didn't worry her and not to interrupt the work. The dress was sliding from the table, the thread kept on tangling itself and the scissors were never to be found when needed. I wondered how Joe was managing without me and then his voice came loud and clear, perhaps to reassure me that all was well. Joe was using a peculiar mixture of Polish and English which was miraculously accepted by his friends. Just then little Chris was yelling to his mother that Joe used to live in a 'p-i-e-n-t-r-o-w-y' house.

'What on earth are you talking about?'

'Mum, Joe used to live in a two-storey house!'

'Why didn't you say so in the first place?'

'"P-i-e-n-t-r-o-w-y" sounds better, doesn't it, Mummy?' I couldn't catch and didn't understand anyway what the mother's reply was, but Chris was absent from our place for the next two days.

Finishing dresses proved to be a nightmare. On the first day Franka and I managed to do three, instead of twenty. Needless to say, Mrs Lloyd wasn't amused, especially when our work proved to be of an inferior and unacceptable quality. With a swift pull of one finger, she undid all the hems, which hurt more than our sore fingers and aching backs. We promised to be more careful and because Mrs Lloyd couldn't change her good heart and nature, she agreed to give us another chance. Franka's dream house was as far from realisation as ever and Joe wasn't ecstatic when I told him I couldn't buy a matchbox car as yet.

'What about the fridge?' he pressed on.

On top of everything else, we had to apologise to our men for not preparing tea.

I also dreamed of dresses again.

We were very stubborn, Franka and I. We kept on sewing, unpicking seams and doing them again. Joe was playing nearby; and I suffered the agonies of rejection. I was absolutely sure that Chris's mother had stopped her son from coming to our place because we were foreigners and because she didn't want him to associate with Joe, who introduced certain impurities into the English language. I tried to tell Joe stories, even interrupted my work to play with him; but it became clear to me that Chris was the one Joe wanted and needed. While he walked around miserable and while I suffered, Chris's and his sisters' voices kept on reaching us. Every time the children giggled, it sounded like a warning signal, a painful reminder of our isolation. I tried everything, I even played cowboys and Indians with my son. But Joe wasn't happy with me. He even told me that 'Chris knows much better how to die because it's not enough to fall to the ground when I say "bang, bang", but before you do, even before you shut your eyes, you have to give a speech.'

Joe was cross because I wouldn't allow him to go and play with Chris. I doubted whether he had understood my lecture on the subject, in which national pride was the main theme.

On the third day, I decided that the matter had to be cleared up, otherwise I would never be able to satisfy Mrs Lloyd's growing demands, or to satisfy myself regarding the role and the place of a migrant in my adopted land. While Joe was taking his afternoon nap, I was drawn by children's voices towards the gate. I was ready to confront Mrs MacAllison. I had already spent two sleepless nights and two miserable days rehearsing words worthy of a major Greek dramatist.

The moment of truth arrived. Mrs MacAllison was weeding.

'Hello, Mrs MacAllison,' I said. The lady in question must have felt guilty, because she stopped her work and even before she got up, she said: 'Hello Mrs Lewitt. Chris, look who's here. Say hello to Mrs Lewitt.' Prompted by their remorse-ridden mother, the children, even the little Pam, said 'Hello Mrs Lewitt.'

'How's Joe feeling?'

'How could he feel? Lonely without Chris.'

'I want to play with Joe, Mum.' The child was obviously moved by my plea.

'I told you once if not a hundred times, you can't.' Mrs MacAllison's voice was very firm. She had to be firm, having three children and while I was trying to phrase my next point and wondering what argument to use to make her see that Joe had a right to play with her children, especially Chris, she said:

'You are sick, Chris. You don't want to pass on the germs to Joe, do you?'

I couldn't believe my ears. Chris was sick, the best news I'd heard for a long time! 'Who is sick?' I wanted to make sure. Mrs MacAllison pointed at her children. 'They all are. Chickenpox.'

'What is chickenpox?'

'Chris, Helen, Susie! Come here. Show your chickenpox.'

Before I even had a chance to recover from the initial shock, the children, helped by their mother, had bared their blistered and spotty backs to me.

'Mrs MacAllison,' I exclaimed, 'your children are sick!'

'Precisely. Nothing to worry about, only a few spots,' she answered in her off-handed way.

'Shouldn't they be in bed?'

'No need.'

'I hope they will be all right soon.'

'But they are all right, as you can see.'

I didn't know how to react. Whenever I was sick as a child, I had to stay in bed and wasn't allowed to go outside for days. I wondered what kind of a mother Mrs MacAllison was. Poor children, denied the right to stay indoors while suffering from some dreadful disease.

'Goodbye,' I said curtly.

'See you,' replied Mrs MacAllison, followed by three young voices.

I went inside, full of indignation, uncertain whether I should allow Joe to associate with the children of Mrs MacAllison. I stood over Joe's bed while he slept, this unique sleep of a child, and I watched him. They like you, I tried to tell him, you are not rejected, my son. He breathed evenly, his eyelids so smooth, every little blood vessel visible. His hair blond, after my mother who introduced the colour into our family. A pang of regret that the grandmother couldn't see her grandson. Joe stared as though aware of my presence. If only our family were with us. In a life like ours, where there had been so much horror and sadness, so little joy, only a child could bring back some meaning into our lives.

Joe opened his eyes and I lifted him up. He smelt of sleep and radiated the warmth of contentment. I told him of Chris. I rocked him in my arms and sang him a song I remembered being sung to me when my mother had held me in her arms.

We are few in numbers
To bake bread.
Only you, little Irena,
Only you can help us.

My mother and I, and then we had sung for my sister Tania, and then the three of us had sung for my father. We had formed a continuously expanding circle. My grandparents had come to join in with us, all of us swaying, laughing, singing. And the governess and my beloved Kazia, our servant.

Here in Australia, our circle was limited. *We are few in numbers* I sang and we turned around, and around, and around, Joe and I.

Joe got his chickenpox all right. Our doctor wasn't concerned and told me that it was a very mild disease, hardly in need of attention, or even confinement in bed. I reminded him of our Polish tradition, at which he smiled and said that the approach to sickness had changed and that one should put trust in a child's instinct to know when to rest and when to play.

'Make sure he drinks a lot; rest is not really important.' I decided our doctor must have been contaminated by the Australian influence. I kept Joe in bed, though it wasn't easy. Whenever I left his room, he would jump out of bed and I would find him next to the window, ready to catch pneumonia.

It was amazing that he recovered. By this time Chris, trailed by his sisters, had rediscovered our backyard.

TEN

Dear Tania,

How good it was to get your letter. If you only knew how much your letters mean to me, you would write every day.

You in love! Congratulations, sister. I loved Jan's letter; he has a way with words; he must be a fine journalist. And a fine person.

You often used to express doubts whether you'd ever marry. And here you are, getting married soon!

I can't stop thinking of you and mother and Jan and the war and of life in general. Sometimes I think there must be something wrong with me. Have you ever tried to trace your thoughts and the direction they are heading? It is an experience worth attention. When I received your letter, guess what sprang to my mind?

Remember that dashing Russian soldier? What was his name? Andrusha, Vanka? I can't even remember. The Warsaw Uprising. Mounting, threatening smoke, the ever present barrage; and that Andrusha, or Vanka, or whatever his name was, stepped in with his squeeze-box, put his legs firmly on the trembling ground, hugged his instrument

*and sang those haunting Russian songs. You and I
stood nearby, watching the tormented Warsaw sky
and wondering why those Russians were so
indifferent to what was going on around them,
singing songs of love and hope, at a time when hate
reigned supreme.*

*'You shouldn't watch Warsaw,' Andrusha, or
whatever his name was, said. 'Look behind the
front line,'* ·he smiled. Tomorrow, tomorrow, another battle, it's our destiny, *he sang. I watched
him, his open, strong face, and couldn't accept that
on the following day, he would go into battle
again, and that every day would take him farther
away from his land. Every day survived would
bring him eye to eye with death and suffering and
madness. He sang, his body swaying, and his
comrades joined in; five, six of them formed a
group and sang together. Their voices were rich,
strong and harmonious, and mother said that the
ability of the Russians to sing stemmed from the
lifelong tradition of the Orthodox Church. I
argued, as always, and thought mother biased and
anyway I wanted to hear their songs.* Fly away
nightingale. I can't sleep because of you. We're at
war, the guns spit fire, you shouldn't be here. You
make me remember my home, the willow where
you always sang. Fly away, little bird, I want to
sleep without dreams.

*I was bewitched by the words, by the beautifully
blended voices, by the scenery, by the agony of
Warsaw and her people, by the pain of every
mother who had a son at the front line.* Fly away,
little bird. I have to rest before the next battle.

*A few days later, the offensive started. Every
regiment stationed in Zielonka moved towards
Warsaw. We never saw Andrusha, or Vanka, or
whatever his name was, again.*

Why am I getting sidetracked in a letter which is meant to congratulate you? Perhaps because I remember how sad you were when that Andrusha left. You hardly knew him, but you were certain you would never be able to fall in love again. I often thought those army men were hardly real. Dashing, full of life one day, killed, or worse, maimed, the next.

This letter is like our never-ending discussions with Franka and Leon. They start in the normal way and then are drawn to the war years. Perhaps it has something to do with the Korea War and the general political unrest. It frightens me that Jozio might be drafted one day. The Cold War, the Iron Curtain, division ... And to think that only a few years ago representatives of both blocs shook hands in victory. I often wonder whether we, the survivors of the war, have a better understanding, a more complete appreciation of life? I thought I had till I met my boss. This Mrs Lloyd and her husband have survived numerous concentration camps, have lost their entire family; nevertheless she is capable of being really mad because Franka and I manage to finish only eight dresses instead of twelve, as though the future of mankind depended on it. Once I found her almost in hysterics because her little boy had smashed a vase which had been given to her as a present.

By the way, Franka and I are getting quite skilful in our work, though I can't see either of us being able to finish fifteen dresses a day, which Mrs Lloyd considers the bare minimum. We'll see. Franka is planning to look for a job in a factory, where the conditions are better and of course the pay is too.

Jozio, whom we call Joe now, was invited to the Lloyd son's birthday party. I sent him dressed in a *white shirt, grey shorts, and a pair of new sandals. When I picked him up, he seemed quite happy, his hands loaded with sweets and a balloon, the party hat sitting on his head ... Remember your birthday parties and how jealous I always was because I never had any? How I resented that my mother gave birth to me in July when everybody was on holidays; it would have been different had I been born in Australia, July is just in the middle of the school year — then you, Tania, would have missed out on your birthday parties.*

Back to Joe. 'How was it?' I asked him. 'Very nice, mummy, but next year I would like to wear my heavy boots instead of sandals.' 'Why, do they pinch?' 'No. They're alright; but John kicked me and when I kicked him back it didn't really count, a sandal kick isn't much. But next year, if I wear boots ...' That's your nephew for you!

I do regret that I'm not with you now. Congratulations, Tania. I wish and trust that you'll be happy. Give my love to Jan and to mother. I'll be writing to her soon ...

ELEVEN

All of a sudden, it was summer. It was hot, so hot that we could hardly breathe. We opened all the windows to let the fresh air in. We just couldn't understand why our neighbours kept their houses hermetically sealed. Our whole street was transformed into a street of the damned, where every house had its curtains carefully drawn. Nothing moved, except for an occasional passer-by, or a car. There was the persistent and ever-present rapid clicking of cicadas, who found our unmade road, with its growing number of cracks, irresistible.

Our greengrocer, as always punctual, arrived in front of our house without his usual vigour. His vegetables were all limp, but the man urged us to buy anyway, because on a day like this, one had to eat a lot of fresh fruit and vegetables. I bought what was needed and listened to our greengrocer's advice that in weather like this, one should keep busy and eat a lot of greens. 'Trust me Signorina, I know.'

Franka didn't feel the best and we decided not to work on Mrs Lloyd's dresses till the evening, when the temperature should drop.

I wanted to do something; and then I remembered our gate. Ever since we had moved into our house,

Julian kept repeating that the following weekend he was going to paint it for sure. Weeks changed into months and our gate looked more and more out of tune with the rest of the house. Today is the day, I thought. I took the brush and the paint. Franka helped me to read the instructions, which wasn't easy even with the dictionary. Seeing how eager I was, Joe agreed to take his afternoon nap and promised to stay inside till I finished my task.

I went outside. The heat, such as I had never experienced before, was intolerable. The footpath felt like burning coal and I had to go back into the house. I was sure my feet had developed blisters; to my amazement, they had not. Summer, warmth, light clothes, barefooted freedom — not in Australia, I thought. I encased my throbbing feet in sandals and braved the outside inferno once again. To save time, I kept on shaking the tin of paint all the way to the gate, which was waiting for me to cover its rusty spots. 'Don't worry, gate,' I said in an intimate tone, 'soon you'll be as white as Polish snow, as clean as a Polish mountain brook.'

I decided to skip the surface preparation, which must have been devised for people who had nothing to do. My time was limited and I was determined to finish my task before Joe got up. After all, the gate was craving to be painted and that was exactly what I was determined to do. To my amazement, the paint looked and felt like cream. Great, I thought. I moved the brush up and down, across and sideways. My hand felt tired. Never mind, keep on working, I reminded myself. The paint got slightly discoloured. It must have been from the rust and the dust. I didn't worry, being more than sure that the next coat would transform our gate into a thing of rare beauty. By the time I had finished the first coat, the paint on the top rod had already dried. Just in time for another layer. I came to the conclusion that hot weather had certain advantages and though it was difficult to breathe, or to move a finger — not to mention the whole arm — one was compensated by the drying properties of hot wind and air.

The paint was getting thicker, but I thought it was even better because it gave a good cover. By this time, my newly acquired skill was showing. I dripped less paint (but I still dripped profusely with perspiration, which turned out to be beneficial and allowed me to thin the paint whenever I thought it necessary).

Our iceman pulled up at the gate. 'What are you doing?' he asked, while balancing a block of ice, wrapped in a hessian bag, on his shoulder. What a stupid question, I thought.

'I'm painting the gate, as a matter of fact, the second coat!' I said, not concealing my pride in a job well done.

'Ain't it a bit too hot for painting?'

'The paint dries more quickly in weather like this.' From our conversation, it became obvious to me that our iceman had little experience of painting. Perhaps he was keen to learn all the tricks of the trade; he watched me for a while.

'D'you mean you painted the second coat on the same day as the first?' he asked, while our ice kept dripping all over his body.

'As a matter of fact, I only started half an hour ago,' I boasted.

'You did?' he asked with obvious admiration, envy and amazement.

'Mhhh.' I looked at him with pride. He opened his mouth as if he wanted to say something.

'Good God!' he shouted, suddenly realising that the ice had melted to half its normal size. He said something under his breath which I didn't understand and for which he apologised. He replaced the quickly diminishing ice with a full-size block and headed towards the kitchen door.

A few more strokes; a touch here; a touch there. Finished! The second coat was finished. The gate was almost dry and ready for the third coat. Thirsty, I was really thirsty and, besides, the flies were pestering me. 'Don't worry, gate, I'll be with you in a few minutes — you really look great,' I patted it. A bit of paint stuck to my palm, but it didn't really matter because the third coat was going to cover up all imperfections.

'I've come in for a drink.' It was very hot inside. Franka was standing at the stove. The iceman helped himself to a drink of water, to which he added a few chips of ice. Then he poured out two more glasses and handed them to Franka and me. The water tasted divine; cold and refreshing. I wondered what my mother would have said had she known I drank water with ice. I knew I was running the risk of tonsilitis, flu, perhaps even pneumonia. The iceman didn't agree and tried to convince Franka and me that cold water had nothing to do with colds. I could have used many examples drawn from my personal experience. I could have told him all about my childhood diseases which were undoubtedly caused by my uncontrollable desire for ice-cream and cold drinks. I could have; but I didn't bother, because my gate was waiting for me.

It was as dry as pepper. I looked at it. It had developed slight wrinkles, which the third coat was going to cover, without fail. Luckily for me, the remaining paint had thickened even more, so I was sure I would be able to solve this ticklish problem once and for all. The paint felt like butter and it was increasingly difficult to spread it around.

'You at it again?' The iceman was going back to his delivery cart. The way he looked at me showed his admiration. He probably hadn't met many women who were capable of painting an entire gate in just over an hour. Three coats, too!

'Pardon me for interfering,' said the iceman, '. . . but if I were you, I would keep all the doors and windows shut till it cools down.'

'The trouble is, you don't understand. We firmly believe in fresh air. When it's hot, you should let the air circulate. You know what I mean? There is nothing wrong with letting fresh air in. If I were you, I would try it. It's the old European tradition. We always keep our windows open when it's nice and warm.'

'Lady, it's not "nice and warm", it's bloody hot. Do as you wish, lady . . . And good luck with your painting,' he called from his cart. He was a nice man, brown and muscular, but I always felt sorry for him. The poor man didn't have one decent shirt. His arms were always bare, the sleeves missing. I decided to look through Julian's shirts. Perhaps I could find one which would fit the man, though he seemed taller and bigger than Julian. Anyway, it was his wife's worry, not mine. I had a job to complete. I waved to the moving icecart and went back to my work. The brush had become somewhat stiff, but because there were only a few last bars to be covered, I persisted. The hot wind was really vicious, but I disregarded my personal discomfort, realising how beneficial the wind was for paint-drying purposes. I looked at my new-looking gate with adoration. The value of our house must have almost doubled. I had to admit there were still some wrinkles left and also some insects which must have found their death in the painted surface, but one shouldn't be too pedantic. There was some paint left and, though the brush felt more like a stick, I was determined to use all the paint. I covered the wrinkles and the insects. On the way inside, I pondered whether I should consider gate painting as my vocation. It was more interesting and challenging than dress finishing. I wanted to discuss it with Franka, but when I reached the kitchen she was not there, and pots were boiling unattended. I turned the flames down.

I found Franka sitting on the hall floor in a state of total exhaustion.

'I can't take it any more. It's a real inferno.' I brought her some water.

'The dinner,' she said in a weak voice. 'The men must have a proper meal.'

'Don't worry, relax. I'll take care of everything. The gate's finished.'

'How does it look?'

'Perfect. All white. The wind helped to dry it.' Franka drank the water and then asked me to open the front door a bit wider, which I did before I went back to the kitchen to attend to the roast and the vegetable soup. Another half an hour and the meal will be ready, I thought. I went to Joe's room. He was still asleep. The whole house felt very uncomfortable. It was even hotter inside than out. Joe was drenched; the sun had invaded his room and the wind, which blew with almost cyclonic force, tossed the curtains. If our curtains had not been made of good continental material, they would have been reduced to shreds, I was certain. I stood in the middle of the room, not sure what to do, where to turn, looking from Joe to the window.

Someone shrieked, someone laughed, someone giggled. Who was it? I walked to the window. I couldn't believe my eyes. Mrs MacAllison was standing in the centre of the lawn and watering her children! No wonder they cried. The woman must be totally irresponsible, hosing defenceless little children. I had never seen an act like this in my life. I looked and looked, and in the end caught Mrs MacAllison's eye.

'Send Joe over,' she called laughing. 'It would do him a lot of good to join in the fun.'

'Very nice of you to ask, but no, thank you.'

'Please yourself,' she answered, and kept on watering her children.

Joe got up hot and exhausted; Louis arrived from school and slumped down next to his mother. By the time Leon and Julian reached home, it was getting overcast and the hot wind was tearing the whole house — and us in it — to pieces.

'What has happened to the gate?,' asked Julian in a weak voice. His question brought me back to life.

'I painted it. Surprise for you!'

'What's that smell?' asked Leon, instead of greeting us in his usual warm manner; which reminded me that I hadn't turned the gas off, which I had intended to do when Joe woke up screaming. Our whole dinner was burnt to cinders.

By the time we were ready to sit down at the table, our backdoor slammed and when I opened it again the wind was cold, as if blowing directly from the Antarctic.

It was the first time we ate a cold tea.

On the following morning, it was raining and cold. The gate had developed blisters. I cried. My career as a gate painter ended before it had started. It was back to dress finishing for me.

Dear Mother,
Immigration is not easy. I don't mean in the material sense, but rather in moral and general terms.

The Australian summer is intolerably hot, the temperature can reach forty plus; we were not prepared for that. Luckily, there exists something called 'a cool change', which means a sudden drop in temperature of up to twenty degrees in a matter of minutes. We have to be on the alert all the time and have cardigans ready at a minute's notice. I remember how at home almost all our woollies were stored in naphthalene flakes for the whole summer.

I don't know, but the first summer didn't worry us as much as this one. Perhaps because we spent it with Ania who persisted in shutting the windows whenever I wanted to let some fresh air in. I was absolutely convinced she was doing it to annoy me. Now I know better and must apologise to her.

The houses here are of light construction and not properly insulated — therefore we suffer. But we have to remember what is more important, that they are within the reach of an average family. Our neighbours are all working-class people. They are buying their houses on small deposits and long-term repayments. For all ex-servicemen, the conditions are even more favourable. Could you imagine Poland or Russia offering benefits like this?

Yes, Australia has plenty to offer, in a material sense, anyway. Once I thought that if the persecution would stop, if the war would end, if we would regain our freedom, if Joe would have enough milk and be healthy, I wouldn't wish for anything else. How mistaken I was! Is greed common to us all, or is this my very own strain of it? I thought I would be less demanding because of what I had witnessed during the war.

I think it was in 1944. New Year's Eve; the carbide lamp; a general state of lethargy among us all. The front was quiet; the Warsaw Ghetto didn't exist any more; and the 'Final Solution' was being executed with German precision. It was freezing. By the way, I can't get used to the fact that in Australia we might celebrate New Year during a heatwave, another aspect we have to get used to.

Sorry, mother, for bringing 1944 back to you, but it's so much part of me that I can't help it. Sometimes Franka and I, not sometimes but, to be precise, quite often, recall the war years. Usually while the men are at work. Leon gets angry whenever we mention the war.

We are halfway through the twentieth century. I don't know why I have to bring 1944 back to my mind. Perhaps because I still remember the hopelessness of our situation and the strong desire to survive, to have the chance to live life as a free person. We sat around the table, 'celebrating' and welcoming 1944. We were cold and hungry and decided to greet the new year according to Moscow standard time, which was two hours ahead of Warsaw. We said: 'only to be free, nothing else'. We were ready to sign an agreement to spend the rest of our lives performing the duties of a caretaker, or a street sweeper, or a rubbish collector. Anything, as long as we were free. That was our dream, our only sincere desire.

The war ended, we are free. We have settled in Australia, where the standard of living is unparalleled by any other country in the world. What puzzles me is this: why am I not completely happy? Why do I moan about the weather? Why can't I get used to gum trees instead of dreaming of pine forests and the crisp whiteness of December, January, February. Is it nostalgia? How is it possible that after only three years of absence, I think of Poland with warmth, being at the same *time totally aware that the Polish authorities issued us a one-way exit visa?*

Julek, though he works as a labourer, brings home enough money to keep us going and to repay the mortgage on the house. What I earn will give us a chance to buy luxuries like an electric refrigerator, furniture and one day in the future perhaps even a car. We have plenty to eat, neither fruit nor sugar is a problem and I have even prepared some jam for the winter. We are decently dressed. And what's more important, Joe has fully recovered. He is a normal, healthy, happy child of four. He spends most of his time playing outdoors with his Australian friends. I do appreciate that, mainly because I remind myself that back in Poland I had to take him for walks which never lasted longer than an hour, two at the most. I remember the queues. I remember my winter coat made from a worn-out army blanket. Here in Australia I have everything. I should be ecstatic with happiness, but I am not. Is it the remoteness, loneliness, estrangement? I went to the city the other day to look at sewing machines (we plan to buy one as soon as Julek sells his camera).

I looked at the strange buildings, the traffic, people, police. The streets have alien names which I can't even pronounce. I looked at it all; the shops were spilling over with luxurious, well-displayed goods; the police controlled the traffic without carrying guns; the crowd hurried with an air of contentment. A vibrant metropolis; but there was not even one familiar face in it all. On the way home, I shared the train compartment with a family. Three generations, including four very noisy children. How I envied them! Suddenly uncle Miron came to my mind. You know I was never too fond of him. He used to pinch my cheeks and his fingertips were stained with nicotine. I thought of him and his tragic end. Perished, as has our whole way of life. And aunt Anna with her cluster of warts. Would you believe me if I say that I would give anything for Joe to have an aunt somewhere near, even with warts, even with aunt Anna's famous temperament.

It's not easy to establish ourselves without the support of you all. I can't reconcile myself to the fact that we have left you behind. I regret that we have parted. To survive the war and then to separate has been an unforgivable step.

We are lucky to have Franka and Leon with us, though Leon laughs at me whenever I bring up the subject. 'You and your wart theory again.'

What worries me is the fact that Joe and Louis are growing in an artificial environment. No one is being born; no one is being taken care of; no one is in need of attention, advice; no one is gravely ill; no one dies. It really frightens me. There is no one to spoil the boys, to pinch their cheeks, except for their very busy and often impatient parents. A child needs this additional warmth, this unreserved adoration not for any special reason but simply because he belongs to a certain clan whose members can't be impartial, nor should they be.

Sorry for all this rambling, but I wanted to tell you how much I miss you. Things are not really as bad as I have painted them. But you know me and my unique ability to complicate the issues.

We haven't received the permit yet. Why hasn't Jan sent his particulars? You must be aware by now how long it takes to obtain the necessary papers.

Please write as often as you can. Look after yourself.

Irena

P.S. Leon met a fellow, also from Poland, who told him that apparently Victor lives in Melbourne. I'll try to locate him. I'm quite excited by the possibility of meeting someone I knew during my teens. If I succeed, I'll let you know.'

TWELVE

Louis celebrated his twelfth birthday. His parents bought him a second-hand bike; we bought him a dog.

Louis was happy beyond description and declared that to have a bike and a dog was all he had ever dreamed about. He spent the whole day outside walking around the backyard, holding the dog with one hand, and wheeling the bike with the other. Joe kept him company. In the evening Louis tried to smuggle his newly acquired treasures inside, but was stopped by his father, who maintained that they were not to be kept in the house. In the end the bike was placed on the back porch, while the dog slept in the laundry. Louis kept on returning to make sure his precious possessions were still there.

The night was oppressive. The cicadas sang their song with the same perseverance as the north wind blew hot air.

Once the children had settled down, we adults wanted to stay outside, but the mosquitoes drove us into the house. We sat around the table, we drank a toast to Louis' health. We drank to all those who were dear to us but far away.

'This was the first proper birthday Louis ever had,' said Franka.

Long after I went to bed, I thought of what she had said. The mathematics were simple enough. Louis had been born in 1939. Before he had turned one, Poland was already engulfed in war. Louis had taken his first steps in the Warsaw Ghetto while his parents tried desperately to make ends meet. Somehow they had managed to survive. They had obtained false Aryan papers, they had lived through the turbulent weeks of the Warsaw Uprising. In 1948, they had been on the move again. Poland, Germany, France, and the unenviable status of displaced persons.

During our stay together, I learned how to finish and sew dresses. Joe went through kindergarten and started at the local school, where I sent him dressed in all his glory, a grey suit, white shirt, tie and shoes which were always shiny. He was the only one attired like a true English college boy, though he was the only foreigner in his class. Louis progressed to high school. Franka found herself a job in a clothing factory, where she earned much more than I did. Julian changed his job once again, this time to a textile factory, where he was put in change of maintenance and was assigned to a foreman who was still studying to improve his qualifications and who sought Julian's expert opinion all the time.

My English was still pretty basic but I didn't mind it too much any more, except when Joe spoke it during the heatwaves. The combination of unbearable sweltering and unfamiliar sounds was too much for me. I still would not recognise the merit of the Australian landscape and constantly referred to the Polish pine forests and rolling plains as the ultimate harmony in nature.

Our life with Franka and Leon was a happy one. Of course we had the normal disagreements. Franka must had dreamed of having her own place, her own way of putting the dishes away and deciding what to cook without endless consultations. The main reason they moved away was my pregnancy; or perhaps it was an opportune moment to part. I was sorry when they left, though gradually I got accustomed to life on our own.

I greeted my pregnancy with mixed feelings. I was delighted with the prospect of having another child, but was unsure about how we would manage on one salary. Apart from this, I couldn't forsee how Joe would react to the prospect of sharing his ever-ready parents with a new competitor. He was almost seven and had been treated as a true Prince of Wales. We explained very carefully that our family was going to enlarge.

'Why?'

'You see, son, there is nobody else in Australia but the three of us.'

'What about Franka? Louis, Leon?'

'It's not what I mean. We are lucky to have them, but it will be nice to have another person whom we can love and who will love us, another member of our family.'

'Is that all?' asked Joe and when I nodded, he ran outside and told his friends that he would have a brother soon, or perhaps a sister.

My pregnancy proceeded normally and I continued with all my usual activities, including sewing, as before. During the winter, we froze more than we had ever done in Europe. The only time we felt relatively warm was while chopping wood for our always hungry fireplace. Only when we bought a slow-combustion heater did our house become bearable and stop smelling of dampness.

Spring came; and Joe was given his first smack at school. I spent a sleepless night wondering why my child was punished in such a way and when a kookaburra greeted the new day with its laughter, I took it as a bad omen. Birds mock at us, teachers hit our small children because we are foreign, I thought. It was an obvious conclusion; I couldn't believe that a teacher would smack a young child just because he didn't put away a pencil when asked to do so. I waddled to the school half a block away — my son objected to my company in the most persuasive way. And I had to admit it was more fun to run with one's friends, instead of being subjected to constant interrogation by one's mother. 'I told you everything, there was nothing else to it. Everyone gets smacks.' My poor, naive son kept on repeating. No matter what he told me, no matter what Julian had to say, I was sure that my son was discriminated against because he didn't belong to this harsh land.

It became more and more difficult for me to move; I was huge, though my confinement was still four months away. I had difficulty in keeping up with the children, when suddenly they stopped. I thought, how noble of them, and then I noticed that they all went through some ritual of spitting and shouting before they set off again at high speed. When I reached the place of their strange activity, I realised it was a convent school. I just couldn't believe it. Australian children spitting at a Catholic school! And then I remembered all the anti-Semitic remarks I had heard throughout my life, and the Catholic Church's policy of non-interference during the war and I was glad I had lived to witness such an incident. What a country Australia is. I thought, what a beautiful country! But then I looked at the children's faces and felt totally ashamed. I was determined to have a good talk to Joe, so that he would never again take part in an incident such as I had witnessed.

Joe's teacher was glad to see me.

'Joe is doing very well, he is a lovely boy, well

behaved, attentive.'

'So why did you hit him?'

The teacher was still well composed though slightly embarrassed.

'Oh, you are referring to yesterday, aren't you?'

'Yes,' I said, and almost cried.

'Mrs Lewitt, if I hit a child, it's for his own good.'

'We never hit Joe. What right have you to do it?'

'I have every right,' she said.

And then I learned that corporal punishment is legal in Australian schools. I couldn't believe it. It didn't exist in Polish schools. I argued with the teacher as eloquently as I was capable; she was eager to hear more about Polish educational methods, but she had to return to her classes. She smiled at me and even shook my hand. I felt much happier on the way home. I realised that the smack hadn't been introduced into the Australian school system in order to persecute my little boy. Had I known, I would have spared myself all the pains of the uninitiated, but then I wouldn't have witnessed the children's behaviour in front of the Catholic school. I was determined that my child, the child of parents whose life had been maimed by blind hate, would never lower himself to the rank of an abhorrent thug.

There was so much to do, there was so much to learn, so much to share. There was so much life to live. My baby moved inside me as if wanting to reassure me that, for once, I was right.

Yet another summer came. The heat, the north wind, the thirsty soil. The season of ice-cream, cold-plate dinners and trouble-free washing days. While I worked at the sewing machine, the material piled up on my belly. I wondered whether my Australian baby would like the heat. I dreamed of a cooler climate and one day when the temperature soared to the forties,

Julian asked what I wanted. 'A pine forest,' I shouted back, and ran to the bathroom where I shut myself in and sat in the bath pouring cool water all over myself. I only hoped my baby wouldn't catch a cold.

On Sunday, Julian took us to the Yarra bank. We sat in the shade of a gum tree. Julian read to Joe, who kept on interrupting him. Obviously he was more interested in what was going on on the river. He had developed an irritating habit of answering us in English and was even demanding that we should buy him English books. I didn't like them. Luckily we had a family in Poland who sent us books worth reading. I stretched out under the tree. Its crown was made of masses of constantly moving silver stripes. I had never noticed this before. Silver stripes, the enamel-blue sky, the splash of the river, which I couldn't look at because my belly mounted to the sky. I was almost convinced that gum trees have something to offer; and then there was a crashing sound and without any further warning, one of the huge, silver-striped branches landed next to me. Julian bent over me, a couple rushed to where we were.

'Joe, where is Joe,' I cried.

'He's all right, over there. He's right,' Julian said in his well-controlled voice. 'And you?'

And the couple asked, 'Are you all right?'

I was, except for feeling slightly shaken.

'Never sit under a gum tree when it's hot,' the woman advised us, 'they crack from the heat.'

On the way home, I questioned the use of a tree you couldn't sit under. But when I went to bed, the silver stripes and the blue sky danced in front of my eyes.

THIRTEEN

At long last Leon gave me Victor's address. I was impatient to see him as soon as possible. Julian was less enthusiastic and argued that he had much better plans for the weekend than to visit a man I had known when I was a child.

'I was thirteen then, hardly a child.'

'Go if you want to. But if you ask me, it's sheer madness. You are not thirteen any more, you're eight months pregnant, it's hot and you should look after yourself.'

'I feel fine.'

'If you call this fine, I dread the time when you'll admit you are not well.'

'Come with me. Please.'

'What for? Give me one good reason why.'

'I was very fond of Victor. You'll like him, I'm sure.'

'There is only one weekend. I have things to do so that the house and the garden will not fall into a state of disrepair and chaos. I'm also entitled to relax a bit before the next working week starts, or am I not?'

'You don't want me to go.'

'Don't be absurd. Go if it means so much to you, but let me be.'

'If I go, I won't take Joe with me.'

'Suits me fine. I'll be only too glad to spend the afternoon with my son.'

'How noble of you.'

'I really don't know what this argument is all about, I'm sure.' Julian looked puzzled, hurt, as though trying to understand. 'If you insist, I'll go.'

'There's no need.'

'What do you want me to do now?'

'Nothing. Show a bit of concern, perhaps.'

Sunday came and we set off to see Victor, my grumbling husband, Joe and I. Victor lived in St Kilda, a seaside suburb. First we walked to the station, which put Joe in a happy mood because 'bus money' was 'matchbox- car money'. On this day we were to save four pennies, which was a quarter of the total cost of the toy. Julian was less happy, rather resigned. I was tired even before we started, mainly because of the weather, because of my pregnancy, or perhaps I was very excited.

Once on the train, Julian looked after Joe. They chatted while I allowed myself the luxury of remembering. When I met Victor, he was already a student at the Warsaw Conservatorium. He treated me as his equal, which made my summer holidays. He never objected to my company, though I was still an awkward teenager who used to come up with a suitable and witty answer only some hours after the conversation had taken place. The people at the guesthouse often commented that Victor was a terrific young man, allowing all the youngsters to pester him.

He used to take us for excursions, hikes. He had that special feel for nature and once, when we went on a deserted mountain track, he ordered us to be quiet. 'Shut up, if only for a few minutes. Be still and listen.' We sat down where we had stopped, some on boulders, some on the ground. I turned away from the others and heard the branches move. The solid shape of the peak mounted in the distance, dark and cryptic. The sky was haze-blue and from one second to the next, the feathery clouds changed their wind-blown shapes. The ground was rough, uneven, and a column of ants marched with a military, well-disciplined precision. I had never seen so much. I was happy. My eyes were ready to see, my mind was ready to absorb. I heard, I thought. A shepherd sang in the valley and the sheep bleated. And then foot-steps. 'Enjoyed it?' I was sure Victor looked at me. I wanted to tell him how I felt and was trying to say how these few minutes had affected me. And before I had time to stop stammering, my elder cousin Janina sprang to her feet. 'It was a divine experience,' she announced in her clear voice. 'I could have stayed like this for an hour, for two, even for the whole day!' Victor laughed, my heart beat hard and then every-body got up and started to walk. The silence and harmony faded away and we went further up. In the midst of the laughter and small talk, I was thinking, why wasn't it I who said what Janina did. I almost hated her; but when on the following evening Victor asked me if I was willing to help him and his friends, I forgave Janina and was on top of the world again. I didn't understand what help Victor had in mind and for a moment was petrified that my mother would stop me from going because I couldn't explain what we were going to do and where we were heading. But then my aunt stepped in and said that my mother should have more trust in Victor because he was such a fine young man. And that she, too, was concerned about Janina and wouldn't allow her to go if it weren't for Victor. And that my mother should have more trust in me and understand that young people are entitled to have their little secrets too. 'Are you suggesting that I am too possessive?' my mother asked in a not very friendly voice, but I didn't even care what else she was going to say because I knew I was allowed to go. And that was the most important thing, nothing else counted.

We set out, Victor, his brother, Janina and I. It was getting dark when we left the guesthouse and Victor explained that we were to fight anti-Semitism. I didn't understand how. My throat was tight. We followed Victor along the rough unmade road until we reached the outskirts of the sleepy township. There were two young men walking some distance in front of us. They stopped for a while, walked on, and then stopped again. 'It's them,' whispered Victor. 'Let's follow them.' Their path was marked with posters. Victor's brother picked up one.

Question: who killed Christ?
Answer: the Jews.
Question: who undermines the role of our Christian democracy?
Answer: the Jews.
Who steals from the poor?
The Jews

The questions varied, but the answer was always the same.

We peeled the stickers off the lampposts, telegraph poles, fences and walls. 'It's easier before the glue dries,' Victor let us into his secret. We followed the route of the two men and hoped that we prevented what they wanted to achieve.

And fifteen years later, I was on my way to meet the initiator of that plan. I wondered whether Victor had managed to complete his musical studies, whether he had settled in Australia together with his family, even whether they had all survived the war. Leon's friend had only mentioned Victor and some vague recollection of unspecified traumatic experiences. I hoped Victor had come victorious from the war and that his sensitivity hadn't become a secondary casualty. He had played the piano with all the passion of the young. 'Apassionata, Beethoven,' he had enlightened me, while my whole self cried out silently. 'Chopin, listen to him. He's Poland, her people, her nature, her character, her struggles and hopes.'

I hoped Victor would have a piano in his flat and that he would play for us and then Julian would understand why I was so keen to introduce Victor to him.

We arrived at St Kilda about 4 o'clock; we were back on the train home by 4.30.

Victor didn't even remember me.

'Am I supposed to know you?' he asked. 'I'm sorry, but I have no recollection.' He turned towards a woman with the face of a martyr. 'D'you remember my mentioning this lady to you?'

'No,' the woman said in a flat voice.

I couldn't accept it. Victor and that summer holiday of long ago were so much a part of me, they lived within me through the war years, they brightened my dark days, they were proof that normal life had existed and would be possible again some time in the future. So few of my friends had survived and the one who had was not even aware that I had ever existed.

All Victor remembered was that he had once gone to the Tatra mountains, and that was about all.

'Sorry for imposing on you. I thought you knew me.'

'Perhaps I did in my previous existence,' he said, and though I remembered his face well, there was something in it, the hardness perhaps, which made me feel uncomfortable. I had the persistent feeling that Victor knew me very well, but didn't want to admit it for some reason which wasn't clear to me.

'It's pointless, then, to introduce my family to you.'

'Oh, please do,' Victor smiled the smile from his previous existence. 'By the way, this is my wife. We met in a forest. After I was rescued by the partisans.' He turned his face towards the window. 'She's my second wife. My first wife and my baby were butchered. And then I met her.'

The woman got up. She was about my age and also pregnant, but not as advanced as I was. She extended her hand to me without even smiling. A mask. Her handshake was limp, as if half-hearted. Joe tugged at my dress. 'Mum,' he said. 'I have to go to the toilet.'

'Second door to the left,' Victor directed us. The passage was dark, the whole place was gloomy, not so much because of the flat itself, but rather because it was neglected. The toilet didn't meet with Joe's approval. He changed his mind and assured me that he would last till we got home, or even longer. He urged me to get out of this 'yukky' place. We didn't stay long, anyway. I was hoping all the time that something would trigger Victor's memory, but nothing did. Victor's wife wasn't too keen on us. She didn't strike me as a hospitable person; she didn't even offer us a drink of water, though she must have been aware of how uncomfortable we were. She kept on fanning her face all the time.

Victor took our address before we left. He seemed to be surprised when I mentioned the piano. No, he had not touched the keys since the war and never would. His brother, yes, his name was Slavek, hadn't survived, neither had his parents. Vanished, they had all vanished during the Warsaw Uprising. He himself had wanted to search for them, but 'Mila', Victor pointed to his wife, '. . . didn't allow me to leave the shelter . . . did you, dearest? Slavek wanted to take part in the Uprising, to fight. When he didn't return, my parents went out too. But when I wanted to go, Mila said no. She cried no. She even said that my family had given their lives so that I could survive . . . Didn't you, my love?'

There was so much malice in Victor's voice that all of a sudden I wanted to leave. Mila stood up, walked to the window, and while she was struggling with the catch and couldn't open it, Victor's eyes were glued to her. And then she let her hands drop. 'If I had known,' she said flatly, '. . . if I had only known, I wouldn't have.'

Back on the train, there was a young man so much like the prewar Victor. His face was alive, transparent, vibrating like life itself. And the girl next to him was radiant, as any girl should be. What had the war done to Victor, what had it done to all of us? I sat close to Julian, I searched for his reassurance.

'What's got into you?' he asked, knowing my reluctance to display emotion in front of strangers. I was happy to have him as my husband and loved him even more for not referring to Victor and the visit.

FOURTEEN

I sent to Hobart for a Tattersall ticket; the win would solve all our problems, the material ones anyway.

Our child was to be born at Epworth hospital. The doctor made all the necessary arrangements. I was happy that he was going to look after me. I trusted him, and he spoke Polish. The hospital gave me a list of items I was supposed to bring along, like cotton-wool, antiseptic, sanitary napkins. It seemed crazy that every patient had to bring her own things, instead of the hospital supplying them. My amazement ended up as the main topic in my letters to Poland and France.

Mrs Lloyd, as usual the expert, shared my view for a change. Her son, too, had been born in Melbourne, so nothing was new to her. She told me that hospitals in Australia didn't have a doctor in residence. I was sure that Mrs Lloyd, once again, was giving free rein to her overworked imagination and her willingness to run Australia down.

'You can believe me or not, as you wish, but the fact is, the hospital is left in charge of the nursing staff.' The triumphant tone in Mrs Lloyd's voice made me feel uncertain.

'Are you sure?'

'Never been surer. And what's more, they don't look after you too well.'

'What d'you mean?' Mrs Lloyd got up. 'Look at my tummy.' She pointed to her huge, protruding belly. 'It's all their fault. They damaged my tummy. I used to have such a beautiful figure. If you don't believe me, you can ask my husband. He always used to say: "Darling, you have such a beautiful tummy, you should be Miss Universe".' She slouched back into her seat.

'I believe you,' I said.

'Good. One thing more. After you have your baby, remember to be regular.'

'What does that mean?'

'You are a scream. Toilet, toilet of course! In the hospital, they don't care if you go or not. I waited for several days, it's amazing I didn't burst open. I wanted to go, you know where, to the place where even kings go on foot. Meanwhile the whole skin of my tummy stretched out. They ruined me. They ruined my beautiful body.'

'Perhaps your beautiful body was a victim of your pregnancy?'

'Rubbish, it was all the hospital's fault. If I had another child, I would know what to do. Two days after the birth you have to tell the nurse that you want to open your tummy. You'd better learn it by heart, it's a special medical term. Your future figure depends on it. Repeat what I say.'

'I'll remember, Mrs Lloyd. Don't worry. I really do appreciate your advice.'

'Another thing you should know. You should work harder. You are going to be in hospital for ten days. Knowing you, you won't go back to work for another week, or two?'

'Mrs Lloyd ... as a matter of fact, I can't promise when I'll resume work. My baby, my children come first.'

'You think work would hurt your children? Work never hurts anyone. On the contrary, it does all the family a lot of good. You know what, I'll do you a favour. I have a new design for which I pay ... Wait till you hear it ... Six shillings and nine pence! I'll give it to you. I'll show you how to sew it; how about it? I'm not such a bad person, eh? You can still make a lot of money before your child is born.'

Mrs Lloyd kept her promise. She showed me how to handle the new design. The creation happened to be a cocktail dress made of black material. It was full of gathers, frills, pleats. In short, it demanded a lot of work. The hot spell didn't help either. I wasn't feeling the best and I spent more time soaking in a cold bath, dreaming of a Polish summer, than making my fortune. Remembering with what ease Mrs Lloyd handled the dress, I felt inadequate, clumsy, good for nothing; an impractical dreamer. Nevertheless, it was dreaming which helped me through the hours at the sewing machine. I kept a constant watch on Joe and his mates through the sleepout window. My mind stopped registering the machine's cluttering for some time then, and was completely absorbed in inner voices and recollections. On this day I dreamed of a win in the lottery. Money. An end to our problems. This surprised me, to a certain degree. In my lifetime I had witnessed the total collapse of a so-called secure, stable life. Money had never meant much to me. All it could do now was to make us more independent, more secure, but at this stage in my life it seemed important enough to me. The cocktail dresses caused me a lot of anguish. On the first day, I managed only five. Mrs Lloyd wasn't amused.

'Ten is an absolute minimum. Otherwise the whole exercise isn't worth the trouble. I need production. The factory is not a charitable organisation. I want to help you, all right? But you must want to help yourself, otherwise ...'

I hated Mrs Lloyd's sermons; they reduced me to some worthless imbecile. What annoyed me even more was my passive acceptance. I should have sent her packing, but instead I kept silent and if I spoke at all, it was to promise to try harder. Oh yes, I held long conversations with my ever-so-well-meaning boss, but only when she wasn't with me. While sewing, I rehearsed. My orations were very emotional, verbose and convincing. I pictured Mrs Lloyd being reduced almost to tears, though it was quite difficult to imagine. Nevertheless, I derived a certain pleasure from those 'encounters', they helped me to get through another solitary day at the sewing machine.

Reality proved to be different. I never had enough guts to use my well-prepared part when I faced Mrs Lloyd in the flesh.

My second day of cocktail dresses seemed like a carbon copy of the first. My hands simply refused to gather the material properly, to pleat evenly, to feed the machine continuously. So when the material kept on slipping to the floor, I had a good talk with my mother. I told her how I felt, the things I had stopped telling her in my letters. She had over-reacted once or twice, so I had decided to keep certain things from her. What was the point of worrying her. There was none.

My belly was constantly in my way. I wondered what my baby would look like. I cursed the dresses. I allowed myself to watch Joe for a while. He raced through the yard with the zest of a true follower of Davy Crockett. His mates were running, shouting, laughing. It was a reassuring sight. And then I wondered what makes the Lloyds of this world tick. I struggled with my sewing and told Mrs Lloyd what I really thought of her. I felt sorry for myself. My baby kicked and someone knocked at the door. I rose up as if I was a tent. A thought flashed — Tattersall, a win, a telegram. I didn't even pick up Mrs Lloyd's dress. I raced through the house as fast as my very pregnant body would let me.

'Who's there?' I called.

'Telegram.'

The voice had answered: telegram! Goodbye, dresses; *adieu* to you, Mrs Lloyd. Welcome, freedom!

A telegram was placed into my hand. A finger pointed to the line where I was to sign my name. I was given a pencil. The telegram burnt my hand. I managed to say 'thank you'. The delivery man smiled — he must have known what good news he was bringing. 'Thank you, thank you,' I kept on repeating. The man jumped on his bike and disappeared. What a pity we were not on the phone. I had to get in touch with Julian! I decided to take a taxi and bring him the good news in person. We can afford it, I thought. Joe, I had to call Joe. I had to change. I smiled at the telegram and opened it with the utmost care. The message read:

DRESSES ALL WRONG STOP PHONE FACTORY IMMEDIATELY STOP LLOYD.

I read and re-read the telegram; over and over till the whole meaning of it sank deeply into my mind. Back to dresses, back to the daily contact with Mrs Lloyd. What a stupid dream to have had. I had wanted things too easy. Life was never like that.

I went to the phone booth on my own; there was no need to drag Joe along. He was much better off in the company of his friends. I dialled the number and felt like fainting even before Mrs Lloyd thundered at me.

'Listen carefully, perhaps this time you'll understand. I can't risk our reputation because of your sloppy workmanship. The dresses must be unpicked and sewn all over again, that is providing the material will withstand your treatment. I advise you to pray that it will. It's very expensive material and I hope that you realise you are responsible for it ... Are you there?'

'Yes. I've got the message.'

'Come over to us in the evening. If you're not sure of what you're doing, I'm willing to give you instructions again. You know me.'

'Yes, Mrs Lloyd. I know you,' and I hung up.

She was right. All the way back home I tried to accept the fact, but somehow I couldn't. I was angry at Mrs Lloyd, as though my lack of skill was her fault. It was hot and dry. I kicked at all the loose stones on the way home, which didn't help much, but only made my feet feel even more tired.

Joe was waiting for me at the gate. 'Where did you go? I was looking for you.'

'Sorry. I had to make a phone call. Where are your friends?'

'Oh, they just went home.'

Heat, my blistered gate. I'd have to paint it again.

'Could we go to the park, mummy? Please, please!'

'Yes, Joe. What a good idea!' I mussed his hair. It was a crazy idea, but it was like a good dream. We went to the park in the middle of the week; after all, it was a school holiday. Joe ran from tree to tree and while I watched him, amiable thoughts chased Mrs Lloyd's words away. This is real life, I thought. Not a lottery win. My son, trees, the harmony of nature and the southerly breeze on a hot summer day. My child running on his strong legs, smiling, face full of freckles. His whole life in front of him, a real life. Joe was our true win in life's lottery; and the child to be born to us soon.

FIFTEEN

Dear Mother,

Congratulations on the birth of your first Australian grandson! Please don't panic. Michael is not premature, he is a well-developed, healthy baby. And he is lovely. The reason I gave you a later date is simple; I wanted you to hear the good news before you began to worry.

The labour went smoothly. I miss Joe — children are not allowed into maternity wards. Joe is staying with Ania and Freda. I can't wait till I go home. The hospital is very good, the only complaint I have is that the nurses address me in English, which, especially during labour, isn't easy.

So now we have a true Australian in our family. I'll have to do something about my English, it's really dreadful not to be able to understand what people want from you.

I'm sending this letter care of you, but it's meant for the whole family. I miss you all very much. I'll write again soon. Michael will be brought in for his dinner soon. I wish you could see him, he is so perfect. When I look at him, I want to cry with happiness.

My love to you all.

My son No. 2 was perfect, the most perfect baby born since Joe.

It was hot on the night before Michael was born. I felt restless. I kept on opening and shutting the windows. I moved from one room to another. Julian was fast asleep, so was Joe. I paced the floor, wondering why, and then I felt a pain. It didn't last long. Was it a contraction? I poured myself a glass of water. I shut the door. I sat at the kitchen table. It was badly in need of a good scrub. Another contraction; or perhaps not? I went outside. The wind plastered my nightgown against my body. My belly was huge. How much longer, I thought. A contraction? No doubt this time. And then I wasn't sure. Perhaps I had eaten something which hadn't agreed with me? What had I eaten yesterday?

The sky was full of stars. Lucky stars, distant stars. The pain passed. I breathed in with ease. Something has to be done about the garden . . . Was I in labour? I wondered whether I should wake Julian up and decided to let him sleep. He needed his rest badly. He was just recovering from colitis, almost a chronic condition, caused by constant anxiety. I wasn't much help either. I was frightened that once the baby was born, I would have to stop working. Our commitments were many: first mortgage, second mortgage, the fridge on hire-purchase. I had cried a lot in the early months of my pregnancy. I had let Julian down when I had carried on airing and exploding all my doubts as to whether we would be able to buy shoes for Joe once I stopped working. And what would happen to us if our fridge was repossessed. 'Back to the ice chest? Is this the future we want for our children? Is this it? Sour milk for our children?'

And then Julian had developed colitis. He had carried on with his work as usual, had seldom complained, had tried to cheer me up and had continuously reminded me that our situation was good. He had lost a lot of weight and the doctor had suggested that Julian's sickness had an indirect connection with his war experiences. My negative attitude certainly hadn't helped, I was sure.

I wasn't going to wake him up. He needed rest. It was only half past three. What a stupid time to start labour. Why this crazy hour? Perhaps it marked the exact termination of the nine months? Big joke. The pains were getting more frequent, the wind was blowing stronger. Julian and Joe were asleep. Birds chirped and twittered, though it was not yet dawn. I went inside, I shut all the windows. This time the pain was really sharp. I held my breath. Steady, steady ... I sat down. I got up. I opened all the windows. The curtains should be washed. The birds stopped making noises, they must have turned to the other side and gone back to sleep. Big joke number two ... The pains had stopped too. Vanished. There was no need to worry Julian.

The sun rose. I went to Joe's room and looked at him. I wondered if my new baby would be like him. I went to look at Julian. His face. I was glad I hadn't woken him and then I felt ashamed. What right did I have to spy on him and on Joe when they were so vulnerable, so unaware? I left the room and before I had even reached the kitchen, the pain, a real sweeping pain, got hold of me and made me stop. I blocked my mouth. I didn't care any more whether the wind blew or not, whether the birds sang or were silent, or whether Julian was asleep or awake.

'W-what, what happened?' Julian's eyes were frightened and half asleep.

'Nothing. We'd better get ready for the hospital.' Julian was ready even before the next contraction again reduced me to a self-centred female in labour. It was almost six o'clock. Julian left me alone and went to the local telephone booth. He returned some twenty minutes later. Not even one taxi was willing to transport me to the hospital. Julian spent his last two pennies on a call to the Lloyds. Mr Lloyd agreed to help us and arrived at our place shortly after. Dressed in pyjamas. By the time I got into his car, the contractions were almost continuous. We went to the farm first. Ania promised to look after Joe, Freda said not to worry. 'How does it feel?' asked Ania while Julian asked her to explain our absence to Joe and to take him to school. 'Everything's under control.' We were on our way. Mr Lloyd kept on apologising for being dressed in pyjamas, I went on biting my fist, while Julian repeatedly asked how I was. 'Never mind your pyjamas, Mr Lloyd, but could you drive a bit faster? Please!' 'Sure,' said Mr Lloyd. I was hot, the weather was really oppressive, though it was still very early. We were going at a good pace, which eased my anxiety. I even started to believe that my child would be born at the hospital after all. I bit my fist and Julian looked at me with the expressive eyes of a loving companion; and then we came to a sudden stop.

'Drive faster. Who cares about your pyjamas? Drive faster,' I moaned.

'I can't. My luck,' called out Mr Lloyd. 'What can I do? Have a look what's going on!'

I lifted my head. We were surrounded by a flock of sheep. *Baa, baa. Baa, baa.*

'Never mind. You'll be fine,' bleated Julian.

What were we to do? I didn't want my child to be born among the sheep. I wanted my doctor. The flock swayed this way and that. *Baa baa* in English, *Mée, mée* in Polish.

'I can't even back out,' méed Mr Lloyd. 'No way.'

'Never mind,' baaed Julian.

A contraction, and another one, and one more.

The rhythm had changed. I bent double. Julian opened the door. A sheep tried to push its head inside. Julian pushed it away and got out of the car. I preferred not to look.

'To think I didn't dare to dress properly, I was in such a hurry to get you to the hospital. I didn't even pick up the dresses. And now we are stranded till God knows when. Dressed in pyjamas. It could only happen in Australia,' said Mr Lloyd.

'Mr Lloyd, would you mind keeping your reflections to yourself?' I delivered the words as if I was giving birth to them.

'You don't like my reflections ... What's wrong?'

'Nothing really.'

'So why should I keep them to myself?'

A piercing pain.

'Why should I?' repeated Mr Lloyd.

'I don't know!'

I heard the dogs barking. Julian came back.

'You'll be all right. Never mind, it won't be long now.' I lifted my head up. The dogs were chasing the sheep away from the car. They flocked together, opening the road for us. Not before time, as far as I was concerned. Julian wiped my face.

'It won't be long. Don't worry ... These Australian sheep dogs are incredible. I explained the situation to the man in charge. He called his dogs, gave a command, and look, the road is almost clear.'

'Who cares?' I cried.

The car moved at a mad speed and soon after I was admitted to the hospital, where my second son was born one hour later.

What I couldn't tolerate was the nurses using English, which I could hardly understand even without being in constant pain. They instructed me to move this way, or that. They forced a mask on me which made me feel dizzy and which hardly relieved the pain. I tossed my head from side to side. The nurses didn't seem to understand that I didn't want to be drugged. Perhaps they couldn't work out what I was saying. Even in normal circumstances my pronunciation wasn't easy to understand. I felt better when my doctor arrived. First, he spoke Polish, the easiest and most beautiful language for a woman in labour. Secondly, he explained the procedure to me without throwing his hands up in a desperate gesture. I accepted the mask from him and the next thing I knew, the sister was bending over me.

'Wake up, Mrs Lewitt. It's all over.'

'What is over?'

'Everything's over. You have a baby boy.'

I smiled at her. She was all flushed, tired.

'I have a boy? A real boy. Sorry. You are tired. You worked hard. Sorry.'

'I'm exhausted. Yours was the second baby today. The hot weather must have brought on labour. I'm tired, but fine.'

Second baby! I panicked. I had a second baby. What had happened to the first? Suddenly I remembered that people were telling me how huge I was, and asking whether I wasn't going to have twins. I felt hot and cold.

'I'll bring your baby to you once we settle you in your room.'

'Sister. Sorry, sister. You speak of one baby. Where is the other baby?'

'The one born before yours? Oh, he's with his mum. Now let me tidy you up.'

'I have one baby, not twins?'

'You are a silly duffer. Did you think you had twins?' When she saw me cry, she said: 'What shall I do with you? Listen, you have one baby. One, no more. A lovely, healthy baby. You understand? Your doctor will come to see you later. Wait, don't move. One baby.'

I blew my nose and sobbed.

'There, there', said the sister. 'Look what I have for you.' She placed a little bundle next to me. My son; Julian's son; a brother for Joe. My baby with all its softness. Making faces. Beautifully formed mouth, huge eyes, long fingers. So tiny. To cuddle, gently, softly.

'He's a lovely baby. Happy now?' said the sister.

'Yes.' I felt tired, and fulfilled, and ecstatic, and I missed my mother, and wished Julian and Joe were with me, and why did they speak English all the time, and I felt sleepy, and my baby was nice, and I had to rest. I felt so sleepy.

The sister said: 'Come on, little man. We mustn't disturb your mum,' and she took my baby from me. And then they transported me to my room and the sister gave me something to drink. 'It's for you, be a good girl. Drink it all up.' She was all right, she smiled a lot and somehow I listened to her. She was about my own age, she could had been my sister. What a pity she couldn't speak Polish. And then she was gone, and when I opened my eyes again, there were flowers and Julian was next to me. He looked at me with so much love and concern and pride that I closed my eyes again. I was afraid I was going to cry, though I was very happy.

'Go to Joe,' I urged him. 'Have you seen your son?'

'He is perfect. Thank you.' Julian kissed me with all his tenderness, my eyes, my whole face, my hands and arms.

'You'd better go,' I repeated.

'I'll see you tomorrow. Happy dreams and don't count sheep ... Our Australian son, ready to join the Australian Natives Association.'

Dear Family,

I can't tell you how sorry I am for not writing before. When your letter, full of concern and wild guesses, arrived today, I really felt guilty, mainly because all is well with us.

Little Michael is now sound asleep, as if he knew that I was desperate for a short spell from the constant nappy changes and feeding. I suffer from what could be classed as a chronic lack of spare time. Apart from Michael, there are Joe and Julian and the household duties. I still try to sew a few dresses a day.

So I could find an explanation or two if I wanted to.

Michael is developing well. Sometimes he reduces me to a sentimental, almost teary mess, especially when I look at Joe talking to his brother with incredible love and when the little one responds with all the trust of a baby. I don't think I mentioned to you that on our return from hospital, Joe insisted on giving Michael his bed and spent the night sleeping on the settee. I regret all the time that you are not with us, because I know how much pleasure you would derive from simply being around.

Michael spends most of his days under the weeping willow which we planted a couple of years ago and which has just grown to the right size to offer him protection from the strong Australian sun. I don't have to walk him. The instant fresh air is just outside our door. So while Michael is peacefully asleep, I wash and boil his nappies in a gas copper and dry them in the sun. And of course I can't stop recalling how it was when Joe was born and the nappies were washed in a communal kitchen to the constant disgruntled chorus of our co-tenants. The first time I washed the nappies,

*they froze solid in the attic after I hung them to dry.
I once described the situation to my Australian
neighbour and she just looked at me with a certain
dose of cynicism. I had a feeling that she didn't
believe me.*

*You ask if we have made any friends. Yes, we
have. Apart from Franka and Leon, whom we visit
regularly, there are a few families with whom we
are in touch, but one couldn't class them as real
friends. Through Ania and Freda, we have met a
Polish woman, Mrs Staszewski, who together with
her husband has transformed her Australian suburban weatherboard house into a miniature Polish
farm, with tall fences, flowerbeds, vegetable plots,
where two chickens, one called Ania and one called
Freda, wander around. I never know which is
which. They are followed by six little Anias and
Fredas. The kitchen, I couldn't believe that a
kitchen like that could be possible in Australia. It
brought back the memory of smells and colours
which I had forgotten ever exist. Plaited onions and
garlic, all home grown, hang from the ceiling. Jars
of salted cucumbers, preserved fruit, wall hangings, ladles, wooden spoons, colourful plates,
paper cuttings, and Mrs Staszewski as plain and as
beautiful as a common daisy . . .*

My daily routine hardly varied. Julian was the first
to leave home, usually soon after seven. Joe didn't
start school till half past eight so I had him with us for
an hour longer.

I often remembered when Joe was born, it had been
so much more difficult. In order to give him a bit of
fresh air, I had had to walk with him through the
dusty and polluted streets of industrial Lodz. It used
to take me a good half an hour to reach the park,
where I usually stayed for an hour or so. By the time I

returned home, I had been simply exhausted and not feeling over-enthusiastic at the prospect of washing nappies, or preparing meals in the kitchen where four other women were trying to do the same. It had been the end of 1945; the war had hardly ended and conditions had been especially difficult. I still remembered it all vividly. It helped me to appreciate Australia more fully.

The letters from our family became uniform and were just about the same. My mother would start with apologies for not writing sooner, followed by assurances that all was well with the whole family. The only complaint she allowed herself to express was a reference to the unseasonable changes in the weather pattern.

Because of this, I often wondered how things really were back in Poland and sometimes felt guilty for writing in the same vein, which said so little about us. Nevertheless I censored myself. I seldom mentioned the things which really mattered. It wasn't easy to keep up a close relationship from one hemisphere to another. I didn't want to cause any worry and then, in turn, I worried myself, wondering if my family was really all right, and how much they kept to themselves, trying to spare us. And then one night I got up, took a writing pad and wrote:

Dear Mother,

I miss you. Joe fell down and hurt himself badly and on top of everything else he collected a nasty splinter which took me hours to dig out. I was angry with myself and shouted at Joe, urging him to behave like a man and stop crying and then Michael started to cry too. I remembered how good you were at pulling splinters out and wished you were with us. My sons formed a crying duet and I didn't know what to do except to shout, which never helps the situation. And then I wished you were with me, Mother, because I feel so very lonely here and lost. Life didn't allow us enough time together — I didn't even learn from you how to pull out splinters ... I met Victor, Mother. He didn't remember me at all. He looked at me as if I had never existed. It hurt me because I was sure he would remember.

I finished the letter and then went back to bed and felt happy thinking that from that night on, I would write all. I was hoping mother would do the same. When morning came, I changed my mind. By the time I looked at the letter again, Julian was at work and Joe at school. His leg had healed almost completely, so what was the point of worrying my mother with something that wasn't relevant any more. So I tore. the letter up and then I felt even more lonely than before, and I wondered whether our family always believed all we wrote.

SIXTEEN

I went to the city, while Mrs Staszewski looked after Michael. Julian thought it would do me a lot of good to go out, to see people, to buy myself something.

It was a cold day with lashing wind and sporadic, needle-sharp rain. I walked from the Princes Bridge Station down to Bourke Street. The crowd rushed by. I looked around and couldn't see even one familiar face. I remembered how it was back in Lodz, where I was certain to meet someone I knew. Melbourne was different. The shops were great, bursting with well-displayed goods, readily available for anyone to buy. But it was a faceless city, lacking in personality. It was too clinical, too smoothly run, too polite. There were no beggars, no small vendors, not even one city fool. I walked down Swanston Street thinking of my childhood and remembered scenes long forgotten, speculating how that well-behaved Melbournian crowd would react if confronted with a man dressed in rags and a top-hat who chanted and talked to himself, danced and ran, followed by a group of young scamps. It was a picture taken from my life, from real life. I wished I could see the man, to experience once again that frightful fascination his presence had offered. For he had mumbled and he had twisted, he had laughed, and he had cursed his young tormentors who called him names. First he had stopped, and then he had turned around, and then he had looked and his eyes had been absurdly frantic and his voice when he shouted had been absurdly thundering and the children who had followed him had kept on taunting him though from a safer distance, just in case, because one day . . . who could foresee what a man like this might do? He had never done any harm. He had vanished from the streets of Lodz at the beginning of the German occupation. The beggars had disappeared too and the small vendors and the pedlars. Lodz had became clean, ready for the new Nazi order.

But Melbourne had never gone through a German occupation, there was no reason why it should be so clinical. People like my fool must have existed in Australia too. Where? Hidden away, so that no one would be upset by somebody's strange behaviour and stench? I was glad I had known this man — I pitied the good people of Melbourne because they hadn't.

Buskers. I remembered buskers. With instruments, or without; voices which were penetrating if not always pleasing. Their songs, sprung from local, even international events, echoed through the streets, through the courts, for everyone to hear, for everyone to learn. How did it go? Mrs Simpson, the Prince of Wales, the Abdication? Crisis facing England?

> *Parliamentarians stood on their heads,*
> *And the mug called Balwyn, especially,*
> *'Bugger it all,' he said,*
> *'It's scandalous,' he said,*
> *'It can't go on like this.'*
> *The poor king scratched his crown,*
> *And the tears glittered in his eye,*

*'I'll be better off with my woman
Than on this hard, cold throne.'*

Our servant sang this song for a long time. It became a part of her rich repertoire and that is how I learned of this great, romantic love.

I was just about to reach Myer's store. I kept on warming my soul with evoked images, and then I saw Victor. A familiar face in a great mass of faces! I smiled and thought that this was just the beginning. Because this city would become more and more familiar. I caught Victor's eye. He looked at me, a hard, piercing look, colder than the lashing rain, more foreign than all the strangers around me. And then he turned his head away and crossed the road. I stood as if transfixed and the hurrying passers-by kept on bumping into me. Rushing, always rushing, without a smile, preoccupied, shut in their private worlds, where there was no room for such as me.

Why had Victor run away from me? Perhaps he didn't see me, not expecting to meet someone he knew? But I was trying to persuade myself, knowing very well that he *had*. All of a sudden I wanted to be home. I wanted to be with Michael and I wasn't concerned with what I planned to buy. And then I bought two pairs of stockings which I didn't really need and on the way to the station I stopped at the Mutual Store, where I bought a loaf of good old rye bread.

Michael was happy to see me and made me feel needed.

In the evening, I told Julian of my encounter.

'Don't worry. Victor didn't even notice you, I'm sure. You and your sensitivity ... He's a strange character, not worth thinking about.'

Julian was right, as in so many other cases, but when I sat at the sewing machine, to fulfil my daily quota, I thought of Victor and felt his penetrating, cold gaze on me. He had turned his head away.

And then he came to see me. Just like that. I was feeding Michael. Julian was at work, Joe at school. Victor entered through the kitchen door.

'I saw you in the city the other day,' he said.

'I know,' I said, while Michael twisted his head towards the strange voice.

'I thought you didn't notice.'

'I did.'

'I wasn't in the mood for conversation. Sorry.'

'Are you now?'

He sat across the table and only then unbuttoned his shabby coat. His shirt looked as if he slept in it and his jumper made me think of the war.

'You have a nice baby.'

'I think so ... I'm sure I have.' I was proud of how Michael ate. His mouth was always ready and open in time for another teaspoonful. He drank his milk from a cup. Not bad for a four-month-old baby, not bad at all. I was glad Michael wasn't breastfed any more, though when my milk had dried up I had been very upset.

'How's your wife?'

'Huge, difficult. Should have had her baby last week.'

'It's quite common, being overdue, I mean. It won't be long and you'll have a lovely baby too. Happy about it?'

Victor looked at me with ... I wasn't sure, but I thought it was hate. He got up. Eight steps one way. Stop. Full turn. Eight steps back. His steps drummed the floor. Michael watched him for a while and then went back to his food.

'I'm not happy about it,' Victor spat out the words. 'The fact is I shouldn't have fathered another child.

It's an act of treason to the memory of my son who was killed.' Victor put his hand on Michael's head. 'See, my baby, my son, was younger than yours is now. Two-and-a-half months, to be precise.' I got up and held Michael very close. I wanted to say something. Victor was waiting for it, I was sure, but there was nothing, not even a single word which would have sounded true in the face of the savage tragedy which had been Victor's.

He told me his story while I changed Michael, put him to sleep, prepared dinner. I wanted to keep busy because I couldn't stand looking at Victor. His voice was bitter and at the same time very clear and it was more than I was able to handle. He told me I was the first person to whom he was prepared to tell 'all this'.

'You told your wife, surely?'

'It's not the same. She dragged it out of me.'

In 1939, Victor married a girl just out of school. He laughed. 'She wasn't even quite eighteen!'

'What was her name?'

'I can't remember any more.'

Victor's parents-in-law lived in Eastern Poland and that was where Victor and his bride settled down. The war started. The Russian occupation, initially a peaceful existence. Victor's father-in-law, who occupied a prominent position, secured a job for him.

'What did he do?'

'I don't remember.'

The town was a small one, surrounded by fields and forests. Victor and his wife whose name he didn't want to remember learned Russian, walked in the woods.

'We sang Russian songs. My first wife had a good voice. We fell in love with Russian songs. I remember one. You want to hear it?' Before I even had time to respond, Victor sang of trees in blossom, of a girl who sang a song, wishing the sound would reach her

136

beloved one. He sang well, melodiously, as if in a whisper and then he stopped abruptly and turned his back to me.

'I think your child is awake,' he said.

Michael was still asleep. I looked at him and wished that his Australian life would be free from haunting songs and events he wouldn't wish to remember. And then Michael woke up and gave me a big smile. I picked him up and changed him, and then I fed him and put him outside under his willow tree, and all this time Victor just stood in front of the window and said nothing.

'Would you like a cup of coffee or something?'

'You're almost as bad as my wife. I came to you to talk, not to drink coffee.'

'So why don't you?'

He looked at me with such pain that I hung my head down. I sat at the table and he sat opposite.

'It's not that easy,' he said without anger. 'See, when the war between Russia and Germany started, we tried to be evacuated. My father-in-law ran from one official to another. On the last day, we all went to the station and waited for a train. People were everywhere, as was the army. It was a warm day, an early summer. My wife was pregnant, very pregnant. Panic. Pushing. Cannonade and a Russian soldier was singing: *And tomorrow, tomorrow we'll go to war again, it's our destiny*. My wife said she wasn't feeling very well and put both her hands over her belly. A German plane circled above and then there was a big explosion which sent everybody flying. My mother-in-law said that enough was enough and that she was going home and would take her daughter with her. The Germans couldn't be as bad as all this. We returned home. In the evening someone came to tell us that the last train had been bombed and so had the station. So we congratulated ourselves for making the

137

right decision. My mother-in-law reminded us that it was her initiative, so we drank to that . . . Seven days later, the Germans arrived and some time later our son was born.'

'What was his name?'

'You don't really expect me to remember, do you?' shouted Victor. 'Is it really so important to know the names of people who don't need them any more? My son, when he was two-and-a-half months old . . . He didn't have a willow tree . . . Anyway, my wife was making plans that one day when the war ended, we'd take our boy to the forest which we knew so well and we'd sing him all the Russian songs we ever learned . . .

'We went, or rather were marched, to the outskirts of the forest. First, the men were ordered to dig the trenches and then the Germans and Ukrainians lined us all up and shot us. We were stripped naked. In our forest . . . I'll spare you all the gory details . . . All I have to add is the fact that the bullet missed me.' Victor laughed. 'It missed me. Why me? I crawled over the bodies of my people. It was dark. I went into the forest. I howled like a wounded animal — I bled like one. And then, a couple of days later, I was rescued by a small contingent of partisans. They took me with them and named me "Lucky". That's where I met Mila and it marked the beginning of the biggest romance of the twentieth century.'

I stared at my hands, not knowing what to do.

'You're amazing! You can ask questions, you know. For example. . . . If I were you I would've asked what makes a person crawl out of a mass grave . . .'

'Stop it,' I said.

'Had you asked, I would have replied that I don't really remember any more.'

'Victor, would you like to stay and have tea with

138

us. Joe will be home soon and Julian shouldn't be later than five o'clock.'

'I'm surprised at you,' sermoned Victor. 'I wouldn't dream of accepting an invitation without my beloved wife Mila. Who can tell, she might even be in labour for all I know. Just this very minute.'

Victor left. I picked Michael up and hugged him, trying to absorb all the warmth of his trusting body, to feel something alive, to chase away the impact and confusion that Victor's visit had brought.

SEVENTEEN

As we settled down, we started to reflect — to sum up — what Australia meant to us. Our sons were growing up playing football and cricket and singing English songs. They showed little appreciation for the beauty of the Polish language.

We still corresponded with the family regularly, but it was less personal, and we wrote carefully selected material considered as suitable for export, rather than a true account of our daily life. My mother and sister were promoted to Dorothy Dixes and from time to time I sought their advice, which amused Julian. He tried to remind me that my association with my family hadn't always been ideal, but I was sure he had simply forgotten how well attuned we were.

And then I received a letter in which my mother painfully informed us that my brother-in-law wasn't prepared to exchange the journalism he loved for some intangible benefits Australia might or might not, offer him. My mother decided to stay in Poland. Tania was expecting a baby and besides, my mother wasn't strong enough to start a new life once more. In Poland she still had a few friends, knew the language. 'And perhaps one day you will visit us, my child. I can't stand the thought that I will never see you again,' she wrote, and when I read it, I cried. It was hard to accept that we were destined to be a nuclear family. The realisation saddened me greatly and as a result, I freed my Polish family from all human vices. I decided never to cause them any worry. My letters fell victim to this resolution. The food in Australia was the best in the world; the climate superb, something like the French Riviera, only better. It was true that we worked, but actually we never felt tired. Our health was thriving; our children, a constant source of joy and happiness.

I mentioned Victor's visit though, to which my mother replied that if she were me, she would stop this association once and for all. 'Can't you see, Victor is a negative character, not to be trusted.' She implied that contact with a man like him could easily lead to disaster. And then she listed all Julian's exceptional qualities. 'It's only the children who suffer in the long run.' This was the letter which prompted me to be even more selective. I accepted that letters could never be a substitute for personal contact. It made me sad, as did the fact that my mother was still capable of misunderstanding me.

The Victorian sunset, the unreal intensity of stripes and bold strokes. Salmon and charcoal, grey and pink. How right the Australian gum trees looked against this background, every leaf sharp and precise as though shimmering with silver and inner life. I learned to love it all. The Peninsula and the Dandenongs; and it was easy to accept that these vast beaches, this dense bush would be a part of Joe's and Michael's lives and I constantly wished that my children would never have to leave the landmarks of their childhood as we had to leave ours.

Michael was growing up, always trailing behind his

big brother and because of his toughness, Joe and his friends bestowed on him the title of 'King of the Kids'.

I became more and more skilful in sewing and Julian changed jobs again, this time to a carpet factory whose owner was a true workaholic. He expected Julian to work overtime. The money would have been handy, but no matter how tempting the proposition was, Julian declined, agreeing with me that it was more important for the well-being of our children to have their father with them in the evening than for us to have more money to spend.

Victor paid me another visit. Michael was two years old by then, so one couldn't class Victor as a frequent visitor. Distant and still the same, with a burning soul, an agile body and bitter memories.

'Look at your boy! Michael? See, I still remember my old friends.'

'You do?'

'He's a lovely thing.'

'He definitely is.'

'I had a boy once, I think I told you. If he hadn't been butchered, he would be twelve now.' He looked at me. I turned my head and in desperation glued my eyes on Michael, who tricycled all over the backyard.

'Twelve years old. A boy. Trust Mila, she had to have a girl.' I felt ashamed for not keeping in touch, for not even knowing of the birth of their child.

'I'm sorry. Congratulations. Your daughter must be over a year old by now, isn't she?'

'No need to feel guilty, it wasn't a momentous event ... Yes, your calculations are almost right. She's twenty months old.'

'What's her name?'

Victor stopped for a moment. 'You have an unhealthy preoccupation with names. I call her Baby. "It's time to change your nappy, Baby," I say. "Stop screaming, Baby." "You're getting on my nerves, Baby." It works very well.'

'Poor Mila.'

'Why do you say that?'

'I'm sure you know why. The baby is your child, she's not a stranger.'

'But *we* are . . . I never asked Mila to have a baby. She has a lot to answer for. In the first place, she shouldn't have nursed me back to health. Had she let me die as I·wanted, she wouldn't have any problems now.'

'Why are you saying things like that? Somehow I feel you have things you enjoy, despite what has happened.'

'Like what?'

'Like making Mila's life miserable.'

He looked at me sharply and then started pacing the floor again, like a trapped animal. Eight steps one way. Stop. Full turn. Eight steps back. What I really wanted to tell him was that he should have shown some appreciation to Mila for all she had done for him, that he should have been thankful for life, for his own, and for the new life which had been born, for Mila accepting him without reservation, for choosing Australia where the start of a new life was possible and probable. For the incredibly beautiful March day, when time seemed to come to a standstill as if it wanted to take pleasure and comfort in nature's serenity.

Unfortunately, Victor wasn't an ordinary man, therefore an ordinary, logical answer didn't make sense. He hurt and he hated using his hurt as a defensive weapon. He shielded himself with cynicism.

'Let's talk,' I said. 'Let's analyse the whole situation.' I felt like a crusader. I'd help the man, I'd lead him to the path of happiness. I felt noble, I smiled. Victor stopped. 'And what is there to analyse?

143

You want to do this! An amateur? A person who is more suited to wash the dishes than, than ... Oh, it's not really important, amusing rather.' Victor spoke quietly. I had the feeling that he was controlling his rising emotions by throwing the words out one by one, trusting that they would hurt me.

'You sit here, in your puny little box, not really knowing, not really seeing. You play with your children, wait for the magic moment when your husband comes home ... You know what you've done? You have created an illusion, that proverbial fool's paradise ... And you have the cheek to question me? You have no right, no right to do it.'

Michael was joined by Mrs MacAllison's youngest daughter. They ran and chased each other and then they started on mud pie production. They used the water direct from the tap; I should have stopped them, but I didn't. If mud pies were to shelter my son from what Victor had to say, good for the mud pies.

'I have no right, Victor, no right indeed, except for the fact that you came to me. After pretending you never knew me ... After ignoring me in the city ... I can't understand you. What do you want? My applause, my blessing?'

Victor laughed, softly, then louder. He covered his face with his palms, threw his head back. 'May I sit down?' he asked and sat down. 'You're right, of course. I came to you first, though not entirely. If you hadn't come to my place ... '

'Wait a minute, Victor ... '

'Please stop interrupting. I'm in the mood to talk. When I was staggering through the forest, naked and bleeding, I was picked up by a group of partisans. You know what nickname they gave me?'

'Lucky.'

'So you remember. I must have told you too much.'

'That's all I know from your partisan days, and

that you met Mila there.' I was speaking quickly, frightened Victor would stop.

'Are you sure you want to listen?'

'Yes.'

'Well. The partisans took me deeper into the forest to where their hide-out was. From then on I don't remember much. I remember crowns of pine trees, cursing their green perfection and wishing for death. I remember pain. And a young girl leaning over me, saying things I didn't want to hear. And then later the girl feeding me, propping me up against the tree trunk. I was physically better by then, but still not quite myself. I wasn't much use to my comrades-in-arms. "Don't worry, Lucky, the time will come." And then, one night, the girl came and offered herself to me. I must have had certain scruples, because I remember the girl saying not to worry. "You're unusual," that's what she said. Apparently every single man from our group had slept with her. "But it will be different once I belong to you. Before it didn't matter. Men are all men. It's war".' Victor watched me and the veins on his neck stood out. He coughed.

'If you had a little bit of intelligence, you might have guessed that the girl was no other than my dearest wife, the mother of Baby.'

My hands, my hands were continuously in my way, and I didn't know what to do with my eyes. I poured some coffee.

Victor had taken full advantage of Mila. His lovemaking had been a mere bodily response to Mila's yearning; he had her because she made herself available. He had been quite certain that the whole group would be wiped out sooner or later. The men themselves had not been too happy with Mila's sexual preference, but they hadn't dwelt on it too much. They had kept on calling Victor 'Lucky'. By then, he had been taking part in a few raids and waiting

145

without fear for death. His murdered wife and baby, and what had happened before, were strangely absent from his thoughts. He just existed, not really feeling, not really giving a damn. Summer and autumn passed, then winter arrived in all its fury. The snow was never beautiful, dry or soft; it was always sloshy-wet and freezing cold. The men became edgy. The group stayed in one place most of the time. There was not much to eat and whenever they ventured out, they were frightened of the footprints they left, counting on good luck or a fresh snowfall. Little by little, the whole group disintegrated.

Next spring, they promised themselves. Most of them were local men with somewhere to go. 'You're all right, Lucky. A broad like Mila next to you.' Mila had chosen to stay with Victor. He had urged her to go and leave him to die. He had told her he had a family, parents and a brother, somewhere in the Warsaw Ghetto. 'So if I change my mind, I'll go to them,' he told Mila. 'I don't love you. You are in my way. You mean nothing to me.'

But Mila was Mila. She just about dragged him to Warsaw. They walked most of the long, long way, though sometimes a peasant gave them a lift. Once they were offered a lift by a German in an army truck. Mila helped Victor into the vehicle, where he shivered during the entire journey. This surprised him; he thought he could no longer be affected by uncontrollable emotions. Mila held him close while he told her to get off his back and out of his life. Mila hadn't said anything, only cried.

'It's a long, messy story,' commented Victor. 'Not many people know of this morbid past of mine. I rely on your discretion.'

'Julian has to know.'

'Is it necessary?'

'In my life, frankly, yes.'

146

And then I went outside to see how the children were. They wanted to transfer their mud-pie production next door for a change and I agreed.

'Another cup?'

'That would be nice ... Where was I? Yes, the Ghetto. We didn't stay long. Mila, remember, always Mila, organised some accommodation for us all on the Aryan side, which was a kind of a miracle in itself. Even I have to admit that. And then the Uprising, the Warsaw Ghetto Uprising, the first Jewish uprising since Imperial Roman times. My brother and I, we, wanted, to, go, back, to, the, Ghetto. But no, our parents blackmailed us into submission. Mila, whom they adored, helped them. In the final desperation, my brother delivered a speech. "Dignity," I remember he said. And some other big words. And my parents told me what a lucky man I was to have found Mila. Anyway, we agonised till the Ghetto Uprising died its painful death and then we vegetated and bickered till the Warsaw Uprising started. My brother, Slavek, you knew him, wasn't prepared to listen to my parents' pleas any more. He just said something about obligations, and of a once-in-a-lifetime chance to do what one really believed in. His Warsaw needed him ... In short, he left and we never saw him again. The shelling was constant and a rebel's chances slim. Don't forget that Hitler's men controlled most of the city, most of the time. My parents, they had always had that irritating habit of thinking aloud. They managed to create an atmosphere of uncertainty. Mila tried to calm them down; but all she managed was to inspire me with an urge to do an heroic deed. I was ready to go in search of Slavek but was physically stopped by my father, while my mother wept openly and howled that I was the only son she had left. Of course, she pointed out how selfish I was. Anyway, what did it really matter? I was dead as I was, which they didn't notice, as though breathing were the only sign of life. I think I even may have stopped communicating. Perhaps not. I can't remember, and don't really care.

Once the Warsaw Uprising died down, we didn't volunteer for evacuation. We chose to stay, being afraid to expose ourselves to the Germans and the Poles. Not many people stayed in Warsaw, as you know. We did. We lived through the almost total destruction of the city. I was still waiting for death. I don't think my parents were and I'm sure Mila wasn't. We lived in an empty, burnt-out Warsaw for four months, from September 1944 till January 1945 when the Russians liberated us. My parents didn't survive. It's not my intention to sing a sad song of hunger, cold, deprivation, of us four, then two, stewing in the same, hard-to-digest sauce. I think I'll spare you the sad tales of chilblains, hunger, filth, not even knowing whether you deserve it or not.'

There were moments when I saw that Victor was good and that he cared and was capable of compassion, and then there was a twist, full turn, as if he wanted me not to like him, as if he was afraid.

'I don't think you're sparing me.'

'At least I'm sparing you all the sordid details, which might prove to be a fatal mistake.'

'I know what war means. I was there too, you know.'

'Not exactly the same, was it? Protected by your mother, if I am not mistaken.'

'You don't have to tell me the war was so much easier on me.'

'Unless I tell you everything, you will never understand what a bastard I am.'

'I hardly know you. I nursed a pleasant recollection of a summer holiday. It's gone. Why do you visit me? It puzzles me.'

'And to think that I was sure I was welcome here. For old times' sake. I will have to add another disappointment to my already long list.'

'You know you are welcome here!'

'That's good. I need to talk. Is it all right for me to talk? For you to listen?'

'Sure.'

'Well, *are* you sure?' he smiled a new — or perhaps an old — smile.

'Come whenever you feel like it. Bring Mila and ... and the baby. What about next weekend, when Julian is at home. Come over for lunch. Next Sunday, if you like. Or Saturday. Michael and Baby could play together. And we could chat, all four of us. How about it?'

Victor was watching me. The short-lived pleasant smile was taken over by the sardonic grin.

'You're not too bright, are you? ... My thanks to you, just the same. Mila and I are greatly honoured. We'll be delighted to accept your ever-so-kind invitation. One day.' He got up, finished his coffee. 'Give my respects to your husband. I will remember to give your best regards to Mila. She will be delighted, I'm sure.' He shook hands with me, kissed my hand and was gone.

He left me totally confused. Luckily there was a lot to do. Joe and Michael arrived home almost at the same time. Joe told me of school. 'It was all right, mum.'

'What did you do?'

'Nothing much.'

I prepared some fruit for them.

I told Julian of Victor's visit. He listened carefully, but didn't seem concerned.

'You shouldn't worry. The man obviously went through hell. It must have affected his whole way of thinking, his whole attitude towards his wife and

149

baby. I feel sorry for him, but it's not really our business, is it?'

'Not really. But I can't see how I can forbid him to come here if he wants to.'

'Don't worry,' said Julian, showing me yet again that he was worth all the love and respect I had for him.

Victor didn't get in touch with us, not on the following weekend, nor a week later.

Winter arrived once again. Our house was quite cosy, and we were pretty well acclimatised by then.

Joe and Michael's favourite meat was lamb, the very one which we had never eaten in Poland.

EIGHTEEN

We spent our summer holiday with Franka and Leon, who lived near the beach. We enjoyed our rediscovered talks and daily contact with the sea. I looked at my sons building sandcastles, digging tunnels, splashing in the water, collecting shells and pebbles. Julian's prophecy had come true. Our boys were healthy and contented like any other children, what else was there to wish for?

I loved the feeling of sand under me and the lazy warmth of the sun, I loved the movement of the sea and its constant melody. I watched the waves with an almost hypnotic fascination. When the tide was in and the waves huge, when there was salt in the air and I heard no other voices but the eternal voice of the sea, I sat at the beach and was grateful to Julian for taking care of the boys, for I needed this time by myself. The white of the seagulls, the blue of the sky, the rising waters, the foaming confusion, and that feeling of well-being from the combination of the freshness of the air and the calm clarity of mind.

Sometimes, I thought of Victor, hitting out with fury, with persistent repetition, over and over again. I felt that if he were ever to visit me again, I would let him throw off all his bitterness, all the pain which had built up in him over the years like a tidal wave. And perhaps then his bitterness would spend itself. That is what I wished. His visits, his sarcasm, cynicism, his bottomless pit of suffering had brought discord into my life. I wanted to forget the war. Perhaps not to forget but, rather, not to remember it every day of my life. We wanted to build our future, to take part in the future of Australia. This land was, if not ours, our sons' land. It was destructive to feel miserable; I had to help my children to look at life in a positive way. Neither Joe nor Michael should be handicapped because their parents had suffered during World War 2. The boys knew we had not been born in Australia, they knew vaguely of the war, they knew of our losses. One day, Joe had asked why he didn't have grandparents, like all his friends. And then he had made the suggestion that he should call Franka and Leon aunt and uncle. Everytime a request or a question like this had arisen, we had talked of our past, or our problems, and it had always made me sad to see Joe being serious beyond his age.

Joe wanted his father to play cricket, or football at least.

'I never played either sport in my life, it's too late to start now,' Julian tried to explain.

'What sport did you play, dad?' continued Joe.

'What sport, dad?' echoed Michael.

'When I think of it, none.'

'None?' cried Joe.

'None?' seconded Michael.

'It was different in Poland; we were not very sport-minded. We had physical education at school ... We played basketball, netball, we followed the soccer. But once I left school, that was it. There were more important things to do.'

'Like what?'

'What, what, what?'

'Can't you leave your father in peace? He must be very tired', I thought that Julian had had enough.

'Gee, mum . . . I want to know. Can't you tell me, dad? Is it a secret, or what?'

'What, what?' giggled Michael.

Yes, it wasn't always easy. We had to explain things to our sons that didn't need explanation in normal circumstances. We were parents, but had to extend our role to grandparents, uncles, aunts, cousins. Victor was complicating our life, mine anyway; he was a constant reminder of our past. And so was the sea, the sky, nature. If not of my past, of someone else's. I picked up a pebble, an ordinary greyish-brown pebble, or was it? Smooth, rounded, flat, it must have been around for a long time. A past, now mine, and that of those before me? Thousands and thousands of years of being picked up, and then dropped by waves. Dragged deep down, tossed, and washed over, and hit, and ground, and then thrown on to the beach again, to be picked up by a migrant, born in a faraway land, whose thoughts were confused because of the cold, calculated, grim brutality which had been committed on her generation. I was looking for an answer and felt it must be somewhere around, perhaps in the eternally rolling waters of the sea, in the grain of sand, in the racing clouds, or in the smooth perfection of my pebble, which I nevertheless left on the beach for someone else to pick up. And then I regretted that I hadn't kept it and searched for it every time we went to the beach. I wanted to find it but, of course, I never did.

The holidays were over. It was back to work and to school, back to the everyday routine. My association with the Lloyds was fully under control. Mrs Lloyd had stopped preaching to me. By then, she had realised for some time that I believed neither in fairytales nor her unselfish motives.

News from overseas was coming at regular intervals. The letters had as little detailed information as ours. Only on very rare occasions did we allow ourselves to write what we really wanted to say.

Dear Mother,

Yesterday, on a train, I sat opposite a young girl who looked so much like Irma that I couldn't keep my eyes off her and was disappointed she didn't speak Polish. It was idiotic: the girl was sixteen, perhaps seventeen; Irma, had she survived the war, would be almost thirty.

I search for familiar faces all the time, although it doesn't really make sense. I know we should try to concentrate on the future, instead of remembering the past. We are tough people, we had to be, in order to survive, not only physically, but also emotionally. Tough, yes, but not necessarily unfeeling.

What amazes me is my capacity to take delight in everyday events. In a sunset, the stillness of an autumn day and the geometrical perfection of a cobweb spun between two rose bushes in our "back yarden", as Michael calls our backyard. Sometimes I think that our appreciation is greater because of what we went through — I hope it is. We definitely have some measure for comparison. A warm house, a clean comfortable bed, two healthy sons, the promise of a safe future. It's more than I ever expected. And yet, sometimes I feel miserable without any real reason.

There is no intimacy between the tongue of my children and myself. I wanted Joe and Michael to know the beauty of Polish. I was very excited about it. I selected the poems, the ones you had read to me. "You know what, boys, your grandmother read this book to me!" The boys watched me with some interest, but plainly wished the session

154

would end. Michael was restless and even Joe kept on glancing at the window as though he couldn't stand being trapped inside. The whole reading proved to be a failure; even Joe didn't understand much. Day-to-day language is one thing, the poetry another. There is a lost link somewhere. And a family without a family. Perhaps because of this I search for a familiar face, if only to remind myself that Julian and I, too, had a past. I wonder how you feel about it?

All is really well with us.

The group of people we knew was growing larger. The whole process of being introduced was like a chain reaction. The only qualification needed was the Polish language. It didn't take us long to realise that the language wasn't really enough to make us close. Sometimes I felt that I understood my neighbouts better than some of my compatriots. Our children shared the same school, the same games. We had something in common, similar problems and joys.

Mr MacAllison came to see me. Till that day, I had never had a proper conversation with him. He even agreed to come inside. He sat down.

'May I offer you something, a drink perhaps?' I asked.

'Very kind of you. Beer would be fine.'

The trouble was I didn't have any beer and when I offered Mr MacAllison something to drink, I simply meant coffee or tea.

'Don't worry. I'm not really thirsty.'

'I'm so sorry. Would you like some tea?'

'Don't worry ... What I came to see you about is my wife ... She has six months to live. Cancer. Four kids! My God.' Mr MacAllison wept. I was wishing I knew what to do. I couldn't tell him not to worry, I couldn't tell him the problem would go away, I couldn't tell him I was sorry, though I really was. I sat still.

'I don't know who to feel sorry for first; for Pat, for our kids, for me?'

'Perhaps a mistake was made. In the diagnosis. It happens.'

'No mistake. Just spoke to the doctor. Six months with treatment, three without.'

'Does your wife know?'

'Not yet. Couldn't face her. The doctor volunteered to give her the news. I think I should do it myself. What d'you think? Pat likes you, and our kids do too.'

'I really don't know. I only wish I knew. Back in Poland, they kept the truth from the sick. Don't ask me if it was better, I don't know ... I want to help. Anything. The children. They know us. They like playing at our place ... Please let me look after them.'

'Thanks ... My mother can help, my sister. We have a lot of friends ... Isn't it amazing how many people will have to be involved in replacing one mother,' and he wept again.

Mr MacAllison was a true Aussie. My whole heart was going out to him. I wondered why he had come to see me. Perhaps because I was a stranger, it must be easier for him to talk to me than to someone he knew well.

When I thought of my life in Australia, Mrs MacAllison featured in so many experiences. The chickenpox and how I had always been on guard, how I had looked for signs of discrimination everywhere and how Mrs MacAllison, because of her down-to-earth, no-nonsense attitude, had cured me, to a certain extent, anyway. Joe and Michael really loved her. She had taught them nursery rhymes which they, in turn, had transmitted to me. Yes, and

156

at Christmas time, though there was no snow in December, there were always presents for Joe and Michael next door. Mrs MacAllison.

'I'd better be going.' Mr MacAllison stood up. 'I have to do something . . . very difficult. Perhaps the Polish way is better, who knows? On the other hand, once the treatment starts, she'll have to know anyway . . . Sorry to have troubled you; hope you don't mind.'

'How can you say a thing like that? We are neighbours, aren't we? If you need anything, remember, call me, any time.'

'Thanks. I might do just that.' Mr MacAllison smiled and left.

I went to the window. Joe and Michael were playing with the MacAllison children. A happy group. I wanted to hold them close, to protect them from the fate which was hanging over them. I felt angry because there was nothing that could be done to change the situation. I felt completely helpless. I wondered whether the MacAllisons would decide to tell their children.

Mrs MacAllison responded to the treatment better than expected. We saw quite a lot of the whole family that year. We visited each other and the children spent a lot of their free time at our place. I taught them a few Polish words, a Russian song or two. I would have enjoyed their presence wholeheartedly if not for that ever present gnashing feeling of something inevitable, coming closer, day by day.

157

NINETEEN

Victor visited me again, again on his own. I told him about Mrs MacAllison and how brave she was to lead as normal a life as possible, not even showing any signs of feeling sorry for herself.

'I'm surprised at you and your admiration!' exploded Victor.

'I don't understand what you mean.'

'Have you ever heard of the Second World War? Of what happened during those six years? Or would you like me to refresh your memory?'

'No need, Victor. But it has nothing to do with the enormous courage of this woman. A mother, whose days are numbered and who can still face the future regardless.'

'I'm afraid I can't share your childish admiration. Everybody's days are numbered. Your heroine is surrounded by loving care, by all the medicos she wishes to have. She has friends. She knows her kids will survive, she knows they have a caring father ... Think of the mothers who were pushed into gas chambers and stop romanticising. There's no glory in death. If someone is lucky enough to die from natural causes, there's no need to elaborate on it.'

'How hard you are. Hard and unfeeling.'

'Not really. I'm a realist, rather, free from hypocrisy and deceit. Think about it in your spare time ...

'Look at yourself, you haven't even asked me how Baby is. You must have lost interest in my family altogether and all because of your neighbour. It's not very nice of you, is it?'

'Your visit is a surprise. I was waiting for you and your wife and the baby to call on us. If you chose not to come, it's fine. But at least you should have let me know. You can't come in whenever you fancy ... You bring unrest into my existence.'

'Oh, that I shouldn't do. Never. Never. Convey my best regards to your husband and your sons, won't you? I trust you'll stay in good health till we meet again ... By the way, don't worry, Mila is well. Baby is well. I'm well.' Victor kissed me, shook hands, and left.

I felt shaken, mainly because of what he had said. I could have cried with exasperation, but I didn't let myself. I felt that this was exactly what Victor was wanting. I felt for Mrs MacAllison with all my being and I was relieved that regardless of what I knew and had witnessed, I was still capable of caring, of grieving, of feeling the pain of someone other than myself.

Mr MacAllison stood in front of me. The children were in the backyard, their noisy, excited voices filled our ears. Mr MacAllison kept shaking his head as if unable to produce a sound. 'Her new home ...' he managed at last. 'It's an irony. Now I would like to give her everything, whatever she wants ... Before this happened, we argued constantly. She was full of ideas. How to improve things. What to buy for the kids. Where to go on holidays .... I ask her now what she wants. "Nothing," she says. "There must be something," I insist. "Morphine," she says.'

Later, when Mr MacAllison had left and when all the children were having their afternoon tea, I asked them how they liked their new house. Chris said that he didn't like it at all, neither the house, nor the school. He said that he missed us all, that the house was too big and, with their mother not feeling too well, it was too hard for them all to keep the place really clean 'which makes daddy angry and in a bad mood. And on top of it all, there're too many New Australians. They jabber-jabber-jabber in their crazy languages, so no one can understand them, all they ever talk about is money, money, money. They're so mean. All migrants are.'

'Chris,' I interrupted because I wasn't ready to hear any more. 'Chris. Dear, dear Chris. We are migrants too and we are good friends. Remember when we met? I didn't know how to speak English at all. Remember how surprised you were, and how I taught you how to say things in Polish and Russian and French and Latin? It was difficult for you, remember? We were laughing? It's hard to learn a new language, but your neighbours will. Give them a chance ... We are migrants too and somehow we managed.'

'It's not the same.'

'What d'you mean?'

'You're a different kind of migrants. Daddy said you're different and mummy said it too.'

'I don't agree with any of you. We were the same.'

'Mum,' interrupted Joe. 'Can we go out now? Please?'

'Yes, of course.'

I was quite upset by this conversation, but Julian wasn't concerned. He saw it as a part of the normal process of acceptance of any migrant by the native-born Australians.

Another visit from Victor. He was quite charming.

He told me that his baby was doing well and was not addressed as Baby any more. Mila had named her after Victor's first wife.

'Halinka. What kind of a name is that for an Australian girl, anyway? Baby can't be Halinka. She doesn't look like Halinka and I won't have it. Mila and her crazy ideas.'

I smiled.

'Why are you laughing?'

'I'm not laughing ... I'm thinking about Mila. Without knowing her, I do admire her. If I were you, I would come up with an alternative name to suit you all, and Australia.'

'Like what?'

'That's not up to me to suggest.'

'You're not much help.'

'I know.'

'I was thinking how strange it is,' said Victor seriously. His voice was deeper, his eyes calmer, his hands still. 'If you lose someone, you remember only the good things. See, Mila, she's not really the worst. You must know I'm not the easiest person to live with. Sometimes I argue with myself. I say to myself that my murdered wife wasn't really as I remember her ... We had our disagreements. She couldn't even cook. She was great when things were normal, but not so great in times of crisis ... Mila's love is different, almost quixotic.'

'That's not fair.'

'Why?'

'The comparison. You shouldn't do that. As long as you keep on comparing, you will never settle down.'

'If I want your advice, I'll ask for it. You just can't understand. I talk and talk. I bare my soul and you don't even know what I'm talking about. You're not too bright, I've noticed it before. Not that it matters ... What I really wanted to say was that martyrdom

161

breeds myths — that's all. But I can't accept that.'

'Why?'

'Never mind why ... Tell me, how's your neighbour? I'm not so bad, see? I still remember you have a neighbour who isn't too well.'

'How noble of you. Unfortunately, she is very sick now. They have moved away and we don't see them too often.'

'Who are your new neighbours?'

'Latvians or Lithuanians, I was told.'

'I bet you must be thrilled.'

'I haven't met them yet, I don't know.'

'But surely you must remember how they behaved during the war? Helping the Germans, taking part in executions, the liquidation of ghettos, guarding concentration camps. Applauding whatever the Germans did.'

'My neighbours are about my age; they couldn't have.'

'In that case, their parents must have.'

'I want to believe they didn't. I can't go on living like this, there must be some sense in life and something better to do than to search for Nazis all the time.'

'The fact is there are plenty of them around. If you want to pretend they disappeared with the signing of the armistice, that's your business. I prefer to know. Nazism exists, anti-Semitism exists, the Irish problem exists, the Black problem exists; the Ku Klux Klan and our very own Australian League of Rights are active and expanding. Nationalism is growing with devastating results. The churches haven't changed either, they're as hypocritical as ever.'

'Australia's different.'

'I wish you could substantiate your statement.'

'Of course I can!'

'Can you really?'

'Look at us. We live in dignity. They let us in. When we stayed in France, we had to register at the police station periodically. We couldn't work without a special permit. No foreigner was allowed to own property. While other countries were considering what to do with postwar refugees, Australia let us in, gave us work and the promise of a more stable future. It gave us back dignity. I'm free, my children are growing into self-confident people, free from complexes.'

'Why d'you think Australia let us in? On humanitarian grounds? Is that your belief?'

'I guess so. The main thing, they let us in.'

'Let me enlighten you a bit. Let me establish certain facts ... They brought us here because they needed us to fill all the perpetually vacant jobs. The hardest and the dirtiest factory work, to build their roads, to extend the sewerage. That's it. They needed us perhaps as badly as we needed their permits. They didn't bring us here because of any great compassion for war victims ... They have more compassion for a dog or a cat ... They don't love us, they need us. As long as they need us, our life might be tolerable here. I hope this prosperity will last for ever, which of course it can't, and once it's over ... then we might feel a slight change in the general attitude towards us.'

'At least they are not anti-Semitic.'

'But they are. Perhaps not in the same way as Poles or other European nations; they have their own ways. They excelled in their treatment of the Aborigines ... They're well known because of their "White Australia Policy" ... I wouldn't be too sure.'

I couldn't take any more. Victor talked and talked and I tried not to listen. I felt like a child who has been promised a dog and when she gets it, finds that it isn't a real dog but a stuffed one. And then I heard Victor saying something to the effect that I must be paid by the Australian Immigration Department.

'I wish I were. I'm sure they wouldn't offer you a job.'

'Why d'you say that? I have nothing against Australia. I look at life in a more realistic way, that's all. And because I am your friend, I want to share my views with you.'

'You're not a friend; you're the most negative person I have ever met,' I said and was surprised at myself.

'At least you can be sure I'm real and alive.'

'You are full of bitterness and hate, you must be real. You feel sorry for yourself, as if you were the only person who has suffered.'

I was saying things I wasn't sure I wanted to say and at the same time I was glad I was saying them. And then Victor got up and I knew it was a sign that he was agitated.

'You have to admit,' he said very quietly, '... there are not many who can match my experience.'

I felt ashamed, so ashamed as I had never felt before. 'Sorry, Victor, I'm really sorry,' I stumbled over the words. 'I didn't mean to say that.'

'All right ... When you apologise, you certainly apologise. I must send Mila over to you for tuition ... Time to go, anyway ... If I feel like visiting you again ... can I come?' And then I think he said — I wasn't sure, but it sounded like — 'please'.

'You know you are welcome, regardless,' I said and then regretted my open invitation.

'That's good to know,' said Victor in his normal, clear voice and left.

I was confused again. I wondered what Victor would have said had I told him of little Chris and his attitude towards migrants. I was glad I had kept it to myself.

TWENTY

We went for a two-week holiday. We rented a small place in Rosebud, a bayside township on the Peninsula south of Melbourne. Joe and Michael played in the sand and water, collected shells and browned their bodies. It was the first proper holiday we had had since we left Poland, nine years ago. We had time to ourselves, we filled our lungs with fresh air, our minds with optimistic plans, and our eyes with new images. We fell in love with Sorrento's back beach, our first encounter with the ocean. The huge waves smashed against the rocks, sending geysers of water high up in the air. The air was invigorating; the sun played on the water, revealing all the hidden colours of the sea. The seagulls glided above, graceful and white, spreading their wings against the blue of the sky. I could have stayed there for ever.

Back home, we learned that Mrs MacAllison had died. It was a sad day for me. I was still full of sun and water, of love and laughter and couldn't believe that this fine woman, my first Australian friend, was gone. I wanted to tell her how it had been and how happy we were, but instead there was that other neighbour who gave me the news and told me that the funeral ceremony was 'short and sweet', except that

Chris had carried on once he learned that his mother had been 'burnt to cinders'.

We went to see Mr MacAllison and the children, but the children were not at home; they were scattered all over with the relatives. Mr MacAllison seemed lost in his wife's dream house. He wanted to sell it. 'I can't stand it,' he said. He promised to bring the children to our place one day and to stay in touch.

I couldn't chase the picture of Pat MacAllison from my mind. I remember her watering the children, singing songs, preparing for birthdays and Christmases. Sometimes shouting, often laughing. She was so full of life; I found it hard to accept that her children were separated from each other now.

And then my mind went quite out of control, thinking of myself and my children and what would happen to them if I were to die. There were not even relatives to take care of my boys if necessary. Franka perhaps would do it, I thought, though she was working hard, frantically saving for the house she had never had.

I watched Joe and Michael with fear. My emotions were running amok and I confided in Julian. He urged me to have an early night and to stop talking nonsense.

On the following day, Victor arrived. I was glad to see him. I felt he was coming to terms with himself and was accepting, though reluctantly, his present situation. I wanted to believe that his own old self would re-emerge one day, though it was deeply hidden. I felt that all his cynicism, lack of consideration for Mila and the baby, were either a conscious or subconscious shield to spare himself more suffering. I felt that as long as I was ready to listen to him, to be patient, understanding, he must pull through. My role, as I saw it, was rather an attractive one; that of a noble woman. Julian smiled slightly when I unveiled my secret hopes.

'What about Mila?' he asked.

'What about her? Obviously she doesn't understand what Victor's needs are.'

'I suggest it's not your business. You have your own family who love you and need you very much.'

'D'you imply I'm neglecting you and the boys because of Victor?'

'I said nothing of the sort. You have your own life. Don't let yourself be dragged into the past.'

'You don't want me to keep in touch with Victor, do you?'

'Not particularly. I wish he would work in the day time as any other normal person.'

'Just now when I feel he's getting better . . . He's the only person in Australia who was my friend before the war.'

'Some friend! He didn't even remember you.'

'But he did! It was just an act.'

'A very convincing one, if you ask me.'

'Act or no act, I feel he needs those visits to preserve his sanity . . . and besides, it's good to feel needed.'

'I wish you would stop exaggerating. I know that after every one of Victor's visits you don't sleep well. All that analysing, trying to understand how the man's mind ticks, leads you nowhere. I don't think you really know how to handle a case like this. And with all your good intentions you might make his wife, his child and all of us miserable.'

'I'm not going to stop him from coming, I can't.'

'I'm thinking of you.'

'I wonder . . . I'll keep on seeing Victor as long as he wants me to, as long as he's in need of talking. Where else could he go?'.

'Good luck to you.'

Julian must have been disappointed in me. Perhaps he didn't like Victor, perhaps he was even jealous of him; if he was, he never spelled it out. Meanwhile, I thought a lot about the MacAllisons and when Victor arrived again, I told him of Mrs MacAllison's death and of the children being separated and living with different relatives.

'Does it worry you?' asked Victor. 'It shouldn't. It only proves what kind of people the Australians are.' I tried to defend Mr MacAllison, pointing out that the man was working and therefore couldn't look after the children properly.

'Have you ever heard of housekeepers?'

'Mr MacAllison couldn't afford one, I'm sure.'

'How d'you know? What irritates me is your rather gutless, illogical approach to people you know. I can assure you that no European working-class family would ever allow a separation like this. And their financial situation would be more difficult than your Mr Mac's. Australian people are cold people, not very emotional. They are unfeeling people, more concerned with their own well-being than with real problems. It must have something to do with prosperity ... It breeds selfishness, egocentricity ... D'you honestly approve of Mr Mac's action, or are you just playing some make-believe game?'

'I'm not playing any games. I feel for them all. Your readiness to judge surprises me ... when your own life is in such a mess. Concern for people! What about your attitude towards Mila and your baby?'

'Can't you ever stick to one topic at a time? We're not discussing my situation. I'm almost certain we never will. I never said I'm proud of myself, or approve of my actions. I know better than anybody else what a bastard I am. But just because I have made a mess of my life, or rather, my life has made a mess of me — that would be a more accurate assessment of my situation, wouldn't you agree? — I still think I'm entitled to criticise. Perhaps it makes me feel more like a human being?'

It became a pattern. Victor would come, Victor would go and in between there was confusion: disturbing, provocative ideas planted in my mind. He definitely was the most blunt person I have ever come in contact with. He would express his views openly, which frightened me because of their force and brutal, naked logic.

Sometimes he would simply come to play with Michael, who liked and trusted him, and then wait for Joe and talk with him of school and how it had been when he was Joe's age. On these occasions, I really liked him. Once I congratulated him on his ability to establish a good rapport with the boys and asked him whether he had a similar relationship with his daughter. He answered that he had hardly any-thing to do with the girl, whose name 'by the way, is Margarette . . . It's not easy to forget once you get involved. I'm still working on Mila. What the woman should do is take her precious Margarette and leave me once and for all. I have told her so many times . . . Had she had a bit of dignity, she would have left me a long time ago. She would have started a new life on her own, or with another man. In the past, she was never short of willing partners; I'm sure she'd manage to pin down someone even now. She has certain basic qualities . . .'

'How can you be so . . . so cynical, so spiteful? I am trying to understand you, you don't make it easy . . . Why are you so . . .'

Victor laughed and covered his face with his hands. I knew that gesture of his when laughter and weeping became one. He didn't want me to see his emotions and though I wanted to speak to him with the same patience as I did when my sons were distressed, I never dared. I told him that if he thought Mila would make his dream come true, he was mistaken. She obviously loved him, for some unknown reason which nobody could possibly understand. I told him that he must feel a certain responsibility towards his baby.

'Not Baby,' he reminded me, 'she has a name, everyone should have a name.'

'All right. Margarette. Sorry. Not long ago it was Baby. "I don't want you, Baby?" ... I hardly know your wife ... She must be a person of rare strength to tolerate your inhuman behaviour. ... And constant sarcasm.'

'You mean she's tough. One shouldn't mix up toughness with strength. Toughness and the Second World War were good partners. Look at me, I keep on living, though, in my opinion the people who perished are more alive than I.'

'When will you stop living in the past?'

'It's the only life I know; nothing has seemed *real* since.'

'Is your night shift a permanent arrangement? Couldn't you change it to a day job? To see more of Margarette?'

'You don't even know what you're suggesting ... I can't risk another child and to trust Mila and her contraceptives would be the same as to trust a bank robber with one's finances ... Don't try to make me see the light, you won't succeed.

You were a funny-looking, skinny, sensitive kid. Once upon a time. You puzzle me, that's why I keep returning. My night shift comes in handy. I don't particularly want to know your husband better, though I wish him well, but you can tell him, just in case, to be on guard ... I wouldn't mind having an affair with you, if I only had the chance. After all, my responses are quite normal, even if my emotions are dead.'

He looked at me like a sharp observer. 'What happened? Aren't you going to spit at me, to faint, to call me names? To throw me out? ... Aren't you going to say anything?'

'I wish I knew what. I don't know. I hope I'll never despise you.'

'Typical, melodramatic answer.

You don't allow yourself to be honest, with yourself, with me. You must be quite fond of me — otherwise you wouldn't tolerate my enlightening monologues. I must hold some fascination for you, perhaps even more now than when you had two long plaits.

Perhaps you are my link between the past and now ... But you hold no physical attraction for me. I love Julian, I love our children.' Victor laughed aloud and then stopped. 'You are naive, aren't you? What I proposed has nothing to do with love, your husband, or your kids, who, by the way, are quite tolerable ... You have made another mistake. If you attract me physically, that doesn't mean a separation from your husband, or other nasty implications. What I have in mind is a rather pleasant physical experience, which we really shouldn't deny ourselves, considering all the horrible things which have happened to us in our lifetime.'

'For me ... Those things ... Physical and emotional, love, consideration, respect, can't be separated — it's all inseparable.'

'Only because you don't think for yourself. You have accepted the so-called values, you have been conditioned to accept them ... I wonder, how d'you see your role in life? I want to know. Don't be frightened, I don't mean any harm ... I will never rape you, that's not my style. You're as safe with me as you must be with your husband. Acceptance on both sides, or nothing. OK?'

I couldn't understand, or explain, why I wasn't

offended. I was exceptionally calm. The whole conversation fascinated me. Instead of searching for words full of indignation, I chose rather to ignore Victor's provocation and tried to answer as if his sarcasm had never bothered me.

'"My role in life,"' I said. 'Those are big words. I have never given it much thought ... I have certain wishes, dreams, expectations ... To see my sons grow up healthy. Without wars ... To have a peaceful life ... Not to hurt the people around me ... To be truthful ... It's difficult to know.'

'How touching ... You don't really know, do you? You repeat what you have heard or read. Or what you think is right. Or what you think is expected of you, so you'll always be considered a good person. You must really like it. I can't stand it.' Victor jumped to his feet, pointed his finger at me in true melodramatic tradition. 'As long,' he recited, 'as women like her exist, the future of mankind is safe ... Listen to yourself. Words, words without meaning, the Pavlovian response to questions. Not even one single thought that you can call your own. You build your life on empty sounds, you don't think.' He was still standing up, looking at me, confusing me.

'What d'you want me to say?'

'You don't understand. It's not what I want you to say,' he laughed, 'it's what you think ... If you ever do.'

'When I tell you, you don't believe me. I don't know what to say. I try. I really try to tolerate your intolerable presence.'

'You want me to go?'

'I don't know. Perhaps ...'

'And to think that I thought you liked me. Nothing physical, mind you, only a purely Platonic relationship. You have a mission in your life. To bring me back to life. To make me forget my gory past. To realise how beautiful life is. To reconcile me with my wife and child. You wouldn't give me up now, would you? No, I'm sure you wouldn't.

Let me tell you something. You tolerate me because you like me, because you like that searching attention of mine. As long as I don't touch you ... You're not one of those, not you. A pillar of society, yes. The righteous woman.' Victor clapped his hands. 'Tell me, my visits, they're all right with you? It never bothers you, the intellectual betrayal, I mean?'

I didn't know what to say, I wasn't prepared to admit that Victor was right. 'If you're so well prepared, if you know what's right without any doubt, how d'you see your role in life?'

'I haven't got one, neither do I pretend that I have. Once I thought I had something to offer, I had this idiotic notion to make our tormented earth a better place for all. The six years that changed the world changed all that too. The war gave me one thing I had never had before. Time. Plenty of time to think. Purpose in life, politics, ideologies, trust, death, religions, polemics, honesty, hypocrisy, love. I had plenty of time to myself. I told you, the partisans, the forest, wounds, and I don't mean physical ones. I wondered why I had been born, what was the sense in all this suffering. The whole world was kidding itself with big words and deadly weapons, with churches spreading good news and "love your neighbour", turning their delicate noses away from the stench of burnt bodies. It was unreal, the crowns of the trees, the blue of the sky and the dark labyrinth of my mind ...

'Man's one and only purpose, his only role in life, should be the reproduction of the species Continuation of life, that's all. And it doesn't always work.'

'Are you trying to reduce human beings to the animal level?'

'I'm not trying to reduce anyone, I'm trying to sort it all out. We belong to the mammals, therefore we should stop wasting our energy on reasoning, on progressing, on inventing, setting ourselves on the course of disaster and complete annihilation.'

'We can't stop thinking.'

'Which is a pity.'

'But we are thinking animals.'

'So is a field mouse.'

'A mouse couldn't write poetry, invent the radio, compose music.'

'And it wouldn't wage a war. Unless its safety, or that of its litter, was threatened. It wouldn't kill for a thrill, it would kill not by the process of reasoning but rather by the instinct which dictates to it to keep life going. In contrast, we pretend. We have brains — there's nothing we can't do. Philosophy, literature, art, inventions, flexibility. We tell ourselves we could change whatever we want. In reality, we progress; but not in a civilised, but rather in a mechanical way. Once we're dead, it doesn't matter. What matters is whether we replace one life with another.'

'What about your daughter, then? I can't accept that. Isn't your life fuller because you reason, because you read, feel, experience?'

'Leave Margarette out of it, all right?'

'Fine.'

'Now. My life is neither fuller nor more desirable because I'm aware of certain things. I think that if man had not philosophised, had not established political systems and ideologies, wasn't power hungry and ambitious, perhaps then the human race wouldn't have to experience some of the cataclysmic events which one can hardly class as being especially beneficial to us all.

Why d'you think we listen to music, or hang pictures on our walls, or buy some useless objects

174

with which we, so to speak, beautify our dwellings? Because we have forgotten how to be honest even with ourselves. We not only fuck — we tell ourselves — we also need intellectual stimuli. Organised society is the answer, the arts. Love for one's country. No need to be timid. We are better than any other nation. Our government knows. We are ready. The country needs us. We have to fight to show those bastards who we are and also for the glory of our country. We don't kill, we just eliminate or destroy an enemy. We don't spy, we are involved in reconnaissance. We are good and honest. The others kill women, children, the elderly — not us. The others spy the others are cruel and barbaric. Never us ... The result is that we are unable to sort out what's what.'

I listened to Victor, not daring to interrupt, frightened to say the wrong thing; and then Michael arrived, loaded with books.

'I want you to read. You talk, talk and you don't read to me.'

'I'll read to you,' said Victor and lifted Michael and his books high up in the air. Michael giggled. 'I'll read you a book, which one d'you want?

'I want my mummy to read.'

'You know what? I'll read you a book and your mummy could get us a drink, milk for you and some coffee for me, OK?'

'I don't want milk. I want my mummy to read my book.'

'Come over here, son.'

Michael ran to me, climbed all over me till he settled down on my knees. I read him his favourite book, which I knew by heart as Michael must have too. I waited for Victor to go, but he didn't. He watched me with such an intensity that my whole face burned. I felt uncomfortable and wondered in which direction his tormented mind was heading. I wondered whether he would ever come to terms with life and with himself. He was searching, that was obvious, asking questions. His answers were distorted, as if seen through the prism of his tragic past.

One book was finished. 'Another one, mum?'

'This one and no more.'

There was a meal to be cooked. Joe was due from school soon. Victor's eyes, burning, searching. Tragic eyes.

'Come on, Michael. Let's go to meet Joe? Would you like that?' proposed Victor. 'That is, if mummy will let us.'

'It's all right with me, if you have time.'

'I have plenty of time.' Victor took Michael's hand and when they were leaving, he said: 'I feel like a pseudo father.'

Victor stayed for tea. If Julian wasn't happy, he didn't show it. He was perhaps a little more courteous than usual. Victor was as close to charming as he possibly could be. He chatted with Michael and Joe most of the time. He was respectful towards Julian and me, and his cynicism was absent. I thought that he must have responded to our kind of evening in a positive way. He left when Julian was busy bathing the boys.

'Say goodbye to your husband from me. He's not a bad man,' he said.

TWENTY ONE

By this time, we knew quite a number of people, mostly of Polish-Jewish extraction. Our group was growing in numbers. All of us were trying to heal our war wounds. Different fund-raising clubs and organisations mushroomed. Polish literary evenings and other functions were organised. So we also received an invitation to a ball which was to take place in the Palais de Dance, in St Kilda.

It was the first invitation to a ball I had ever received. The war had started when I was fifteen. When it ended, I was pregnant. Joe was born by the end of 1945. There had been neither time, money, nor the desire to attend balls. But I had preserved a mental picture of my parents getting ready for an occasion and then greeting us the next morning in their bedroom with paper umbrellas, masks, balloons, fans — all those ravishing and stunning things which made our day and which evoked some nostalgic feeling towards balls and their obvious magic. My mother's ball gowns were exquisite. I remembered how once, when my parents were away, I had gone to my mother's wardrobe unnoticed and had changed into her gown. I picked the one which glittered and tantalised the most. It was too long for me and much too big. I was slightly disappointed that it looked so very loose on me, though I straightened it out by gathering all the surplus fabric behind my back. I was determined to match my reflection in the mirror with my preconceived image of myself. I stuffed the bodice with handkerchiefs and stockings, which proved to be very effective. I put on my mother's high-heeled shoes. I used my father's tie as a belt and drew the bodice of the gown over it. I looked tremendous. Mother's cosmetics transformed me and her perfumes made me slightly dizzy. I looked at my reflection and had to admit that I was the most beautiful creature I had ever seen, even more beautiful than our beloved dog. Though perhaps I didn't quite match my mother's poise, so perhaps I was the second most ravishing beauty in the world.

I had certain difficulties in keeping my balance. Whenever I moved around, the shoes had a tendency to twist and were hard to control. The only solution was practice, that's what I was always told. 'If you don't succeed the first time, keep on practising till you do.'

I tried to walk as gracefully as possible; I even managed to keep my feet in the shoes; most of the time, anyway. I was confident that I was just about to conquer my problem, when the right shoe turned to the left, while the left one turned to the right and I fell down. There was a tearing noise. I closed my eyes and wished I didn't have to open them ever again. And then someone came in. 'What on earth are you doing?' I heard my sister's voice. 'Look at you! What a mess. Your cheeks! What have you done to your cheeks? And the smell, what's that? It makes me want to spew! Whatever possessed you to do it?' grumbled Tania while she was helping me to get untangled.

'Do I look beautiful?' I asked timidly, hoping that Tania would appreciate all my efforts in full.

'Beautiful!' she screamed and let me drop back to the floor. 'You look ... awful. You look ... like a tart!'

'What's a tart?', I asked.

'Never mind.'

And then Tania discovered the tear. It was really ugly. It made a repulsive, threatening gap in the silver glitter.

By the time Tania had stopped screaming and telling me what a wicked, horrid girl I was, never to be trusted, vain and clumsy, our governess, obviously attracted by our raised voices, had rushed in. She started all over again, which was normal. She told me that this time nothing would save me, that I'd have to dance to the music, or something like that. She told me that I had ruined my mother's best dress, the most precious one, and as a matter of fact, she was quite certain that my mother was planning to wear it this coming Saturday. She called me all sorts of names I had never heard before and because they were new to me I couldn't judge whether they were bad or good, though it was enough to look at her, even without listening to her high-pitched voice, to conclude that she was very angry.

What surprised me was the fact that I didn't even cry. While my governess was pulling the dress off me, I even urged her to be extra careful, because she might tear the gown still more if she wasn't. This quiet observation evoked a new wave of abuse. My governess was more than disappointed in me; I was the most outrageous child she had ever had the misfortune to work with. To think I didn't even cry made her want to cry herself.

I watched her with interest. It would be fascinating to see her cry. To my disappointment, she didn't. She marched me off to the bathroom instead. When I saw myself in the bright light, I had to admit that my cheeks were slightly too rosy and my brows slightly too wide and black. Even my lips, which I had covered with lipstick with the utmost care, were smeared. My nose was whiter than a well-whipped egg white. When I looked closer, I thought I really looked funny, a bit like a clown, so I started to laugh, which in turn brought on a new facial expression in my governess. She went all white too and then she started scrubbing my face. She showed me no mercy. The harder she scrubbed, the louder I laughed. I didn't want to cry.

When my parents arrived home, I was still in the bath. My governess rushed out to meet them and left me alone. I could hear her high, excited voice telling my parents what a horror I was. My mother said that she fully agreed. It had definitely been wrong on my part to do things like that, but as far as my mother was concerned, the tear in the gown didn't necessarily make it any worse. What surprised her, my mother said, was the fact that I had been left to myself for such a long time without my governess realising that I was missing. My governess cried. I wasn't absolutely sure, but I thought she did. And then my mother said that she was sure I hadn't done it on purpose, so in her opinion the matter should be closed. 'As you know,' my mother concluded, 'I don't believe in putting a child to bed without forgiving her.'

I heard a few more super screams coming from Miss Lotte and then my father said that if she wasn't happy with us, she was free to give notice, or even leave straight away.

'That is exactly what I will do,' cried Miss Lotte. She slammed the door, though she was always telling me not to do it. My bath was getting cooler and cooler.

And then my mother came to the bathroom and I cried. She said: 'You will catch a cold. The water is absolutely cold.' She turned the hot-water tap on and then she put her arm in the water to stir the water and when it was nice and warm, she washed me, and her hands felt soft and loving.

'You understand what you've done was wrong?' she said.

'I'm sorry. I'm really sorry. I wanted to look like you ... I didn't mean to spoil your gown.'

'I know. You promise not to do it again?'

'Yes.'

My mother put me to bed. Before I went to sleep, I heard my father telling her that she shouldn't be too soft with me. Then I cried for a while longer and then I went to sleep. In the morning Miss Lotte was gone. I wasn't sorry; her hands never felt nice.

I remembered all this when I making preparations for my first ball. I bought a piece of material. I bought a pattern and tried to copy my mother's ill-fated gown. I was really excited. While I worked, cooked, or whatever I did, the idyllic picture of balls I never went to floated around me. Scenes I remembered from the movies, from books. Blue girls, and girls pink, and white, smiling, turning, gliding. Full skirts, small waists, the immortal music of Strauss. That's what I was hoping for. When the day arrived and I was dressed, Joe and Michael looked at me.

'Gee, Mum,' they said almost simultaneously. I felt great.

The ball itself was a different story. People drank a lot and talked nonsense all the time. They pretended to be very gay and *bon vivant*. My bottom was pinched several times. In the end, I danced only with Julian and worried whether the boys were all right with Mrs Staszewski. The wine was lukewarm, and so was the orchestra. They played prewar Polish tunes. The singer looked ancient, his voice wobbled together with his body and he sang of broken hearts, of passion, of never-ending love, of love and yearning. The tunes didn't mean much to me, though they meant quite a lot to many people who sang along with the orchestra.

I enjoyed dancing though, and told Julian that once during a school social I had been given a balloon for being the best waltzer. He said that I wasn't a bad dancer at all and that made me realise that this was the first time we had danced together. It made me feel good, because we were free and together, with our life in front of us. Julian didn't enjoy waltzing too much, it made his head a bit dizzy, so we danced other dances and gazed at each other. Julian didn't pinch me even once.

Had Victor danced with me, I was sure he wouldn't have pinched me either.

TWENTY TWO

Mila came to visit me by train and bus and foot with little Margarette. The weather was really bad, it was raining hard, and the wind was cold. I wondered what had made Mila choose a day like this.

'I wanted to see you,' she said. 'Not the best kind of a day. But one never knows. It might improve later, don't you think? One never knows in Australia.'

'Yes, one never knows.'

Michael was happy to see another child. Since the MacAllisons had moved away, he missed his next-door friends very much. He took Margarette by the hand and wanted to go outside, but even for him the sky looked too threatening and before I had a chance to stop him, he changed his mind and took his new friend to his room.

'I have wanted to see you for some time now,' repeated Mila. 'The weather, not the best, but I didn't want to wait any longer. You think I should've?'

She was saying things as if she had prepared and repeated them for some time.

'I'm glad to see you. Michael and Margarette should be good friends. She's a lovely child. Her eyes, she reminds me of prewar Victor.'

I wasn't sure why I said that. Margarette's eyes

were very dark and very big, they were like her father's, but I wasn't sure if it was the right thing to say so.

'D'you really think so? Margarette's a good child. I only hope Victor's going to see it one day.'

'The last time he visited me, he told me of Margarette ... you know he visits me, don't you?'

'I know ...

Where did I go wrong, do you think? See, all our neighbours know Margarette. You ask anyone in our flats: "You know Margarette?" and the answer is yes. They all know how many teeth Margarette has and whether she put on weight or not. You ask Victor, and nothing. He tells me to leave. I don't know how much longer I can take it. Even a stone gets worn out.'

I hardly knew Mila. I had only met her once, on our first visit. I hadn't been impressed. But since Victor had started his periodical visits, I had rather changed my mind. His lopsided view of Mila and their life together had made me think.

Mila's face was broad, with widely spaced, very blue eyes. Her nose was sharp and upturned and her lips full. Her hair was cut, or rather butchered short, it was mousy in colour. As for her figure, it was difficult to distinguish because of the oversized jumper and loose, shapeless skirt. Her shoes were dirty, perhaps because of the rain, though if my memory served me right, her flat hadn't been spotless either. She had an irritating habit of scratching her head all the time. But when she looked at Margarette, her face would change, become warm and quite pretty. When she smiled, she exposed her upper gums and two rows of very white, healthy teeth. It wasn't difficult to guess why she had come to see me. Even the weather hadn't stopped her, nor her pride.

Victor's visits to me bothered her, she told me in a flat voice. Apparently since the end of the war he had been involved with several women. She knew, and Victor had never denied the fact.

'It was nothing,' smiled Mila, not even looking at me. 'Not much feeling in this world, is there?'

'Not much,' I said, because I wasn't sure what else to say.

'You know, I hoped ... How I hoped! That once our child was born, Victor would stop pretending that he can't love. It's funny, I never knew him to be more distant than he has been since Margarette was born. He didn't even want to give his child a name. Baby, he was calling her.'

'I know.'

'You see, he told you.'

Mila asked once or twice whether the children were all right, so we brought them to the kitchen where they played together with their toys, interrupting us from time to time, or rather all the time, making conversation quite difficult.

Mila told me that she had been a fighter and a battler all her life. 'I never gave up. Never.' She had joined the partisans because she hadn't fancied working in Germany as a slave labourer. Many girls from her district had been sent to work on German farms. She had asked her mother what to do. Some girls had been quite content to work away from home. 'My mother wasn't much for talking. She wasn't much for giving advice. I often wonder if she loved me ... She must have ... Life was difficult. Plenty of hard work, not enough to eat. There was no time to do much apart from work ... My mother didn't even care if I finished primary school or not. She rather saw me helping on the farm. Life was harder for us after my father lost his leg. Early in the war. He wasn't much use to anybody...

My mother was glad when I left home. She was keen on a fellow I didn't like ... Anyway, it has nothing to do with what I wanted to say.'

'You were telling me about the partisans.'

'Yes. The partisans ... They were good to me. They fed me. Even brought me some warm clothes. So I didn't really mind. I lived with them. See, it was war. They looked for some comfort ... It didn't worry me. I liked them, I wanted to help them... They were good men. Their lives were so uncertain ... We lost seven men. A lot for a small group... You must be shocked,' she said and looked me straight in the eye.

'Not at all. I understand.' And I really did.

'One day, the partisans returned to the hideout and reported that all the Jews from the area had been shot. "No more Jews," said one man, and a second added, "Good riddance". They all laughed, except the one who had joined them from the city. He said that once the Germans had finished with the Jews, they'd start on the Poles. "The fact that we are living through a relatively quiet period could be attributed to the fact that the Germans are too busy liquidating the Jews and the Gypsies".

His name was Tom,' smiled Mila. 'He never slept with me ... He was fond of big words. We always laughed a lot, whenever he said "attribute", or "relatively", but apart from this, he was all right... Funny, but all right.

Anyway, in the afternoon three of the boys went down to the village. To have a look what was going on. And to bring some food too. One of our men said it would be good to look in Jewish houses. It was a well-known fact that Jews were rich. They returned in the evening with Lucky, which means Victor. That's what the men christened him.'

'I know.'

'You know?' Mila was surprised. 'Victor told you?'

'Yes.'

'He told you how it was?'

'Not much. Glimpses here and there, nothing much.'

'He was a mess. Not really as lucky as the men said. His wounds were bad. He could hardly move and he didn't want to speak at all.' Mila blew her nose hard. 'It wasn't easy for him. My mates were good, helped him a lot, but they were not too happy once I told them I wasn't prepared to sleep with them any more ... You see, as long as it didn't matter, I didn't mind, but once it started to matter, I just couldn't do it any more. They teased me a lot and told me that it wasn't fair for a Polish girl to prefer a Jew to her own kind. And that Jews were strange lovers and I had better think things over ... Perhaps they were even right. Victor was strange. He stayed under a tree, staring, without seeing, not even noticing me. But I loved him. I don't know why, but I did ... Ever since ...

I heard the men saying that they were sick and tired of sheltering a Jew. And that it was against the German law and we could all be butchered once Lucky was discovered. And besides, why should they look after him when he only ate and slept and because of him they had lost me, and where would they find another girl ... They must have really liked me ...

I told Tom what I had heard and then Tom reminded us all that being partisans wasn't really acceptable under the German jurisdiction, so it wouldn't matter much once we were apprehended. When he said "jurisdiction", the boys looked at each other. When he said "apprehended", everyone screamed with laughter. Tom looked at us, annoyed, and then he explained what the words mean. Tom was more and more of a leader from day to day, though he talked funny ... And then, a day or two later, Tom said that he was not going to tolerate it if any of the men forced themselves on me. I still remember how he said it ... You want to hear?'

'I would very much like to hear it.'

'Tom said: "all of you had a good time with Antosia". My real name is Antosia, you see. I was Antosia then. Victor didn't like it. He told me once that it reminded him of Poles and anti-Semitism. So I changed my name to Mila. After all, what's a name?' And then she wrung her hands and said that it hadn't really changed the situation.

I had never come face to face with a love like Mila's. The odds were against her. The whole picture became clear to me; the forest, the harsh conditions, the danger and the strange love. Every word spoken, every gesture, every look, spelled only one thing: Mila's unreserved love for Victor.

'When I was small. My mother ... Every Sunday, we used to go to church. It was beautiful. Pictures and statues. Singing. People dressed in their Sunday best. Our priest ... He knew how to talk. I wish I could speak like him. Victor would listen if I did. I always listened to our priest. He told us of heaven and hell. I even wanted to die. The young go straight to heaven, you know?

... He told us about the Jews and that they killed our Lord Jesus. He told us not to buy from them and not to have anything to do with them. Once he said that because of them, the war started ... I'd never spoken to a Jew before I met Victor. I knew them by sight. They dressed differently to us, they looked weird. We saw plenty of them on market days, when we went to market. I saw Jews and they were always afraid of us. Once I picked up a ribbon from a Jew and ran away without paying. He didn't even chase me, just stood there and said nothing. My mother was pleased, so I thought that I had done something good.'

Mila talked and talked. Little Margarette cuddled up to her knee. Mila picked her up and held the child

in her strong arms. I put Michael to sleep and
returned to the kitchen. Mila kept on rocking
Margarette to the tune of an old Polish lullaby, which
I remembered being sung to me in my childhood.

> *Looli, baby looli,*
> *Cuddle to your mother,*
> *You'll be safe,*
> *In your sleep.*

Margarette closed her eyes - Victor's eyes. And then
Mila continued in a half-whisper.

'I came to you. You know why ... I worry ...
Because of you ...'

'Mila, let me ...'

'No. I want to tell you what it means ... When you
came to our place, Victor said he didn't remember
you. He lied. Something he does for me. To make me
feel better, I think. When he does, I tell myself that
perhaps he's beginning to like me and then he tells me
to go away, so I don't know what to think.'

'He must care for you. You went through so much
together. It binds people.'

'Sometimes I think so. But then he's mean to me.
It's hard to know. First he tells me he doesn't
remember you. Then he tells me he remembers you
and that only because of me he couldn't tell you. And
that I don't even know how to speak properly, not to
mention the way I dress myself. And that he hardly
has anyone whom he knew before the war and now
that he has found someone he can communicate with,
a person who can understand him, he has to call it a
miss because of me ... "I wish you were not
pregnant", he told me a few weeks before Margarette
was born. "I'll never love this child, anyway," he told
me. I told him it's his child ... D'you know what he
said? Did he tell you that too?'

'I don't know. I don't think so.'

'He told me that he couldn't be absolutely sure,

because with someone like me, one could never be sure. He didn't say sure, he said certain ... It hurt me. I don't often think of being hurt ... I'm a good wife to him. One day he'll see ... One day. If you don't take him away from me.' Mila hung her head down as if exhausted.

'Mila', I said. 'I may call you Mila?'

'Sure,' her body was moving from side to side; she never stopped.

'Mila, listen to me. I don't want to take Victor away from you. He belongs to you, to Margarette. I want to help. There's why I won't stop him from coming here. He has been badly hurt. You know it better than I.'

Mila cried silently and cuddled to Margarette.

'He needs a lot of time. To heal, I mean. He comes here. We talk, or rather he talks. I think it's important. The hell he went through still rules his life, confuses his emotions ...' Mila stopped rocking Margarette. 'You tell me that? You think I don't know? You think I'm an idiot?'

'Sorry, Mila, I didn't mean to upset you.'

'You can't upset me', she smiled. 'Nothing can upset me. I'm Victor's wife ... You say things. You know nothing ... His nightmares. He wakes up screaming, calling his wife's name. He calls for his little boy ... Cold and wet with fright and real pain ... That's why he took the night shift. He's afraid to sleep. The night shift is only an excuse, it's not because he's frightened of me having another child ... It didn't stop the nightmares, anyway. When he's full of anguish, when his eyes bulge, then he needs me. For a moment or two, and that's all.

And then he goes to you. You talk the same language. I know. You remember things from his life when it was free from pain. It must be attractive to him ... He tells me to take Margarette and go. No, not to go, but to disappear from his life ...

'I think he loves you. If you love him, if you care, you must send him away ...'

'Mila,' I tried again, but she didn't allow me to say more.

'You, you don't even know what love means... Don't let him think you care. It's not a game. Margarette needs a father.' She looked at me, her eyes the colour of cornflowers, shining with indignation, hope, despair, but above all with inner life, with acceptance of what life is, with courage.

'Mila,' I said. 'Victor and I talk. I have a husband, two children. I love them very much. There's no room for an affair. But there's room for friendship, for feeling, for concern ... Julian knows of Victor's visits. He doesn't like them much.'

'See!'

'We just talk. Victor and I, we talk, nothing else. I hope these talks might help. It's important for you. You're great, Mila, you must win, Victor must see you as you are, he only pretends he doesn't.'

Mila got up, pressed Margarette against her heavy breasts and cried aloud, unashamedly. Margarette woke up, opened her dark eyes and cried too. Mila was choking with words and tears.

'Hush, hush, my precious,' she cried. 'Daddy, daddy ... Daddy will love you.' She handed Margarette to me. 'You don't mind?' she wept. I didn't. The girl was soon comforted. Victor's daughter. Mila blew her nose, dried her eyes and stopped crying as suddenly as she had started. She didn't stay much longer, she didn't want to and perhaps she felt there was not much more to say. I asked her to come again. She agreed but I wasn't convinced she would.

TWENTY THREE

Winter went away, spring came, and then summer and autumn. Victor hardly ever came and when he did, his visits were brief and impersonal. Meanwhile, Julian was planning our future, assessing our situation and comparing it with that of other migrants. He was working hard, I was working hard, the boys were growing. They were going through their shoes and clothes with the same speed as European rabbits would go through a field of Australian cabbage.

Quite a number of our friends had ventured into retail businesses, mainly milk bars.

'It's ridiculous,' Julian planted a seed. 'What about it?' he said seriously, though initially I thought he was joking.

'We could sell the house and buy a milk bar too. Work there for a couple of years...'

'And then what?'

'And then we shouldn't have any financial problems.'

'I don't know ... Our home, it means a lot to me.'

'We could always get another one. A better one. With a garage, internal toilet. On a made road.'

When we had bought our house, it had never

occurred to us that one day we might be in need of a garage. Eventually, we became the proud owners of an Austin A 40. The trouble was we had to park it outside, which didn't improve the rusting problem and no matter how much time we spent polishing it, we could never bring the duco back to its original glory. The car started from second gear only. The gear itself had a tendency to switch to neutral without any warning. Apart from that, we had a lot of fun with it and put it to good use.

'It would be nice,' continued Julian, 'to have a new car one day.' The seed of temptation was taking roots. 'I'm sick and tired of taking gallons of water whenever we go for a drive, it's maddening.'

I had to agree.

We consulted Franka and Leon.

'It depends on what you want from life. Australia is a land of opportunity. Perhaps you should take the plunge.' By then, Leon was already swimming in his own business waters.

We consulted other people and were introduced to experienced milk bar owners. They seemed worn out and I hoped that their finances looked healthier than they did. Exhaustion or not, they initiated us into all the secrets connected with the right selection of a business.

'You have to buy a shop which sells a lot of milk and bread.'

'Why?'

'It's a lot of work, but it means a lot of people come to a shop like that, which indicates good trade prospects.'

They showed us how to make milk shakes and spiders.

'Spiders are the best line: the lemonade foams before you start pouring it in.' Meanwhile our boys stuffed themselves with jelly babies. And then

Michael wanted to go to the toilet, but changed his mind once we reached the outside dunny. So on the way home Julian and I decided that if we were going to buy a milk bar, it would have to have a proper toilet and a habitable dwelling.

The milk bar alternative never left us in peace. It cropped up whenever we needed a new pair of shoes, or even more urgently when I dreamt aloud of a washing machine or a larger fridge.

'You'll be able to stop sewing, once and for all,' Julian was taking on the image of a serpent, while the well-established plant of temptation was thriving.

Another year went by. Michael started kinddergarten and Joe proceeded to Grade 6. By then, we heard that milk bar prices had soared and the money we were hoping to get from the sale of our house, less what we owed on the mortgage, wouldn't be enough to buy a good business. There was a way out, we were told. One could always borrow money.

The decision wasn't easy. It disturbed us till, in the end, we accepted that a milk bar was our destiny, something inevitable, like measles.

We resigned ourselves to the fact that a fever, the desire for security and financial freedom, was raging in Melbourne. The most susceptible people were the migrants. Before they succumbed to the sickness, they were pestered with images of plenty. Huge fridges and trouble-free cars, children's music lessons and houses with internal toilets, shower recesses and subscriptions to the theatre, concerts and holidays. And more effective assistance to the family back in Europe. All these dangled in front of the affected people like a carrot in front of a donkey.

In the end, just when spring started, we managed to sell the house and we bought a milk bar which had a decent toilet, a bathroom and a backyard for the boys to play in. It was also selling some milk and bread.

With the help of the experienced 'milk-bar-ers', we calculated that it should take us one year to repay the money we had borrowed, provided that we ran the business properly. Our friends were not entirely happy with the amount of bread and milk the place was selling. They had shown little interest in the toilet and the dwelling and no admiration at all as far as the bathroom and the backyard were concerned. They told us to concentrate on the running of business and to try to repay the loan in the shortest possible time. We were fully aware how generous our friends had been. Even the Lloyds lent us a hundred pounds. Somehow the whole process of borrowing money wasn't very difficult; the difficulty started with the repayment of the loan. From the very beginning, we were not absolutely sure how long we would last. Yet it was the length of time we were prepared to run the business which was going to determine whether or not we were going to establish and consolidate our financial stability.

I didn't much like this period in our lives. We didn't make a fortune — very few people did. I wondered how many customers were aware that their corner milk bars were often run by people who in their previous existence had worked as technicians, lawyers, chemists, teachers, opticians. 'A golden age of milk bars'. I was angry with myself and with Australia, looking at Julian wasting his productive years in filling fridges with milk and soft drinks, replacing items missing from the shelves, and sorting the empty bottles.

I resented the fact that we never had a meal together, that is Julian and I. We usually took turns to eat with the boys, so that they would remember who their mother and father were. The other party looked after the shop. If the person on duty wasn't able to manage alone, the call would go out: 'Shop, please', which used to start the adrenal glands working hard. While both of us worked in harmony and unison, saying 'Yes, please' and 'Anything else?' and 'Two-and-sixpence, thank you', Michael would charge towards the lolly counter, grab as many sweets as possible and disappear from the shop before we had a chance to tell him what we thought of him. We suspected that Joe was behind this. He certainly displayed a very strong ability for guerrilla tactics and training.

Our new life caused a number of previously non-existent problems. Julian studied the prices with the same determination with which he must have studied for his final exams. The boys knew very well which moment to choose to disappear from the house in pursuit of pleasure. So once the mini-stampede was over, I would have to go in search of my sons. Experience taught me that the boys would be found in a house equipped with a television antenna. I would follow my instincts and it usually worked. In the end, we gave in and bought a television set, something we had never wanted to do. Another compromise, another principle thrown overboard. For we were the parents who wanted to keep the dialogue with their children going. We were the parents who used to criticise others for not even knowing where their children were at any given moment, for not knowing what their children thought and did. We were supposed to be such parents as no other parents had ever been. All of a sudden, we were letting our boys, our unique sons, get away with murder, or just about.

It was strange to discover what physical exhaustion and mental apathy could do to one's principles.

I hated the milk bar from the very day we started, when I was asked for a block of chocolate and didn't have a clue where it was kept. The customer kept on pointing it out to me but I couldn't see it. And then all the people in the shop pointed their fingers at the chocolate, saying : 'It's over there' and 'Can't you see?' and 'Gee-whiz' and still I couldn't locate it. I felt like a jelly and then Julian, who was performing miracles serving all the customers, urged me to hurry because it was bad for business to keep customers waiting. And as if that wasn't enough, Joe walked into the shop on his long legs. So instead of looking for the chocolate, I asked him why he wasn't looking after his brother and what he was doing in the shop.

'We're starving, Mum,' he said and left the shop with dozens of Violet Crumbles.

I stood there not knowing what to do and then the man who wanted the chocolate must have lost his patience, because he said 'Permit me', walked behind the counter, and helped himself. It was very decent· of him and I wondered why he hadn't done it in the first place.

Our milk bar was located in Malvern. We were the first foreign intruders into a lolly-shop in the area. The previous owner, a true-blooded Aussie, had warned us that the suburb was a very conservative one and that the milk bar had never been run by anybody but Australians. 'So you can appreciate, I'm sure, that I can't guarantee how my customers will take to you.' We took the risk because the toilet was irresistible and the Spring Road Central School meant that Joe would be able to proceed to Melbourne High School.

We stayed in the shop for a little over one year. On weekends, during the school holidays, or whenever the temperature soared, we simply shut the shop in the afternoon and took the boys to the beach. We felt that spending a couple of uninterrupted hours with our boys was more important than making money. Whenever the air became hot and the ice-cream lost its firmness, Julian and I would look at each other, and one of us would say what was to become our proverbial sentence: 'We'll start making that fortune one day later.'

Our opposition was happy with us. So was our dentist. And so were the local boys who collected the refund money on empty bottles. Their never-ending procession puzzled us because they had bought hardly any soft drink from us. But because they usually spent the refund money on milk shakes and 'spiders' and chocolate bars, we valued them as good customers and didn't mind. And besides, they were funny and laughed a lot. Their ingenious scheme wouldn't have been discovered if not for the fact that Julian, thanks to the thriving summer soft drink's trade, developed a hernia and, once the season ended, had to undergo an operation. Two weeks in hospital, followed by a period of recuperation at home. He started on the job of sorting the empties and made himself comfortable between the laundry and the bottle shed. There he discovered that we had partners in profit. He watched our valuable customers helping themselves to the empties from the lane. The partnership was dissolved almost immediately, though little by little, the boys returned to us. One even apologised and proposed to repay the money by sorting the empties after school.

While Julian was in hospital, Franka decided I shouldn't stay on my own, especially at night. She organised that she, Leon and Louis would sleep with us in turn. I tried to reassure her that I wasn't frightened. If someone was stupid enough to risk his freedom in order to rob us, I argued, I would simply pretend to be fast asleep. Franka didn't accept my reasoning and one morning, the ever-so-eager Leon let the milkman in. The milkman's eyes almost popped out of his head and I had the feeling that he had lost his shaky belief in fidelity and good marriages.

The shop. Children. Husband in hospital because of the business I had never wanted in the first place. Lost reputation. It was a handful for me. No wonder that I wanted to sell our goldmine as soon as Julian was feeling better. But we had to wait for a while longer. Apparently I had done a criminal thing: I had overstocked the shop. All I had wanted to do was to show Julian that I was capable of running the shop. So that he wouldn't have to worry. When he returned from hospital, he found well-stocked shelves and a statement from our friendly bank, all in red.

'Forget about selling. We have to stay till we repay the overdraft. We must get rid of some of your stock at least.'

Michael started at the local State school and didn't fall in love with it as we had hoped he would. The school was old and dilapidated; and so was the infant teacher. 'She spits on my blackboard,' Michael complained, 'and then she asks me to wipe it off.'

School apart, Michael was fine. He established friendships with boys from the neighbourhood. All his new mates lived in normal houses, set in gardens. I held the secret hope that from that time on, Michael would be spending time in the right surroundings. My hopes were short-lived. Michael's friends preferred our yard to their own envy-evoking properties. Their parents were unconcerned; they didn't object to their children playing with the children of the local shop-keepers. Australian democracy at work.

When I was a schoolgirl, there existed well-defined boundaries which were dictated by snobbery and ignorance. In the house where I lived, there was a small delicatessen, run by the parents of a girl who attended the same school as I. The girl was on a scholarship, devised by the nosy, though well-meaning parent body to assist poor children with scholastic potential. The girl was assuredly more mature, more serious about her work, than I. At that stage, I wasn't even absolutely sure what school was for, except perhaps that I saw it as a place where all nice girls should go, and also where one should have a bit of fun.

To my shame, I never walked to school with the shopkeeper's daughter. Whenever we met, we just greeted each other and each of us went her own way.

Australia was different.

Another incident. A Baptist minister, a customer of ours, took pity on Joe and Michael and one Sunday morning, when he saw them stuffing themselves with lollies, invited them to come to his Sunday school.

'It's impossible', I said and felt that because of what I was going to disclose, I was throwing our whole future to the lions. 'We are Jewish, we're Polish Jews.' My heart was beating hard, and I wondered what the consequences would be, for I had disclosed our own and our sons' capital crime.

'It doesn't matter,' said the man. 'The Gospel is the same everywhere, isn't it?'

It was well worth coming to Australia to hear words like that. It was even worth while running a milk bar. The fact that we were Jewish didn't stop people from patronising the shop. By the time we left, people were sorry to see us go. I was amazed how many of them were prepared to share their thoughts, their experiences, with a shopkeeper. I was hoping that the new owner would find time to listen. There were so many lonely people around.

TWENTY FOUR

When we sold the milk bar, we rented a small flat in East St Kilda. We bought a car, a brand-new Holden, on hire-purchase. The dealer took our beloved Austin plus twenty pounds and left us with a new station wagon and vouchers for the twenty-four monthly repayments. So instead of owning the car, the car owned us. This fatal vehicle kept us in its clutches for two long years. It was the first and the last time we bought anything on hire-purchase.

The chase for a job started all over again. And then Julian was offered a position at the Gordon Institute of Technology in Geelong. Initially, we were very enthusiastic. We went to Geelong. Julian disappeared into the Institute where conditions and his pending responsibilities were discussed, while I waited with the boys in a nearby park and wondered what Julian's decision would be. He was away for a long time, or perhaps it only seemed so very long to me. Loneliness crept all over me again.

The realisation that I didn't know one single person in the whole sleepy town was devastating. If Julian would accept the job, we would have to go through the same agonising process all over again. Another migration. I remembered Mrs MacAllison and didn't want to tear myself away from the few friends we already had in Melbourne. I felt desolation. It was present in my thoughts, in my short breath, in sweating palms and in the urge to run away.

The boys were quite unconcerned, they played as any other children did and when I called them over, they came reluctantly.

'How d'you like it here?' I asked them and my voice wasn't like my own.

'It's all right. We haven't seen much, have we?' said Joe.

'Dad promised we'd go to the beach.' Michael was the one who really loved beaches, water and sand.

'If we settled here, wouldn't you miss Melbourne, your friends, school?' What I was saying wasn't really fair.

'I don't know . . . I suppose I'd miss them all.'

'I'd miss them all, except for school,' said Michael.

'Oh, you'd better go and play. I don't really know...'

'You don't know what, Mum?'

'I don't know what to think about it all. Geelong, I mean. It would be a welcome and a long overdue change for your father to work in his field. On the other hand, we don't know anyone here.'

The boys were standing in front of me, almost at attention. They must have felt my confusion and unrest, otherwise they wouldn't have listened to me with such patience. My poor sons. Having migrants for parents could certainly complicate life.

'Oh, never mind. We'll think of something. Run along now.'

'You all right, Mum?'

'Of course I'm all right,' I forced a smile. The boys ran away and I thought how easy it was to fool them.

How unpredictable my moods were. Only this morning, I had been happy. I wasn't sure what had got into me now. My thoughts rushed uncontrollably. My mother, Tania and her two children who I had never had a chance to meet. Regrets, sickness, death, migration. Had it been such a good idea, this new life-dream, to tear ourselves away from the remaining members of our family? Was it fair to our children, to ourselves, to them? That absurd milk bar venture, how had our family reacted to it? Oh, yes: 'What a crazy way to earn one's living! Can't you find anything else to do?' that was what they had all said in one way or another. But for us, when we had bought the milk bar, it had seemed to be the only logical solution.

What were we to do now? To move miles and miles away from Melbourne would mean to end friendships we had established over the years of loneliness. No one could keep a close association with stretches of highway in between. Weekends were designed for gardens and children, not for trips. Letters, even letters tended to be less frequent with time. Even the letters from my mother, or to mother . . .

The park was lovely, which seemed to be the norm for Australian parks. Huge trees, endless lavish lawns, a paradise for birds and children, perhaps the answer to disturbing thoughts.

Julian was walking towards me in the company of another man. His walk was, as always, springy and trusting. He introduced me to his companion, who apparently worked in the Institute.

'It would be tremendous to have Julian with us,' said the man. 'Geelong is a nice place, not as big as Melbourne, but I venture to say that the people are more friendly. A good place to bring up children.' The man was smiling.

'I'm sure it is,' I said more abruptly than I had intended and then I turned to Julian. 'You've made the decision already?'

'Not yet.' Julian looked embarrassed.

'I would love to go home.'

'What about Joe and Michael?' said Julian. 'I promised the boys to show them the place. The beach, the football grounds.'

'I'd rather we went home. I feel tired. I have a headache.'

'I'm sorry to hear that,' said the man.

'Don't be, it's really nothing. It's up to Julian, if he feels like staying, we'll stay.'

'I was planning to show you around, so you'd have a better idea of the place. To take you to the local estate agent, who could give you some idea regarding the cost of houses.'

'Surely there's no immediate hurry. Julian hasn't made up his mind as yet.'

I wished Julian would step in and say something, if for no other reason than simply to stop me from saying things I shouldn't say. I looked at him. He must have been aware of my plea, but somehow chose to ignore it. The silence was building up.

'You have thought of everything, George, haven't you?' said Julian.

'Not really', said George.

'There's plenty of time, though. Thank you just the same, George. You've been a great help.'

'Don't mention it ... When do you think you will let us know?'

'Within the next three, four days. Is that all right with you?'

'Fine,' said George. 'I hope your headache will go away soon.'

'Yes,' I said and wished I had been more polite to the man. It wasn't fair to blame him for our own problems, but I was frightened because of his good manners and charm, I was frightened that because he was so very polite and helpful, he might sway my opinion and force me to reconsider my stand. Julian looked quite happy. The offer must have given him satisfaction. Why was I spoiling it for him? George must have seen me as a cold, selfish bitch, which I really wasn't.

'Once more, thanks, George. You've been a great help,' Julian repeated, which for him was a sign of nervousness. 'Time's getting short; we'd really better be going.'

'Sure', said George. 'Are those your lads?'

'Yes. Joe and Michael,' Julian smiled, as always when he mentioned the names of our sons.

'They are about the same age as our children, though we have one more, a girl, in between. Next time they'll have to be introduced. And my wife, of course.'

'That would be nice.'

Julian didn't call the boys to come over. I myself didn't know what to say. Perhaps it would have been better had I said that I didn't wish to leave Melbourne, that I didn't like Geelong. That I couldn't stand the thought of leaving my friends behind once again. Even George would have understood. For how many times could one start a new life over again? All the pain, all the spent emotions weighing against a better job, job satisfaction, that ever-so-elusive security. Was it really worth it?

I didn't even hear what Julian and George were talking about, till George said: 'Goodbye.' He even shook hands with me.

'We're not really savages,' he said and his eyes smiled. 'Once you'll give yourself a chance to know us better.'

'I never thought you were,' I said and shook George's hand firmly.

When he walked away, Julian looked at me.

'What's the matter with you?'

'Nothing's the matter.'

'You can pretend in front of George. You can't fool me.'

'I told you, I have a bad head.'

'I don't believe you.'

'Suit yourself. I wish I were home and had never come to this godforsaken place.'

'How can you know, without even giving yourself a chance to look around?'

'Would you like me to pretend I like it? It's not the place itself, it's the whole idea. To leave Melbourne, our friends. It's like another migration.'

'Not exactly, is it? Opportunities like this don't knock on one's door every day. Especially on a migrant's door. I don't understand you. You always moan what a waste it is when a person doesn't work in his own field. I thought you'd be happy with a husband working in a tertiary institution. I thought you like the idea. You did in the morning, didn't you?'

'Yes, I did. And then when you went there and when the boys were playing their stupid games, I couldn't stop thinking how lonely it would be. In Melbourne, the shopkeepers are already used to my pronunciation. I don't have to start all over again. Where we came from, and poor us because of the war, and not to worry because we'll be all right... And I was thinking what would happen to you if something happened with me ... Nothing morbid, simply a stay in hospital or even the flu.'

'If you don't want to move ... You thought of a lot of problems, haven't you? The people I met were friendly enough, even though I didn't know the latest cricket score ... I felt we should give it a go. But when I think of it, it doesn't really mean that much to me one way or the other. I think I buried my professional ambitions during the war. You know what I want

206

from our life. Peace of mind and a certain amount of security for you and the boys. I don't care what kind of job I do. Sooner or later they all become routine, no matter how interesting they are to start with.'

'I thought you were taken by the idea and the place.'

'Sure I was. But it doesn't really matter. Job satisfaction became a shaky concept a long time ago. Job and fulfilment, another utopia. Job and income, that's more realistic. One could always find an interest in books, in music, in family life, in the theatre. Geelong has nothing like the Melbourne Theatre Company, anyway.'

'You know what else I thought?'

'Tell me.'

'You really want to hear?'

'You know I do.' If Julian's voice was flat, I was trying to persuade myself that the only reason was the fact that he was slightly tired; after all, it had been a long day, rich in events.

'D'you realise that Geelong hasn't got a University? Which means the boys would have to study in Melbourne!'

'That's a long way off.'

'But it's a fact. I couldn't live without them ... You know, I thought how my mother must have felt when we left Poland. Her children ready to start on a new life, away from Europe. A new life at the end of the earth. I wonder if my mother will ever meet our children, if I will ever see her again.'

'You will. One day. Let's go home. I'll write to the Institute ... I rather like Melbourne.'

I was happy and frightened. I knew that if I were to say anything else, I would cry. I didn't trust myself, so instead of saying anything to Julian, I called to the boys, urging them to hurry because we were going home and then I threw my arms around Julian.

'What has got into you? Be careful, we are living in Victoria.'

Julian was right. A job offer like the one from the Institute didn't repeat itself. I was full of remorse, which didn't help the situation nor restore Julian's missed chance.

Being a realist, he didn't dwell on the lost opportunity. It didn't take him long before he bought a cake shop. The reason he decided on the shop was mainly because the hours were good; that was for me. Julian needed my assistance between ten o'clock in the morning and half past two in the afternoon, which meant that I was at work only when the boys were at school.

The shop was easier to run than the milk bar, though Julian worked pretty long hours. He used to leave home before seven in the morning and never got home before seven in the evening. But at least we had the evening together, half of Saturday and all day Sunday — unheard-of luxury to any milk bar veteran.

It took us over two years to repay the money we had borrowed for the business, and then we started to save for the house. Ever since we had sold our first house, the dream had always been close to the surface, though hardly ever mentioned. The flat we rented was a very tight fit and the boys kept on dreaming of a dog, but they weren't allowed in the flats.

I don't exactly remember how long it took us to buy the house, but I know that our whole life changed once we bought it. It was a brand-new house, with a garage, a shower recess and three bedrooms. For the first time in their lives, the boys had their own rooms. We spent every spare moment on the garden and once a week we bought a plant which we planted with the utmost care. The problem was that whenever I arrived home, our backyard was full of dogs who showed little consideration for our gardening efforts. Michael always offered the same explanation: the dogs had followed him home, therefore they must like him. As far as the side gate was concerned, he didn't have a clue how it came to be locked. It must have been a sudden wind, or perhaps one of the dogs hit it with its tail. It was never easy to get rid of the dogs and after the chase our garden looked a poor sight.

'Michael', I tried to explain. 'One day you'll have a dog of your own. We must let the garden establish itself. We will never have a proper garden as long as you keep on bringing all those dogs ... You want a garden, don't you?'

'I want a dog. You promised. You never keep your promises.' And then Joe arrived from school and said it wasn't fair.

'Another three years and my school years will be over,' he said. He wasn't my little Joe any more. He was big. A tall young man. How quickly it had all happened, or perhaps there had not been enough time to see it all.

Joe was a good son, he never caused us any problems. We didn't really know what was going on inside that young man. He was doing well at school. He wasn't particularly keen on reading books recommended by us. 'I haven't got enough patience with Balzac. You have to read two hundred pages before the plot starts, and then another fifty before you start to know who the main characters are.'

'If you don't want to read him, don't,' I retorted. 'Don't do me any favours. If I suggested Balzac, it was because I wanted you to be aware of the world's literature and to do something constructive besides being preoccupied with sport.'

'Mum, what are you talking about? It has nothing

to do with sport. I simply said that I find Balzac boring. Tolstoy too, though not to the same extent.'

I was speechless. Our son, the child of migrant parents, the son of people who were raised on European literature, to pronounce that the giants of letters were boring.

And then, when I thought about it, I had to admit that I, too, had found certain passages in these books tedious. I used to skip over them, though I would never admit it. So my son was a more honest man. I had never dared to question the virtue of the written word until I grew up. Joe's generation was so much more open than we had ever been. I was glad.

We bought the boys a dog. He looked like a sheepdog, only his coat was rusty, which inspired us to call him Rusty. We all fell in love with him, though he made the task of establishing the garden almost impossible. He was a true digger. He kept on digging holes, big holes, small holes, holes for the north wind, holes for the south wind, and for the westerly, of course. He was fully aware that he shouldn't do it. Whenever Rusty wouldn't run to me on my return home and greet me with his passionate devotion but crawled on his belly instead, I immediately knew that our precious animal had dug yet another hole. Then one day, while visiting the zoo, we observed the same kind of holes in the dingo enclosure. Then we appreciated Rusty's problem and his atavistic practices. We allowed him to keep his holes. In gratitude, he offered us his unreserved love and devotion and it was enough to hear Joe and Michael speak to Rusty to forgive him his inheritance. He definitely had filled an important need in our children's lives. They addressed him with a warmth and tenderness I had never suspected them to have, and I thought that if one day they would speak in the same way to their wives, there would be two very happy women on earth.

My mother sent us some old family photos, apart from the new ones which we were always getting.

Joe and Michael were impressed. My mother as a young girl, at the beginning of the twentieth century. Sitting on a bench, her legs dangling. The background, birch trees and a lace-finished country house. A graceful figure of a woman, my sons' great-grandmother. And a small dog. A scene from a life long forgotten, preserved in sepia print, as if taken directly from a play by Chekhov. My father, at eleven, twelve perhaps, with a group of five friends. All dressed in severe, high-buttoned school uniforms. End of the nineteenth century. The boys' faces all turned in the one direction, hands either folded across their chests, or placed modestly on their knees. A no-nonsense photo, projecting the values and general attitudes of the time. But then we discovered that the boys' eyes were really full of life. So we speculated that once the photo had been taken the boys had started to laugh, and perhaps had even started to chase each other.

We spent the whole evening looking at the photos and introducing the previous generation to our children. We mentioned the war and the raging emptiness which it had left. All that was left of the once large family were these worn-out, fading fragments of moments in the lives of the people who had given us life. We were lucky to have photos. It was only because my mother, my impractical, loving, not always reasonable mother, had never parted with the photos even in the darkest moments, maintaining the importance of links with the past.

'Tell us more,' the boys insisted.

It was a rare moment, when we felt that Joe and Michael were eager to establish some kind of link with their forefathers.

After all, Rusty dug holes, didn't he?

TWENTY FIVE

Someone told Julian that Victor had taken Mila and Margarette and had left Australia. I couldn't believe that he would do such a thing without seeing me first. It was a disturbing thought which stayed with me for days. In the end, I decided to go to Victor's place. I was informed that the family had moved out more than a year ago. No one seemed to know where to. They hadn't left a forwarding address. On my return home, I spent some time looking up the telephone directory without any success.

'It should teach you a lesson not to allow yourself to get involved with people who don't give a damn about others.'

I was annoyed with Julian and his logic; with myself and my lack of it. With my whole life. I blamed the milk bar, the Boy Scouts and swimming lessons, music lessons, school projects, the garden, Sunday School, dog's obedience school and Adult Education classes, the cake shop, guitars and my boys, for monopolising me and making me neglect my friends.

I felt depressed.

'There is nothing the matter that a week away from the constant rush won't cure,' advised my doctor. 'I strongly urge you to go. Your family will survive without you, I am sure.'

Julian booked one week's stay for me at Mount Buffalo. The boys assured me that they didn't mind. My friends promised to keep in touch with them.

I travelled by train to Wangaratta. It was my first long-distance train trip since our arrival in Australia. It was a strange feeling to sit there with nothing to do except to look at the passing scenery. It was mid-December and the train was taking me to a place I didn't know. To go on holidays seemed such a peculiar thing to do, when I knew that Julian was working himself to death in the cursed shop, and that the boys must return home to an empty house.

The train sped through the vast stretches of the Victorian countryside while I slept, worried and admired the scenery. At Wangaratta, we, the Chalet guests, were given cups of tea and then loaded onto the bus which was to take us to our destination. The bus climbed the mountain in darkness; it swayed and twisted. People were silent. The driver told us that we should reach the Buffalo plateau about eleven o'clock. The air was pure though the windows were barely open, and then the driver drew our attention to a wombat which ran in front of the bus. Some people jumped to their feet. 'Where, where?' And a triumphant voice announced that he could see the animal, and then all was silent again. I looked at the darkness and at my reflection in it. The trees moved. I tried to follow a telephone wire. One moment I could see it sliding among the trees and then I couldn't. Boulders would appear, standing out in the dark with their night-white glow. The stars were very bright and the sky mahogany black. Not like the city sky. I thought of Joe and Michael and wondered what they had eaten and wished they were with me to see what the true night sky should look like.

There was a bright light in front of us and the driver told us that it was the reflector which was attached to the roof of the Chalet and that we should be there any minute.

I went to bed almost immediately. The bed was cold and strange without Julian. It was hard to go to sleep without checking whether Michael and Joe were well covered. My first holiday on my own, not that we had many.

I woke up to the sound of a bell and didn't know where I was. I didn't have to prepare breakfast. I worried whether the boys managed without me. There was nothing for me to do except to get ready for breakfast and stop worrying, which had been the main purpose of going away in the first place.

The Chalet was a big place with long corridors, a never-ending stream of holidaymakers, chambermaids busy polishing and cleaning and an impressive dining room. High ceiling, panoramic windows, tables set with silver and with white cloths starched to perfection. The woman next to me asked whether it was my first stay at Buffalo, to which I answered 'yes'. All eyes turned towards me. By answering, I must have given away my foreign descent. I was waiting for question number two — where did you come from? — and was surprised when the woman expressed her disappointment with the weather instead.

On the way to my room, I heard people referring to the weather, how disappointing it was, and stressing that it wasn't the best kind of a day for walking. I wrote a letter home, full of questions and exclamation marks, and I went for a walk. I was in a melancholy mood, so the mist and the moist air suited me fine. There was no one in sight. The air was pure. There was quiet, only my steps on the wet gravel made a grinding sound. I couldn't see much, only a few trees which kept on reappearing from the dense fog to disappear again. My hair was all wet and so were my clothes. It was a feeling of *déja vu* and then I remembered a far-away holiday in prewar Poland when I had gone to a mountain resort with my parents and Tania. The weather had been just the same as on this day. We had gone for a walk and mother was in one of her moods. Because her hair had been all wet, because she had felt we were all risking one sickness or another, because there had been nothing to see, and because the ground had been so very slippery. Father had tried to humour her, which had been even more difficult than walking in the fog. Father had said: 'Let's check the visibility. I'll walk forward. You stay where you are and call out when you can't see me.' Mother had said that it was a crazy idea but Tania and I had been quite taken with it. 'One step,' father had said, 'two, three'. His voice getting more and more distant with every step, and his body less recognisable. Mother had complained that she felt really cold and then we hadn't been able to see father any more so we had shouted: 'Father, we can't see you any more!' and 'How many steps?'.

There had been silence. Father hadn't answered. 'Father,' we called. 'Father?' And then mother started to run and Tania and I had run, too. Mother had cried 'Keep to the track, you two. All I need is for you two to get lost too.'

'Father can't be lost,' I had said very loudly.

'Borys,' mother had shouted. 'Where are you?'
The fog had been even denser than before, actually we had been in impenetrable clouds. We had been forced to stop. We had clung to each other. I had been very frightened. How long it had lasted I wasn't sure. And the wind had sprung up from nowhere and the clouds had moved. We could hear someone playing the flute and sheep bleating. 'A tree,' I had said. 'I can see a tree.'

'Yes,' mother had said. 'A tree and the path in front

of us. And look, a valley. Only your father is missing.'

And something had come towards us. It wasn't father for sure. Father's suit had been light. The figure in front was dark, even the face, though the walk was familiar. 'Borys,' mother had said, 'If it is you ... I don't know what I'll do with you.' And then when we had been sure it was father, we had run to him and he had burst out laughing.

'Just wanted to find out how much you missed me. Apart from that I fell down, therefore you must forgive me for my appearance.'

'You are totally irresponsible. Worse than a child.' The fog, the clouds had almost disappeared, as if drawn apart. A valley, green and lavish had lain in front. An idyllic picture as if painted by a very romantic artist. The distant huts had been there and the sheep and the shepherd boy. Chains of mountains around and when I had watched it all, spellbound, father had kissed mother and had left some of the mud on her dress and face. She had looked funny, so Tania and I started to giggle and mother had said: 'Thank God you're all in one piece.'

I walked and thought that I had to come to Mount Buffalo to recall an event which I had never suspected I remembered. I was pleased it was foggy. It had been a long time ago. When I thought of it, it was a long time since I had eaten at a properly set table. Our boys, our two savages, seldom ate with a tablecloth.

A few years ago, my mother's friend had come to visit us. She wasn't happy in Australia and always ready to criticise, at the expense of the positive aspects of life here, which she used to ignore completely.

I had tried my best and had prepared a nice meal. I had even put on a tablecloth, which had immediately been observed by the boys. They had asked the reason and whether they had forgotten someone's birthday. I had told them not to be stupid and had set the table with the utmost care. My mother's friend had been watching me and then she had produced a handkerchief. She had pressed it against her eyes. 'If your poor mother only knew...' she had almost sobbed. 'I remember the way your mother used to arrange the table. Flowers were a must.'

My gracious guest must have forgotten that there had been a war in between, when we had eaten without flowers, and often hadn't eaten at all. I didn't have much time for the woman. She had left Poland at the outbreak of war. Now she urged me to remember 'the values' implanted in me by my parents. To make her happy, I promised to use a tablecloth, which I did for some time; but then I reached the conclusion that the custom, though very pleasant, demanded too much work. So I revoked the decision and had never regretted it.

And now Buffalo and the crisp, freshly starched tablecloth. I would have to bring Joe and Michael so they would learn how a real table should look.

Whenever there is mist, there is this unique stillness and quiet. I stopped at a huge rock. The water trickled down. The rock was very cold, slippery and wet. The pebbles were smooth and full of colours, as if waiting to be picked up. The mist was all over me. The birds were silent, though from time to time one would leave a tree in mute determination to disappear into the fog. A unique day. I couldn't recall when I had last felt like this. This was what life should be like. I had almost forgotten the feeling in this crazy, bustling existence of ours.

I hadn't thought about my father for a long time. He had loved the mountains and used to take Tania and me for many hikes. The Tatra Mountains are rugged. Father never rushed, he always insisted that we should allow ourselves enough time to look, to feel, to observe. This is what he has offered me, I thought. A moment of experience in time. Till then I hadn't thought much about it.

I would have to bring my boys here, all three of them. Not only because I wanted to show Michael and Joe a properly set table, but also because I wanted to share the feel of a mist with them, to look at the moist pebbles playing with colours, to feel the chilling coldness of the rock and to farewell the bird disappearing into the fog. To hear our footsteps on a mountain track, and to imprint on our minds forever a tree wet and heavy with moisture. And to listen to the silence of a foggy mountain together. And to store all those memories, so they could reappear again whenever badly needed.

I walked and walked and then it was time to go back. I felt happy and calm. So what if Victor had left the country without seeing me. It was good that he had vanished from my life before he had managed to bring an even greater confusion. I had my three men to share life with. I thought of Joe and Michael with a great tenderness, a feeling I had almost forgotten. And of Julian, my down-to-earth, stable and trusted companion.

I was glad I had that time to myself.

On the second day, it rained. I went for another walk on my own and discovered that Albert Namatjira's colours were true, a fact I had been reluctant to accept. As for my defence: whoever had heard of a tree trunk with pink, purple, orange, yellow, brown, red and black stripes and patches? On a white background. It certainly had been news to a European migrant.

On the third day, it stopped raining and the mist disappeared. The Australian landscape is not dull! It's alive with colours and movement. I had never seen a place like Buffalo before. Its beauty hit me like an unforgettable piece of music or poetry. On the plateau where the old guesthouse was situated, there were roads, tracks, meadows covered with an abundance of wild flowers, creeks with freezing clear water, rocks to climb, endless walks, birds galore, the high sky, the lake, the pure air and the Australian bush with all its mysteries. Never-ending new impressions: a snake with Aboriginal motifs on its back, a vivid colour, a bird calling, clouds bumping into each other; and purified by fire, bleached to perfection by snow, sun and rain, the ghost gums. Sheer drops of rocks, waterfalls, and the endless horizon. Chains of mountains, yet another one, and one more. The distant farms in the valleys down, down below and the absence of shops and traffic lights. I wrote home:

My holiday is coming to an end. I feel so well. I had forgotten how well one should feel.

Mount Buffalo: how can I describe it? It's as inspiring as Beethoven's Ninth, as soothing and as true as Vivaldi's Four Seasons. If Joe and Michael don't exactly know what I mean, they should listen to the music. Perhaps we will do it together.

I hope that next time, we will all go together and then I will be able to show you all my favourite spots.

My table companions proved to be all right. They are extremely polite, seeming to understand my need for being left to myself. One man gave me a list of Australian writers: it's quite impressive and long. The people I met are more discreet than our neighbours. Surely my pronunciation must bother them, but somehow they pretend there is nothing out of the ordinary. They didn't ask the usual questions as soon as I opened my mouth. They waited patiently till I was ready. On the third day, I volunteered and told them where I came from, and when. I informed them about my marital status and the other vital statistics, like the number of children we have and my attitude towards Australia. They, in turn, opened their hearts to me. They are all from British stock and all have visited England (which they call 'Home') at one time or another. It amazes me that Australian people after so many generations of settled life maintain this romantic attachment to England, Scotland, or Ireland. Anyway, they are nice people and good company. I am quite determined to follow the list the man prepared; it must have taken him hours. I feel that perhaps through reading I will be able to sort out my own feelings towards this land.

I am returning to you fit and well. Thanks for giving me this holiday. My thoughts are clear, my eyes full of new images.

The fragrant scent of the bush is incredible. It depends on the time of day, the temperature, the stillness, the wind, the moisture. It's hard to describe. But no matter what, it always smells like the Australian bush. I'll tell you all about it. I'm bringing back pebbles, a piece of a ghost gum and some gum nuts. Michael will be able to show them at school.

My return home was as any other happy homecoming. Julian and the boys were glad to see me. They had managed well without me. They didn't look undernourished or neglected. The house was clean, the clothes washed and folded away.

'Soon you'll declare me obsolete,' I jested, feeling a bit sad.

'What rot,' responded the boys, and Julian put his arm around me.

TWENTY SIX

I was determined to look after myself. A run-down mother isn't much use. I wished I knew how to relax. Julian mentioned yoga. And then I thought of Joyce.

Joyce lived near us. On the day we'd moved into our house, she had arrived at the door with a broad smile and a bunch of flowers.

'Hi!' she had said. 'Welcome to the district. My name's Joyce.' She was tall, big and very well proportioned.

'Hi!' I had responded, though the expression wasn't necessarily me.

From that day on, we had seen each other constantly. Joyce was full of life and energy. We were the same age. Joyce was wanted, Joyce was needed, Joyce was ready to give and help. She was involved in a thousand activities, ran her home efficiently, looked after her four children and helped her husband in the family business. She had a stopwatch when a stopwatch was required, and a lot of understanding and patience when necessary. She supervised Michael together with her own children in swimming and athletics, and was happy to spend the whole night sewing minute doll's clothes as a part of Christmas preparations.

Shortly after we met, she became what Mrs

MacAllison had been to me, a vital part of my Australian existence, but even more so. It was a peculiar friendship. Her background was as remote from mine as Australia was from Poland. A strict Anglican upbringing, a middle-class home, sports galore. She had been a growing girl during the war and remembered how difficult it had been to keep up clothing her developing body on the ration coupons. She had finished Domestic Science with flying colours. Her husband had been taken prisoner of war during the Japanese offensive. 'He never talks of the war; must've had an awful time. I was told he weighed only eight stone when the war ended. I met him later, at the yacht club.'

That was Joyce, easy to relate to, bubbling over with vitality, always-on-the-go Joyce.

'So what about yoga, Joyce? I would love to do it. We should do it, both of us. Relaxation is very much in demand. It would be good to know how to do it, don't you think?'

'Why not? It's fine with me. Have you heard of any classes?'

'Someone told me that "Eemka" classes are good. Would you enquire, please!'

'Why don't you?' Joyce smiled because she knew the reason but wanted me to spell it out once again.

'Joyce. My pronunciation, you know.'

'Phooey,' she said with passion. 'Nothing wrong with your pronunciation. I can understand you. You have to start talking to people. No one's going to snap at you.'

'Joyce, please. This one more time and no more.'

'That's what you always say. I'm too soft with you.'

'Don't you want me to learn how to relax?'

'You're impossible. I'm wasting my breath on you

. . . Oh, all right. What's the name again?'

'Eemka.'

On the following day, Joyce arrived and told me that she couldn't find any Eemka in the whole telephone book, had never heard of the institution, and wondered whether I would spell it for her.

'Sure,' I said puzzled. As far as I knew, Eemka was a worldwide organisation. 'I'd better write it down for you; it's easier for me than to spell the Australian way.'

I wrote the name down and handed it to Joyce.

'Good God,' she exclaimed. 'It's the Y.M.C.A.! Why didn't you say so in the first place? "Eemka", indeed! I looked under E and no wonder I couldn't find it.'

'I'm sorry, but it's not really my fault. In Polish, you form a word from the first letters. I think it's done in English too. UNESCO, you don't refer to it as U.N.E.S.C.O. all the time. It's phonetic spelling versus the English. YMCA, you pronounce eemka. It's logical and simple.'

'Perhaps for you, not for me. Why won't you give them a call, then? I'm running late. Have to feed the horse.'

'Joyce, it takes only a moment for you. I would really rather you did it.'

'You're stubborn, aren't you?'

'I have a reason.'

'What can I do with you?' she said. 'See you after I've fed the horse. In half an hour. Keep the kettle boiling.'

I waited for her and wondered how one could explain to an Australian woman that the Polish branch of the Young Men's Christian Association had been an anti-Semitic organisation. When the Y.M.C.A. had been established in Lodz, the people had been happy that at long last, the town was going to have a swimming pool in the heart of the city. The good citizens of Lodz had responded favourably to the building appeal, regardless of whether they were the Poles, Jews, or Germans who made up the population of the city. My father had given a donation. Money had been collected at my school, but when the complex was finished, it was made clear that Jews wouldn't be admitted. So while the Poles and the Germans of Lodz had taken advantage of the new facilities, Jews accepted their exclusion in the same stoic way as they had been accustomed to accept so many previous discriminatory moves: with passive pain and growing awareness of being second-class citizens. We tried to persuade ourselves that, after all, it was a Christian organisation, and therefore it was only proper that there was no room for Jews in it. What was incredible in retrospect was that the whole event had taken place in 1937, when the world should have been aware of what was going on in Hitler's Reich. Given two more years, the Poles would also be barred from the Y.M.C.A. in Lodz, a fact they didn't forsee in 1937.

I had been deeply hurt by the rejection. It hurt me when I was told that in the United States, Jews were allowed to use the Y.M.C.A.'s facilities. I didn't care for America; I cared for Poland. There was no other music, no other poetry, there were no other people, no other national heroes. My language, my landscape. No other forests, no other bread, no other flowers, no other mountains.

A Pole because I was born in Poland and because
my mother told me that I was. A Pole because
I love Chopin better than any other composer,
for the reason I can neither justify nor explain.
A Pole because the poetical creativity, which
proved to be the pinnacle of my life, could express
itself only in the language of my forefathers and

proved impossible in any other, no matter how
well I knew it. A Pole, because a pine is dearer
to me than a cypress, for reasons I can't even
explain. A Pole, because my aversion
to the Polish fascists is greater than to those
of all other nations and I consider this as the
best proof that I am a Pole.
A Pole, because, when the time comes, I want to
be buried in Poland, so that my bones will
nourish her soil.
A Pole, because I feel that I am one.

This is how Julian Tuwim, the Polish poet, felt about
Poland; some Poles called him 'a Jew writing in
Polish'.

As a child, while watching a military parade, I had
heard shouts of 'down with the Jews'. My father had
said 'never mind' and had smiled sadly. My father,
who had fought for the independence of Poland, told
me that we shouldn't pay any attention to 'an
isolated, extreme voice like that'. It had hurt, but it
had been easy to take my father's advice, because I
had desperately wanted to believe it was true. Only
when the so-called isolated voices had gained in frequency and volume, only then had I allowed myself
to question why. It never affected my love for the
language and the country, though my attitude
towards the people changed. The trust was gone.

I wondered if Joyce would understand what it had
all meant to me. Perhaps even the yoga classes were
an excuse to find out for myself whether Australia,
too, was going to push me away: a test case. I was
trying Australia out, not so much for myself, but
rather for Joe and Michael. I timidly hoped that my
sons would never experience what racial hatred was
like, that Australia wouldn't hurt them as Poland had
hurt me.

Joyce. Where was I to start, how was I to present

the issue about which I felt with such a desperate urgency? Joyce and her war recollections; Joyce and her sports. Her problems and my problems; her life and mine.

I told Joyce about Poland and the Y.M.C.A. as soon as she arrived, even before I poured our coffee. She was astonished. 'If it wasn't you who told me, I wouldn't believe it,' she said.

'One thing is certain, it couldn't happen in Australia. I'm sure.'

'I wish I was as sure as you are.'

'And so you should be.'

'It's not easy. With time you lose trust.'

Joyce placed a cup of coffee in front of me, she wanted to say something, she looked at me, once, and then again. In the end, she sat down and said: 'What d'you want me to do?'

'Just ring the Y.M.C.A., ask them about the yoga classes and make sure they accept Jews.'

'It's not the easiest thing to do on the phone, is it? I have a better scheme. Why don't we both go there together to enrol? And if they object to you, I'll make the biggest fuss in the history of the Southern Hemispere. And, naturally, I would resign. You know that I'm that I'm a member, don't you?'

'I didn't know.'

I wasn't absolutely sure how Joyce really felt. She was obviously stirred, though I wasn't certain whether it was because of me, or because the horse hadn't fed well.

'Don't worry,' she said. 'I want us to go and enrol tonight. I want to prove you wrong.'

'That's fine with me.'

We went to the sub-branch of the Y.M.C.A. after tea. Joyce greeted a few people; I was given a form. Surname. Christian name. Address. Age. Religion. 'See?' I whispered to Joyce. I filled the form out and handed it to the receptionist. She looked through it. 'That will be three pounds,' she said. I wondered whether she had noticed and, if not, whether the blow was going to follow.

'My friend,' said Joyce, 'is worried that you won't accept her because she's Jewish.'

'On the contrary,' said the woman. 'We're glad to have people with different backgrounds.'

And that was that — better than yoga classes. On the way home, I was grateful to Joyce for keeping a chatty conversation going, without referring to what had happened. It was difficult to say, but I thought she did it on purpose. Parting, she said:

'One day, you'll have to tell me more about yourself and Poland. I hardly know of the war and how you survived.'

'One day, perhaps. I'm washed out tonight. Tonight was the moment of truth. My greatest Australian discovery. Our children's lives will be less complicated. Thank you, Joyce.'

'What for? You're a funny duffer, aren't you?'

Joyce was absent for nearly a week. I was convinced she had decided to end our association. One moment I wanted to go to her and apologise; the next, I decided not to run after anyone. She knew where I lived and, either she was going to accept me for what I was, or to retreat to her suburban existence.

I spent days re-examining what I had told Joyce. I had no regrets. I had been honest with her, without being apologetic. It was a good feeling, something which I had discovered in myself not long ago. I was hoping Joyce would understand.

When she came to pick me up for the yoga classes, I greeted her in a typically Polish-Jewish way — I hugged her.

'I thought you were cross with me. The whole

week! You never came.'

'I had to help my father, it never occurred to you? The simple reason! You're a duffer if ever I knew one. Cross with you, whatever for?'

Joyce told me her parents were so strict she hadn't been allowed to go out with a boy till she was seventeen. And I told her that during the war that hadn't been my main problem. When the Jews knew they were condemned, some desperately tried to secure Polish identity papers. There had been a black market for Polish birth certificates and the prices had been exorbitant, so mainly people of means had been able to afford to buy time. It had all been very difficult. One had needed to look like a Pole. Black eyes, dark hair, long noses were 'out'; blond hair, blue eyes and upturned noses were 'in'. The main difficulty had been to find a place to live. German law hadn't helped either. To help a Jew, to offer him shelter, had been punishable by death. Some people were ready to risk their necks for money. Others simply because they were appalled by the total destruction of a nation, but those had been few. Not that I blamed them. Inexcusable were the professional Jew-spotters, who had always been eager and ready to denounce their quarry to the Germans, which meant either instant or slow death. For their trouble, the professionals had been paid in money or vodka.

'I didn't have a clue how it was,' said Joyce. 'I'm sorry. It must be terrible to talk about it.'

'Talk is only talk.'

'A thing like that could never happen in Aussieland.'

'I wish I could share your confidence; we never believed that it could happen in twentieth-century Europe.'

'I see your point ... What can I say? Listen, if a calamity ... If a calamity like that would ever happen here ... Not that I believe it ever could ... You must know that you and your family would be safe; I'd hide you and save you.'

'You don't know what you're talking about,' I responded, and then realised that I had hurt Joyce. There was no point in apologising, a steamroller pays no attention to a flower.

'What we're discussing now is only a hypothetical exercise. I believe that you like us. You're ready to help every single underdog around. It's a good feeling, isn't it? But just think about it. If the situation were to arise again. You wouldn't only be going against general opinion, but also against the law. Remember, to help a Jew was a capital crime. A person who was willing to do it, for whatever reasons, was executed together with her Jew. Not only the person, but all who lived in the same house, including children. A law is a law ...

'Did I mention the neighbours? I don't think I did. The neighbours were to die too. A good deterrent, don't you think?'

'I ... I don't know what to think.'

'Would you be willing to help us and not only risk your own life, but also the lives of your family and neighbours?' Joyce was silent; she had tears in her eyes. I knew I wasn't being fair. I was bringing tumult into her uncomplicated, Australian existence.

'You shouldn't be so sure and dogmatic,' I continued. 'My expectations are more realistic and less demanding. If history should repeat itself, which it often does, I hope and trust that you wouldn't denounce us.'

'How could you,' said Joyce. 'What you said ... Just now ... It's ... It's almost insulting!'

'I'm being truthful with you, that's all. If it will make you feel any better, I never felt free to say things like this to a Pole. So perhaps Australia has loosened my tongue and clarified my thoughts. I'm not afraid to say what I mean. Frankly, I don't give a damn what people might think. You don't have to agree with me, but if we are to continue being friends, you have to know how I feel, what I think.'

'Sure.'

'The wrong that was done to the Jewish people ... I have a friend, I don't even know where he is now. He still suffers, I wonder if he will live a normal life ever again ... Sometimes I think, how was it possible? How come the world didn't stop it?'

'It's over now. It won't ever happen again. Don't think about it any more ... You look down on sports, perhaps it wouldn't be a bad idea if you started doing something apart from living in the past.'

Joyce and I. Southern Hemisphere and Northern.

'Pope John XXIII, I think, was the first pope in the long history of the Catholic Church who thought it proper to remove the curse from the Jewish people.'

'Whatever for?'

'For killing Jesus ... It never occurred to any other descendant of the Apostles to remove the curse, if for no other reason than in the name of Christian principles of brotherly love.'

'Are you sure? You must be mistaken, surely?'

'Don't you worry. I know my facts only too well. *I* was considered guilty of the crime. *Michael* was fully responsible for it. So was Joe; and Julian; and the Jewish children whose heads were skilfully smashed by the representatives of the pure Aryan race; and the Jewish children yet to be born.'

'I can't believe it.'

'Your knowlege of Christian practices must be very limited. Better ask your minister.'

'I will ... It doesn't make sense. The Pope and the Vatican, I don't subscribe to them, but I wonder if you have your facts right, or is there a bit of Jewish bias?'

'Joyce, for your information, the problem's not new. For us, it's a matter of life and death. The future, or another slaughter.'

'It doesn't make much sense, does it? Jesus was born a Jew.'

'You know it and I know it, but if you went to Poland even now and repeated what you just said, you'd be stoned. You'd be considered a heretic . . . As long as I lived in Poland, I never allowed myself to acknowledge the fact.

I don't trust churches. I hope I'm not offending you. It's not a crime, or it shouldn't be, to choose to worship God in a different way.'

Joyce got up. 'It's interesting', she said. 'Heavy stuff, though. I'd better be going. The horse has to be fed. Steven and his swimming practice, you know.'

'Yes, I know.'

Joyce left, looking puzzled. Not for long. A vigorous swim might help her, or a ride on her horse.

I wasn't very proud of myself. I was aware that I was changing Joyce's peaceful existence by introducing some strange, disturbing problems. I wasn't even sure whether she wanted the introduction, whether she was ready for it.

I even thought that perhaps I was doing to her what Victor had done to me. I was repeating facts which were, or should have been, well known. It was my bid to promote a better understanding between different people. What I was saying sounded almost like a well-mouthed cliché. Except that for me every word was synonymous with futile, senseless suffering, no matter how stereotyped it might seem to others.

TWENTY SEVEN

There are certain things in Australian life that I could never get used to. Skin on hot milk. People leaving rubbish on beaches or public grounds. Adults treating children as lesser people. Rhetorical manipulations of issues and beliefs. Lack of control over my own thoughts and emotions. People leaving tables without replacing their chairs. Public toilets. Hypocrisy. Lack of humour.

To this long, but very incomplete list I now had to add something else: Joe driving a car, Joe going out, Joe's girlfriend stroking his beard and complimenting him on its 'savage beauty'. One thing is certain, time hadn't stood still. Our son, our little Joe, had finished school. His school years had gone smoothly, except for that first smack and an incident which had happened in fourth form. Joe had come home disturbed, had gone to his room and hadn't wanted to talk. Hadn't even said hello to Rusty, and when Michael had proposed cricket practice, Joe had sent him out flying. 'What did I do now?' Michael had wondered.

'Never mind,' the wise mother had consoled. 'Why don't you go and play with Steven?'

Michael had looked at me with annoyance, then said 'all right' and left, and I had known that I had failed him once again by not responding, not discussing, but simply sending him away.

And then the whole story had come out into the open when Julian and I had been almost ready to go to sleep.

'Hi, Mum,' Joe had said.

'Yes!' I had yawned.

'What's going on?' Julian had opened his eyes.

'It's all right. Turn around and go to sleep.'

Julian had turned to the other side and Joe had sat on my bed.

'In our form, there's a boy ... He said the Jews are scheming to dominate the whole world. That America's infested with them, banks, the press, industry, Congress.'

'You shouldn't listen to rubbish like that. You should know better.'

'I do, but do the others? ... He said the Jews are getting more and more powerful in Australia. They want to corrupt the Australian Christians and totally destroy the whole system.'

Turbulent echo from the past. My child, born at the end of 1945, not in the year of the dog, not in the year of the moon, but in a year of optimism, of euphoria, when to give birth to a child had been justifiable by the general trust in a bright future. A year of 'all people are equal', 'United Nations' and 'nothing to do with the League of Nations'. The Charter as no other Charter had ever been produced by the human race.

That had been Joe's year. Our year. Sixteen years later, and our son was confronted with the problem we had wanted to bury, we had hoped would never re-emerge. And here it was, in its destructive enormity, in the land we had chosen for our children to live in. Julian was asleep, lucky man. Joe kept his eyes — his hurt, questioning eyes — on me. 'It sounds to me like typical Nazi propaganda.'

'The boy is German.'

'So it must be his home, his parents, his background.'

'Perhaps it is, though that doesn't necessarily help. My other mates don't know much on the subject. The boy is clever, intelligent, persuasive. He knows how to present the case.'

'We'll write to your form teacher. Better still, to the headmaster.'

'That's not what I want.'

'What d'you want?'

'To speak out ... I feel rotten. I've never felt like this before. He quoted from *The Oxford Dictionary* to prove his point. The definition of *Jew*. You must know how I feel.'

'Yes.'

'What about Michael?'

'What about him?'

'Perhaps you should send him to another school, to take him out of the State school system?'

'There's no guarantee he won't be confronted with the same problem at another school.'

'I mean a Jewish school. I'm serious, Mum.'

'It means running away. Government schools. You know, in Poland, Jewish children were barred from secondary schools except for a very few, perhaps one or two to a form. It was private schools for those who could afford them and no schools for the others. When we came here, your father and I, we were jubilant. A school system open to all children. I still believe in it. It's good to meet the cross-section of a society, even if there is a price to pay, the realisation that anti-Semitism hasn't vanished ... It's late, son. Tomorrow's a school day. We'll decide what steps to take. I won't let it go unnoticed. The headmaster has to know.'

'They'll think I'm not to be trusted. A Jew spying

on others, undermining the pillars of Christian unity.'

'Stop it, Joe! You should trust us. We won't do anything to undermine your position at school.'

'If it comes out into the open, how can you prevent it?'

'We'll find a way . . . Before you go. What was your other friends' reaction?'

'It differed. They were not impressed, but two giggled and found it quite amusing. "Jewish piano" and how noisy and show off the Jews are.'

'What's Jewish piano?'

'A cash register.'

'All right, Joe. It's time to sleep. School tomorrow . . . Another day.'

Joe still sat on my bed for a while and then he got up.

'Why us, Mum?'

The same thought, the same feeling, separated by more than twenty years, and the Second World War.

'There's no answer. There never was.'

I was wide awake. I didn't think about how lucky we were to have settled in Australia, or about our house, or how good it was for our children to grow up in a country that had never known foreign occupation. I didn't think how wonderful it was to have all that fresh food and to feel free to tell Joyce what I really thought and wanted from my life. My thoughts clouded by reflections, and no matter how hard I tried not to make a final balance, past events, the statistical evidence, history kept on pushing me into reaching a conclusion. I tossed in bed, wanted to share the burden with Julian, but decided not to wake him up. The memories stored in my mind kept me company till the Australian dawn lightened my Jewish speculations.

We composed a letter to the headmaster of Melbourne High. It was difficult to keep our emotions out of it.

Our background was there, and the reasons why we had settled in Australia. Our dreams were mentioned, and the plans and expectations for our sons' future. And, of course, the incident. There were two sentences to which Julian objected, and on which I insisted, something like:

You have to appreciate how deeply we feel on the subject. We didn't choose to exchange Europe for Australia for our son to be subjected to Nazi propaganda. We ended with the hope that appropriate steps would be taken and we signed the letter *Faithfully Yours*, though the formula seemed pompous to me. 'This is the proper form', Julian insisted.

We received a quick reply. Though the news 'on hand' was disturbing, wrote the headmaster, there was nothing he could do until Joe was prepared to name the boy. '*I remain, sincerely Yours*, he ended. Joe wasn't prepared to disclose the boy's name, though he insisted that the name was so typically German that had the headmaster wanted to find the boy, he shouldn't have had any trouble.

I don't think we wrote much in the second letter, we only informed the headmaster that Joe wanted to keep the name of the boy to himself. To which we received a short note to congratulate us on Joe's strength of character. *Don't hesitate to get in touch with me whenever in need* . . . There was *I remain* and *sincerely Yours* and all that rubbish. I had been flying too high, I had let my dreams form themselves unchecked. I had put too much trust in our Australian existence. The feeling, this long-forgotten feeling, when as a child I had heard the yell 'down with the Jews', was present in me once again. Not exactly a welcome return.

The day passed, a quiet day, when we talked little and thought a lot. Joe arrived home from school. He told Rusty how much he loved him, he arranged with Michael to go to the sports ground for cricket practice. He kissed me between a glass of milk and an apple.

'Everything all right, Joe?'

'Great,' he said and smiled.

I reported it to Julian, 'What d'you think?'

'You can't expect the young man spend his life on gloomy reflections just because one of his school mates is an anti-Semite. Even we had our share of joy in the Polish conditions, or have you forgotten?'

That must be it. If we didn't have resilience, our life would be an endless misery. Hurrah for resilience and the Jewish sense of humour.

When we were just about ready to go to sleep, Julian and I, Joe knocked on our door. 'May I?' he asked.

Julian moaned, and I quickly reminded him how precious moments like this were, and how much longer did he think Joe would be willing to share his thoughts with me? 'Come right in,' I shouted, and advised Julian to turn over and go to sleep. Joe sat on my bed. 'You're not too tired, are you?'

'Not at all.'

Julian said something under his breath, so I repeated once again that I wasn't tired at all, on the contrary, I felt well rested and was in excellent form altogether, not to mention that it gave me tremendous pleasure to have a little chat with him.

'Yeah? It's all right, then?'

'Of course it's all right.'

'We had a good practice with Michael today. I'll be surprised if he doesn't make the school team — he's really good at it.' Cricket was a joy we could never share with our boys. The fact that they became cricket fanatics was something we just couldn't understand. Joe knew it only too well. He didn't come in order to keep me awake, to tell me just this. Perhaps they kicked the German boy out of school, I fantasised. He must have done something dreadful, something despicable, something atrocious.

'How was school?'

'Fine.'

'Anything exciting, interesting?' I was sure there was something to do with the German boy. Perhaps his parents had decided to return to Germany, who could tell? Perhaps it was disclosed that they were well-known Nazis ... Once they were unmasked, they were given a dictation test in ... in Hebrew. I wasn't sure whether Hebrew was accepted as a European language. Anyway they couldn't have passed the test and thus have been deported. Who can tell? ...Only Joe could tell me, but somehow he wasn't ready. He looked at me, at the ceiling, at his father, with a slightly bemused expression.

'Well?', I pressed.

'Nothing that would interest you ... The headmaster has organised a new set of lectures for the senior classes.

'What kind of lectures?'

'He has invited a number of experts on the Second World War...'

'What for?' I interrupted, not daring to anticipate.

'Let me finish, all right?'

'I am sorry.'

'You should be, too. You will never learn to listen. You always have to say your bit, regardless of whether it's relevant or not.'

'Sorry. I'll be quiet. I promise.'

'I sincerely hope so.' Joe looked at his nails, annoyed. He kept them well, which pleased me a lot. I wanted to comment, but bit my tongue.

'The headmaster, in his introduction, explained that he feels we should be offered unbiased information regarding the Second World War, because of what took place and because it changed the political structure of the world, dividing it into zones of interest ... What d'you think of it, Mum?'

'I think your headmaster is a very clever man. Do you think we should write to him, to thank him?'

'That's up to you.'

'We might.'

'One more point in favour of our school, ah, Mum?'

It was difficult to sleep. I thought how lucky we were to have settled in Australia, how good it was for our boys. I was even prepared to forgive Australia for cricket. I tossed from side to side till Julian woke up and then I told him everything. We talked and we laughed and we made plans till the Australian sun warmed our dreams.

Michael made the school cricket team, and the swimming team, and the marching squad. After the competitions he returned home displaying a row of blue and red ribbons. He took as much pride and joy in them as any competitor would. We were happy for his sake and Joe showed all the admiration expected by the champion.

Meanwhile, Joe started driving lessons as soon as he turned seventeen. The reason was simple. Both Julian and I felt that ten lessons were not enough to let anyone loose on the road, even if they passed the driving test. Therefore we proposed to Joe that after a couple of lessons with a reputable driving school he should drive with us whenever he had time. We were assuming that a year of driving under supervision would make him a responsible driver. We presented him with a brand-new set of L plates and received a warm hug in return. And then all of a sudden Joe was spending more time with us than he had in the last two or three years. His school friends were full of respect for us, our car and Joe, though not necessarily in that order.

Joe would take us to our friends, though after a while he stopped. He was sick and tired of listening to how much he had changed since they had seen him last, which had been ... years and years ago.

Joe *had* changed.

He matriculated and spent the summer holidays hitchhiking with six of his friends. They travelled as far as Townsville, while I kept on worrying from one postcard, scanty in information and frequency, to another. He returned home with tousled, long hair. It was difficult to see whether he looked well; half his face had become invisible behind a mass of unruly beard. But he was brown and happy. He bid farewell to his schoolbooks and school cap and declared that our objections to his new look were without substance; and in the case of his balding father, it was an obvious display of jealousy. We let Joe be, feeling that there were more important things to discuss with him than his untidy looks. We also hoped that one day he would become bald, the sooner, the better.

The main worry was Joe's driving. As long as he was under our supervision, all was going well. He always reacted with amazement and verbal indignation towards the maniacs behind wheels. How he was performing on his own, or in the company of his friends, was impossible to know. We allowed him to use our car whenever we didn't need it. Joe became very popular with his non-driving friends, as well as with a few girls, mostly from the Methodist Ladies College, a top Melbourne Girls' school. They all frequented our home. Joe was happy and in constant demand. One day, when he arrived home later than we had expected, I told him that all his friends ever wanted was for him to drive them around. 'It's not you they care for,' I said. 'They want your car, and that's all. And as far as your girlfriends are concerned, it amazes me that all of them have been to MLC. If you ask me, they are almost illiterate.'

'I'm not asking you and, frankly, I don't think it's any of your business.'

At which I almost cried; and in a voice full of pain, I informed Joe that his business was my business, our business, whether he liked it or not. I told him that I would always tell him what I thought of him, even at the risk of losing my popularity ... And then I went to my bed, and he went to his. Julian was upset too, but not to the same extent. He told me to calm down, because after all the main thing was that Joe had come back well and unharmed. And then Julian reminded me that when he had finished school, he had gone to England to study.

'I was the same age as Joe, left for a foreign country, with limited money and, what is more, limited knowledge of the language. My mother never knew what time I came home and with whom I went out. Somehow, I survived. Joe is a good kid, we must trust him.'

'D'you think I don't? I don't want him to be hurt, that's all.'

'He has to learn to choose his own friends. To live.' I continued to overreact regardless of what Julian said.

'It's all Australia's fault. The family doesn't count. Nothing counts. My son tells me that his life is not my business! Did you ever dare to say a thing like that to your mother?'

'Times were different.'

'That's not an excuse! I'm concerned with his well-being ... And besides, what kind of an example d'you think it is for Michael?'

'Don't exaggerate.'

'That girl, whatever her name is. The MLC girl. Sitting in full view, stroking his beard, telling him how lovely it feels. Not even embarrassed by our presence. MLC, my foot!'

'Joe is not a little boy any more. You can't check on him all the time...'

'What about his jazz trio?'

'What about it?'

'Where do they practise? At our place. Drums, double bass, piano! Show me another home, another mother who would tolerate it all ... All of them great virtuosos, trying to deafen each other. And the double bass player, in a trance, spinning the blasted instrument around and around. He has ruined the carpet!' Julian was calm while I was boiling, erupting.

'Joe's a happy, normal young man. Calm down. Don't poison his carefree days.'

The normal carefree youth! Perhaps I couldn't comprehend, identify with, because when I had been fifteen, sixteen, seventeen, eighteen, nineteen, twenty, there had been war and the problems had been so different from those of my son and his generation. How good it was that he and his friends, those from his school and MLC, were preoccupied with cars and hitchhiking, dances and jazz, the discovery of the secrets of life and the mystery of human relationships. Joe and his pals, the pioneers of long hairstyles and beards.

'In other countries,' I told them one night, when two of them stayed late and talked, 'students start revolutions, overturn governments, are involved in politics. Students are the social conscience, the voice of progress, of reason...'

'Like in Hitler's Germany?' smiled Stuart.

'I didn't mean that', I said, sadly.

'Sorry, I apologise.'

'No need,' I said, '...it's time for me, anyway.' When I went to bed, I heard the boys talking; and then they were silent to the powerful, disturbing voice of Odetta.

Sometimes I feel like a motherless child.
Sometimes I feel like a motherless child,
Sometimes I feel like a motherless child,
A long.long way from home,
A long long way from home.

TWENTY EIGHT

A war was taking place in an unknown part of the world; unknown, that was, for me. Two, three generations, I wasn't sure, had never known peace. 'It's dreadful,' we commented, watching the reports from the war zone on our television screen. We drank coffee, sent Michael out of the room and watched, passive, in silent acceptance, the never-ending stream of people on the run. Different features, foreign scenery, but the same feeling of aimless urgency. The faces, the slanted eyes, the figures dressed in oriental fashion. It was Vietnam, but I thought of Poland. In such a situation, people seldom walk, they always run, I remembered. They seldom talk, seldom cry, even the children. The same the world over. I could see my friends, I could see myself, from another war. The bare feet, the huge loads on their backs, were they Vietnamese or Polish peasants? It was irrelevant whether their hair and eyes were dark or light — that haunted, vacant look was the same. And the running feet, running away. The troops were the same, too. The guns were more advanced, more sophisticated, but the faces, the swift, rectangular gestures, the commanding voice of an officer, as dry and impersonal as a shot, were all the same. Young soldiers, who only a little while ago had kicked a ball, had worried their parents with long hair, untidy beards, the company they kept and acne, were boys like Joe and his friends, conscripts for search-and-destroy missions. Silent people, and the screaming, jumping troops. Guns like sticks of wood, pointing, probing, threatening. Flames shooting out, and the people herded together. Not a word, only a mother turning her child's head away. Ruins, and so-very-dead bodies all around. They were guerrillas, the war correspondent reported, while an army boot turned the tied-up body over. A camera zoomed at the face, or rather, at what had once been a face.

'Shall I change the channel?' Julian offered temporary escape.

'No, wait.'

'Not much point in watching, is there? We know it all, at first-hand. Unless you want another nightmarish night.'

Blindfolded boys, hands and legs tied up. Deadly, dangerous, desperate men, must have their brains blown out. Absolutely needed for the security of the future of mankind. And their grain must be burnt to cinders. 'We'll starve them out of their holes.' And their forests and rice paddies must be thinned out. 'We'll drive them out from their hiding places. Defoliation is the answer.'

My nights were full of images, old and new. I lived, I cooked, I ate, I was glad to see a nice flower. I was mad at Joe and his long hair, I felt pain, I laughed with Michael, argued with Julian. I was angry with my butcher for giving me the wrong cut of meat. I enjoyed the taste of an apple. I worried because my mother had not written for a long while.

'It's not the first time, is it? The letter will come. Starting with apologies for not writing sooner... Sometimes I feel you enjoy being, or making yourself, miserable '

'This war, I can't stop thinking about it. Letter or no letter.'

'So stop thinking about it. You can't help much, can you?'

When Julian said that, I cried. Because I realised that it must have been the same during the Second World War. Perhaps some people had felt sorry for us, and had said how dreadful and cruel it all was, but it hadn't really altered their lives. The women had applied lipstick and the men had drunk beer in their locals. They had suffered because of the ration cards and been glad that the depression had come to an end. Except of course for those families whose sons and fathers had been in the army. Their wives, mothers, sisters, brothers, children, fathers, friends, they had known exactly what the anguish and the agony felt like.

'See,' I sobbed, '...even we, we care so little.'

'What can you do? If you would come up with some reasonable proposal, that would be different. Then worry. You can't change a thing.'

'No one really knows ... No one really spent one single sleepless night, no one really cared about us. In the same way as we don't care...'

'The war won't be over any sooner because you cry. If you stop, it will still take its unnatural course until the time is ripe for negotiations. It will not end one single day sooner.'

'It's terrible.'

'It is. What worries me are our double standards. On one hand, we teach our children to be honest, loving, caring — in one word, good — and then we let them loose unprepared into a hostile world. Honesty can't fight deceit, decency is no match for corruption. When love confronts hostility and aggression, it always becomes a victim.'

'What do you propose to do? Teach our boys that

one has to be a bastard in order to survive? That there is no time, no room for trust? All people are bad? They will steal from you and hurt you because you are a Jew? So don't be a sucker, my sons. Beware?' I stopped crying. I was angry.

And then Julian said that what he had meant wasn't necessarily applicable only to us. 'Take an American boy. One who doesn't get excited at the boxing stadium. One who doesn't rush to see every horror movie, but rather listens to Bob Dylan, reads and responds to poetry. Our boy doesn't belong to the Ku Klux Klan, but rather mourns the death of Martin Luther King. He thinks, he cares. America and its Star-Spangled Banner, Vietnam and its complex problem, and our American boy in the middle. Conscription. The boy is drafted, sent over to Vietnam to fight for democracy, freedom, our way of life . . . He has never smelled decomposed bodies before and has never seen the hostility in the eyes of the people whose liberty he is supposed to defend. He has never walked through rice paddies before . . . How could he have guessed that mildew would be so difficult to eradicate? How could he have known that an explosion would be so frightening and deafening? He would never have suspected that he would be ready to buy a few frenzied minutes of copulation. Or that drugs — he'd never tried them back home — were good too. And mainly, he would never have believed that after a while he would get used to it all, send snaps home, laugh and sing songs.

To carry on, to live. Because life was rushing by, and he was never sure what tomorrow might bring.

'But if you didn't kill the bastard, the bastard would try to kill you, so you had better be quick . . . And that good American boy might be your own son, one day in the future.'

'Joe will never go into the army.'

'Says you.'

'Says I.'

'We have conscription, too.'

'The war will be over by the time he has finished his studies.'

'And that's how all the parents of this year's conscripts reasoned.'

'Joe will object.'

'I hope he will.'

'He must, I know he would.'

'Will you go to the Moratorium?'

'Yes, I will.'

Nights were the time to think, to prepare a defence for Joe in case the date of his birth was drawn in the ballot. I thought of Victor and how the war had changed him. I thought of all the young men whose parents didn't know better and treated war as a big adventure. Was it enough to protect only one's own child? I knew it wasn't.

I had to accept what Julian said. No matter how I felt, how thousands felt, the war was going to go on until the politicians were ready to end it. And meanwhile young lives were to go on being lost and bodies maimed.

The whole idea of toughening myself was repugnant to me. I had no regrets that Joe and Michael cared and in the process might get hurt. I remembered my fears that once the war over, I'd become an unfeeling person, stripped of human emotions.

A long-forgotten picture comes to my clouded mind. A Polish village in summer, the whole family having lunch under an enormous tree. The sunlight, diffused by the leaves, caresses rather than warms. My mother wearing some light, moving dress. 'Dresses don't move, silly,' says my governess. Wild strawberries and cream. Grandfather's grey moustache that tickles. Tania's pet chicken, more obedient than mine. The leaves transparent when looked at against the light. Some of them eaten up. All the green stuff. Only the skeleton left. 'Have you heard this? Only the skeleton left. The skeleton of a leaf.' Why do they all laugh? I don't like it. And then that noise, a horrible noise, as if of someone crying, wailing. 'It must be the puppies,' says my governess. 'Pups don't cry like that,' says Tania. And I know that she knows. Grandmother calls her 'the mother of all dogs'. And then Tania says that she is going to see, so I ask her if I can follow her. And she says that she prefers her chicken. 'You must love your little sister.' I follow Tania. The ground is uneven and the grass full of burrs; they cling to my dress but don't cling to the chicken's feathers. 'She's a very special bird.' I didn't know a chicken was a bird. 'You are an ignoramus'. I don't know what that means. Someone is crying with pain. The sun is warm. I trip over. My crying is nothing to compare with the other. Our landlord is smoking a pipe and scratching his head. He wears shirts without collars. He has big veins all over his neck. 'Can we play with the puppy?' 'Ask my wife. She's frightened you will spoil him rotten and he'll never make a watchdog.' Wailing. 'Ask my wife.' We find her under a pear tree. The pears are small and dark green. Her clothes don't move. The awful noise is where she is. She is pinching and kicking and hitting the little pup we wanted to play with. 'It's your fault,' she says. 'I have to toughen him.' We back out. 'Can we play with his brother?' 'He died.' I feel cold. Tania offers me her hand. The pup yaps at us. 'He's buried in the dunny.' Tania says that I am too small to see. There is a hole in the centre of the turds and the huge flies buzz and buzz.

TWENTY NINE

I can't remember what the weather was like on the day of the first Vietnam Moratorium. Had it rained, had it been excessively hot or windy, I would have remembered; or perhaps the weather wasn't important and my attention was drawn elsewhere.

I left the shop earlier than usual. Some shopkeepers were closing their shops. There was a feeling of expectation, both negative and positive. Police were everywhere, the largest number I have seen since I had left Europe. The crowd was lining both sides of Bourke Street. There was a continuous sound of voices, feet, and a metallic vibration of shutters being pulled down. 'Bloody commos,' someone shouted. The traffic stopped and I thought how wide and empty the road looked. 'They have no right to shut the city. Who do they think they are?' The voice belonged to a well-dressed woman. She almost choked with indignation. 'You didn't have to come shopping today, did you? You have plenty of time to spend your filthy money any other day.' The voice was young, and came from somewhere above; from a lamp post, a veranda top, I wasn't sure. But then there was a commotion and a few policemen ran to the spot and commanded the people to get down.

'This very moment,' one of them said in a very polite and yet very official voice. 'General conscription is the answer, not this ballot business. We're getting too soft. The Anzac tradition's dead,' someone said, and the young man next to me snorted a few times and winked at me.

'Here they come!'

The crowd moved, swayed. At the very top, in front of the Houses of Parliament, there was a dark line. The line moved and quivered like hot air above the road.

'Don't push!'

'Where, where?'

'You up there, get down!'

'Can you see? My eyes used to be so good. I always knew what number tram was coming — not any more.'

'School kids shouldn't be here. Should be expelled, if you ask me.'

'No one asked you.'

The single voices were being drowned in a sonorous resonance. The line, still pulsating, increased in massive magnitude and formed a tight, well-bonded, complete unit, filling the entire width of the road. There were banners and flags, but above all, the human chain, streaming down in unison. Row after row. Thousands and thousands.

'The Australian flag and the Vietnamese!'

'Ho, Ho, Ho Chi Minh.'

'Bloody Commos.'

They were coming closer and closer while the elusive line at Parliament House continued to quiver. The tightly knit crowds responded to the need to express their feelings and moved with the unalterable certainty of a river. And then row after row sat down and I spotted Michael. Just then the clock struck a quarter to some hour and Michael held someone's hand and they were trying to sit down simultaneously without breaking ranks.

'My son is there,' I said aloud and the young man who had winked at me smiled.

'Good on him.'

'He is supposed to be at school.'

'Good on him!'

And there was silence. The most vocal silence I had ever listened to, more meaningful in its manifestation than all the great speeches put together.

I didn't go to Michael. Soon after, the crowd dispersed and the people were urged to make their way to the City Square, to listen to the speakers. I wanted to go home. The mood of the city had changed; there was a lot of pushing and shouting, while the police directed people in the most exemplary way. I had the feeling that if someone were to insult them, to try to provoke them, they wouldn't respond. On this day, there were no arrests. Who had instructed them, I wondered?

In the evening, we all assembled in front of the television.

'I was there', I said.

'I was there too', said Michael.

'What about school?'

'I went to school. I even asked permission to attend the Moratorium. From the headmaster, if you must know.'

'Did he give it to you?'

'You must be joking! He wears an RSL badge and dreams of another slaughter.'

'How did you manage to go, then?'

'We just went, Pete and I.'

'D'you think it was wise', asked Julian.

'I wanted to go, Dad. It's important. I'm ready to face the music.'

'Such as?'

'Not sure ... Unless ...'

'Unless what?'

'Unless you back me. You must understand how I feel ... I was thinking. If during the Second World War the people had gone to the streets ... Perhaps the war would have ended earlier. Some people would have been spared ... I don't know. I don't want Joe to go. I wouldn't like to go myself. It's not as if our freedom were at stake.'

I wanted to go to Michael and kiss his head overgrown with hair and reflections, but somehow I didn't. He suddenly seemed so grown-up. I wanted to tell him that I had also thought of the impact a protest like that might have had on the duration of another war. I wanted to say more, but I didn't trust myself.

'I will see your headmaster tomorrow,' I said.

'Thanks, Mum.'

Joe arrived home late. He said that the protest in front of the US embassy hadn't been so peaceful. I told him of Michael.

'My kid brother is growing up', he said and smiled.

The headmaster didn't share in our feeling of pride about Michael. He wasn't amused, either. He was full of past glory, discipline and 'my country for better or worse'. He was polite enough, though I left with the impression that he was blaming our methods of upbringing for Michael's disobedience. Nevertheless, he was ready to take our European experience into consideration and allow Michael to come to school without even suspending him, which he certainly deserved. For which I thanked the headmaster from the bottom of my heart.

During the Warsaw Ghetto Uprising in 1943, there had been one protest made. A Jewish member of the

Polish government in London had gone to the British Foreign Office and commited suicide. This act had made as much impact on the fate of the Jewish people as the man's endless reports on the German atrocities which he had dispatched again and again to the heads of the Allied States.

The Vietnam war went on and on and seemed as though it would never end, despite all the protests in the world. We stopped talking in terms of 'the war will be over by the time Joe finishes his studies'. He was just completing his last year and was summoned for the medical. 'I'd rather go to prison than Vietnam,' he declared. He had fallen in love, deeply, seriously and joyfully. 'As soon as I start earning money, we'll get married.' Anita was beautiful, we all fell in love with her. There was a special serenity about her, and she didn't consider Joe's rugged beard his main distinction.

Joe was exempted from the Army on medical grounds: his early lung infection, my nightmare during his early childhood, in some ironic way had proved to be a blessing. We commented how idiotic it was that only the totally healthy and fit were drafted, in order to be exposed to injuries, disabilities and death.

As someone observed, that was 'military intelligence'.

How different the Australian practices were from the European ones. Julian had been called to the army twice. First before the war, by the Polish authorities; he had been deferred indefinitely for a curious, Polish reason. According to the law, every matriculant had been eligible for officer's training, but Polish authorities had not been too keen to produce officers of Jewish descent. So while there had been plenty of Jewish conscripts in the Polish army, there had been no Polish Monashes. Thus the deferment for Julian.

The second time had been during the war, when Julian had lived in the Russian-occupied zone and had volunteered for service when hostilities had broken out between Russia and Germany. Julian had been summoned to appear at the military centre for the medical. He had been asked to strip naked and when he had done so, his clothes had been put away, except for one single item belonging to him, his passport. He had been ushered into a long hall and joined a queue almost as long. All the men had held a passport in one hand and had hardly known what to do with the other. Recorded music had blasted from the P.A. system and Julian had been grateful for the harmonic beauty still miraculously preserved in Russian army songs. From time to time, the music had been interrupted by a pep talk, or an announcement. 'Conscripts! Before you leave the centre, you'll be able to purchase certain items which have been especially flown in from Moscow, like underpants — long and short — all offered at minimal prices, in a variety of colours, from practical khaki to daring purple. Toothpaste, soap. A limit of two cakes per person. Safety pins, the recruit's best friend!'

Every now and then, a group of ten nudists would be called out and disappear behind a tall door, to be replaced immediately by a new contingent.

The next room wasn't an examination room. There were ten chairs and ten zealous barbers. The floor was cushioned with a thick layer of hair. The men sat down, and the barbers threw once-white sheets over them.

'What are you trying to protect, my suit?'

'Don't be funny with me. It's a regulation.'

They all got a real crew cut and had felt even more naked than before. One even covered his head with his passport.

The next room had been set up as a surgery. Six

doctors, uniformed officials, six desks and six chairs for the conscripts. All were examined very thoroughly: eyes, ears, lungs, heart, liver, tongue, penis, blood pressure, teeth, bum, feet. All were proclaimed fit for service, though one kept complaining that he couldn't see, and another had shamelessly declared he was suffering from syphilis.

'For Christ's sake, are you blind?'

'Yes, Sir! Ready for active service!'

Julian's passport had been examined with even greater care. Name, address, occupation, education.

'Are you a permanent resident of our territories, or a refugee?' The officer who had asked the question had had a sharp face and a voice to match.

'I'm a refugee, I suppose. I ran away from the Germans.'

'Where d'you live?'

'With my sister and her family, at Stryjska 17.'

'Are your parents alive?'

'I hope so. The last time I heard, they were. It was before the German invasion.'

'So your parents are not with you?'

'Unfortunately not.'

'Unfortunately or fortunately. Keep your answers brief and to the point... Where are they?'

'In the Lodz Ghetto.'

'Where is that?'

'In the part of Poland annexed to Germany.'

The officer got up and left the room with Julian's passport. He was absent for a short while, and when he returned, he had written something on the documents and had said that Julian was free to go home.

'When should I report for service?' Julian had asked.

'Never. There's a clause which doesn't allow anyone whose immediate family lives in German territory to be drafted.'

'My parents ... my parents are not Germans; they're on the priority list for destruction by our mutual enemy. Yours, mine, theirs. They are one of the reasons I volunteered.'

'Sorry, my friend.' The officer's face had dropped its mask and lost its harshness. 'Regulations are regulations! Next please!'

'There is a human intelligence, an animal intelligence and a military intelligence': I wish I could remember who said that.

THIRTY

After twenty-six years, we decided to visit our family in Europe. Our sons were grown-up, Joe married and a father.

'You'd better go before it is too late,' Joe urged us.

'What d'you mean, "too late"?'

'No one's getting any younger.'

Joe and Anita had spent a year in Europe and had visited our remaining family. 'Vitek's very old,' they said. It was hard to imagine Vitek as old. Not Vitek; he had had so much energy, his mind had always been so full of provocative thoughts, ideas. No, not Vitek. Inka and Vitek had retired to Paris, to be close to their son and the grandchildren. All was well with them, except it was hard for Vitek to lead an idle life, to learn a new language. And both of them missed Poland very much. But apart from that, all was truly well. And my mother? When I'd left Poland, she had been forty-eight, three years younger than I was when we decided to visit them all. When I would see her, she would be almost seventy-six. For the twenty-six years, we had kept on writing how well we all were and there was nothing new to report. Everything was always the same, we suffered no hardship, no illness. One year, and another, and another, five, ten, fifteen, sixteen and twenty. My loved cousin Marek had married and now had three children. His wife was French and everything was always well with them. Simon and Genevieve, they must be in their sixties! Simon over sixty? Marek had become bald like his father. Tania's boys were both just about finishing their studies.

'I'm going to see my nephews for the first time in my life. Perhaps they'll even call me 'aunt'. D'you think they might?'

I knew nothing of them, except that they were *all well*.

They knew nothing of us. Oh, yes, I had told them about the lump in my breast, but only after the operation, and only when we had confirmation that it had been a harmless cyst. The initial shock, the regrets, the panic, the anger had first of all been mine, and then they had been shared with Julian. I had written how good Joe and Michael had been while I had been in hospital, and later when I had come home and had still been ordered to do nothing . . .

'It amazes me,' wrote my mother. 'Your boys can cook and wash and clean! It certainly shows the great change from one generation to another.'

Anita promised to look after Michael, who didn't really need any looking after. There was a girl on the horizon. Of course, Michael was terribly young, only twenty . . .

'When you left Poland, you were twenty-three. And a migrant with a two-year-old child,' Julian reminded me.

'True.' How had my mother felt then?

We were informed that the weather in Europe was dismal, six degrees. We wouldn't be able to see the Alps. We were advised, once more, to keep our safety belts on. We were to arrive in Paris at 6 a.m. Poor

Marek, I wished he wouldn't come to meet us and then I wished he would. What would I say to his wife, to his children? *Bonjour*, that was good. *Bonjour Lise, bonjour Francoise, Sylvie, Jean-Michel*. It had always seemed funny to me how the French called their little children Victor-Robert, or Marie-Antoinette, and now my cousin's children were the proud bearers of the French tradition ... All right, *bon jour*. What then? *Ca va? Ca va bien?* That was ridiculous. Some conversation. I needed a topic of conversation. SOS. I wanted to tell them something, like what? We live in Australia. They knew all that. I have two grown-up sons! They knew of that too. They had even met Joe and Anita and had been impressed ... *J'aime les livres*. And who didn't love books?

I must have slept again and then I couldn't think of a single French word, and then some French songs came to my mind. Great, I thought. Just great, as soon as I see Marek's wife and children, I will burst into song. *Frère Jacques, frère Jacques. Au clair de la lune*. And perhaps even *Au près de ma blonde, il fait beau, fait beau, fait beau,* and I couldn't even remember the rest. I was thinking that singing was the best method of teaching. I started to think of what I had learned at school and came to the conclusion that I knew the songs best, better than history, better than mathematics. And then my ears were giving me hell, so Julian gave me another lolly. My tongue felt like a grater.

The customs officers didn't even look at our baggage, thanks to the miracle called an Australian passport. They saluted and let us go. We were put on a conveyor platform which went up and down, and twisted, till we noticed Simon and Marek and the three children next to them, waiting for us. I forgot all my French, English, Polish, Russian and Latin. I ran to them and hugged them.

Paris was veiled. *Les Temps Tristes*, but beautiful. It was somewhere outside the window and our main reason for coming had been to spend as much time with our family as possible. We didn't want the Louvre, we didn't care if the lights of Paris were the most splendid in the whole world, and the Christmas decorations stunning. We wanted a few quiet moments with Simon and Genevieve, Inka and Vitek. Vitek had aged and even his voice had lost its familiar melody. His hands would shake and then he would try to steady them...

My French and Julian's was improving from day to day. I devised a new technique. Whenever I wasn't sure of a verb, I would add an 'er' ending to the English word. Sometimes it worked. We even discussed politics.

I spent a week with my mother, sitting next to her bed. Her legs were all swollen and the snowflakes whirled behind the window with the same crazy confusion as the thoughts in my head.

'I'm having a little rest. When I stay in bed, my legs get better,' she said.

Her hands were still beautiful, not like mine, 'What have you done with your hands?' She wondered. 'I bet you didn't use glycerine and lemon.' A whole life gone. Hers was coming to an end while her daughter, her son-in-law, her grandsons, were building a new, brighter life, somewhere beyond the seas, beyond her reach.

'I had a happy life,' she said.

Had I met her in the street, I wouldn't have known her. She dozed off and on and in between smiled at me. 'Tell me about the children, your children ... My little daughter a grandmother!'

So many missing pieces.

Tania told me that when Mother had felt better, she used to go to the coffee house, order a cup of coffee and then look at the photos sent from Australia. 'She would spread them all over the table and sit there smiling at them. She was well known there and the staff was aware of your existence, as were the permanent patrons.'

A mother carrying her family in a handbag for a quarter of a century.

'Tania promised not to send me to an old people's home. She is good to me. I take up a lot of space.'

There were three rooms in Tania's flat. My mother had given her room to her grandchildren. 'The boys must have privacy.' Tania's and Jan's bedroom was next to the living room where my mother's bed stood. Because there was no space in the kitchen, they all ate, watched TV in that room.

'It's good like this; they always keep me company.' Mother dozed off.

Tania wasn't the best organised person in the world. The place was untidy. I wanted to have a word with her, to advise her how to run the house, how to look after my mother better, but then I had lost the right when I left them. It was Tania who was looking after my mother, not I. It was Tania who shopped and queued, and washed, and ironed, and listened, and fought for every miserable day in her life.

'We are grateful to you and to Julek for all the help. Twenty-six years is a long time.'

Money versus grey days and my sister's courage.

I went to the mental hospital to visit a school friend of mine. One had to ring at the entrance and the patients, dressed in dressing-gowns, ran to the door to see whether someone had come to visit them. I couldn't even say whether my friend knew me. She was sitting on her bed, other inmates formed a circle around us. 'You came from Australia, really!' an old woman asked, and then she sat and kept on repeating 'Australia, Australia', And then she sang:

> *In our garden,*
> *In our garden,*
> *There're red roses,*
> *And the blue bluebottles.*
>
> *There 're a hundred petals in a rose*
> *And only five in a bluebottle*
> *I'll make a spray*
> *And give it to my beloved.*

A male nurse arrived and took the old woman away. This was my first meeting with my friend since the war. She thanked me for coming and for a scarf, though Tania felt it would be better to take it home, because 'good things are known to disappear'.

I hardly slept during my stay in Poland — it was a small price to pay for the naked truth.

'I prayed to God to let me see you. My wish has been granted.' My mother, she hadn't really changed. Perhaps she had lost her active involvement with people and issues, but she still trusted and believed in God. I didn't argue with her that it wasn't God, but rather an opportune moment when we felt we could spend money. It was I who had changed. I promised mother that I would come again.

'I know God will see to it that you do.'

Back to Paris, to a more normal situation with Marek's children. A new life was being built for another of our fragmented family.

We promised to come again. 'Make it soon,' said Vitek, and his voice trembled.

We spent two weeks in Israel. We toured the country for a week and spent the rest of the time seeing friends. It was just after the Yom Kippur war. Had we settled in Israel, which had been a strong possibility, both Joe and Michael would have been in the army, fighting. When I mentioned the war, a friend asked

263

'Which one?' and then I realised that there had been more than one in the lives of the Israelis.

The ancient sites impressed me, the kibbutzim, but above all the people and their determination to live a normal life in a most difficult situation.

'Any regrets that you settled here?' I asked my friend. He lived with his wife in a small flat and his son, Joe's age, was somewhere on the Suez line. Though he wasn't sure. Every hour, on the hour, my friend would turn on the radio. 'Excuse me,' he would say, 'it's news.' News time, the sacred Israeli hour. All was quiet on the Northern and Eastern and Southern fronts.

'You asked me whether I'm happy. No one calls me a dirty Jew. My son has no apparent problems. Of course, he would like to finish his studies without another interruption — that is, another war ... Life is hard. Galloping inflation, constant threats. This is the second war for our boy ... We mourn every young life lost, but at least it's not a ghetto situation. Perhaps one day our neighbours will recognise our right to exist.'

We were very excited on the way home. We were loaded with emotions, overpowering impressions and optimistic anticipations. When the plane started its descent over Melbourne, I felt we were close to home. 'It's good to be home,' I said to the customs officer.

'Welcome back,' he said.

Our little grand daughter gave me a bunch of flowers.

'Nana, Nana,' she said.

Joe and Anita, Michael and Karin, the faces of my children, a bit further back, and later, the face of Melbourne. Speeding cars and the changing sky-line of my children's and my grandchild's home town. The crowded city, the easy run through graceful St Kilda Road, down the Nepean Highway, car yard after car yard, and then the ridiculous shape of Moorabbin Town Hall. Home!

I was thinking constantly of our trip and for a while our letter writing improved. We were more direct and honest in sharing our thoughts, but after a while the letters became less frequent again and reverted to the old pattern.

And then a letter arrived from Poland. It hadn't been written by Tania. It had been written by my mother's friend. *It is my painful duty to inform you that your mother is dead.* When, how, I thought. The words were jumping in front of me and it was difficult to read. I hadn't thought much about my mother in the last few weeks. Anita had given birth to another daughter and we were all happy and busy within our Australian orbit. Joe was to be posted to England as soon as Natalie was allowed to travel. My mother would never know of Natalie, she wouldn't add her photos to the family in the handbag collection. I had written to her only a week ago. Too late for her to know.

I sat at the table and wanted to cry aloud and painfully, but my throat was tight and no sound broke through. *Tania isn't ready to write as yet. She is quite well, but you must understand how difficult it is for her to send the news.*

Tania. It was I who was considered as being a good daughter, well organised, the one who knew where to go, how to plan. Tania was the one who never managed well. A dreamer ... And it was Tania who had had to face my mother's old age, who now had to face my mother's death.

Your mother felt better after you left. Seeing you must have given her a new lease of life. She was going out a lot, visiting her old café. She was telling everybody that next year you would certainly come to visit her again, and this time, she wouldn't be in bed, but would show you around instead. She was hoping you would come in the spring and that the opera and the theatre season would be interesting. I'm writing all this so that you will understand and realise that she was well and full of happy thoughts. She died suddenly. She was visiting me and towards the evening she asked me to take her home. 'I feel tired,' she said. When we arrived at Tania's place, your mother looked up to the window and said that Tania must be washing the dishes because there was a light in the kitchen. And then she quietly slipped down and died. One couldn't wish for a better death.

What had I been doing when my mother died? It had been evening in Poland, it must have been three or four o'clock in the morning. Asleep, dreaming. Three weeks ago. It must have been one of those beautiful autumn mornings, crisp, slightly foggy with the promise of a quiet, sunny day. I didn't know, I cried. I didn't know. Had I been planning my day, to visit children, thinking what seedlings to plant before the cold weather set in, hoping that Julian wouldn't be late from work so we could go to see our friends? Had I thought how cosy our house was and that I would rather have a house with a bathroom and a toilet than to live surrounded by the relics from the past and do without, as so many Europeans did? Perhaps I hadn't thought at all. I didn't know. And meanwhile Tania. Tania must have rushed down and dragged my mother upstairs. A doctor, an ambulance? Dead, they had pronounced. And Tania? Had Jan been with her? pronounced. And Tania? Had Jan been with her? What about her sons? Had they been with her, or had there been only herself and my dead mother?

My mother's friend wrote what a wonderful person my mother had been. Had been, I thought.

There was quite a large funeral, some people I didn't even know. There were plenty of flowers, being spring, you know.

'Quite a large funeral', without the daughter, that good one, who had settled in a faraway place, and who hadn't even known, hadn't even felt.

What should I do? Ring Julian, ask him to come to me? It had happened three weeks ago! Let him be. My mother hadn't been a young woman, she had died a natural death. She had survived the war, had protected us all. We had been saying during the war that if someone died of natural causes, one shouldn't make any fuss about it. Or was it Victor who had planted this thought in me? I wasn't sure.

If my mother had been happy that I had come to visit her, I was glad I had gone.

Autumn that year was even more splendid than usual. It hurt me.

One Sunday, we drove to see the autumn colours in the Dandenongs. We left the car and went for a walk. The red and the gold, the yellow and the orange drew my attention but couldn't dim and distract my thoughts. I cried and cried because I knew my mother would never see the autumn colours again. The days when she had introduced me to nature were gone.

'What's got into you now?' asked Julian.

'Nothing,' I sobbed. 'Everything is well and lovely.'

'I will never understand you as long as I live.'

'Just keep on living, keep on living . . . Whether you understand or not.' I wept.

Another letter arrived, this time from Israel. The handwriting was unknown to me and struck me as being raw. I turned to the last page; it was signed Mila. Mila, Victor, little Margarette, what were they doing in Israel? I lit a cigarette, though I had promised myself to stop smoking. I was too excited.

Dear Irena,

I hope this letter will find you all in good health, which, thank God, we are.

I have wanted to write to you for a long time, but Victor didn't remember your address, and then he met someone who told him that you had moved away from the old place, so it didn't really matter that he lost the address because you wouldn't have received my letter anyway, even if I had written to you.

You must have noticed I am writing from Israel where we have lived for the last fifteen years. Victor was restless in Australia, as you may remember. And then someone asked him why he is working on the night shift? 'It's not a Jewish thing to do. All Jews love money, they all have a lot.' It happened at work. So Victor returned home in a real state. He told me he was leaving for Israel as soon as possible. He told me to take Margarette and get lost. I remembered what you told me, that one day he would understand how much we need him, so I said to him that wherever he would go, we'd follow him, so we'd better go together. He looked at me with such disgust that for a moment I thought he would hit me, or something, but he didn't. He said: 'What shall I do with you?' And then he left the house in a great hurry. I thought he must have gone to you, though it was perhaps ten at night, so it was pretty late, and I didn't think he would, knowing that Julian would be at home. Victor stayed away the whole night. It was raining too and when he arrived in the morning, he was wet and worn out, so I knew that he must have walked the whole night through, but I didn't ask him where he had been. I only said: 'Did you have a good time?', and he said 'I certainly did'. His hair was wet right through and so were his shoes and his clothes. 'You better put on something dry,' I told him, 'before you catch pneumonia.' 'I'm not cold,' he said, 'mind your own business.' He looked so much like he had looked in that forest. So then I didn't say anything because I knew it was better that way. He went to sleep, Margarette was still asleep, I would have been asleep too if I hadn't been worrying. It was a long, hard life together that we had. Everyone had told me that I should have left him straight after the war. I couldn't. I don't know why I stayed. Victor never showed me he cared. He told me things which really hurt, though I am not a softy. Maybe I will write to you another time to tell you everything. It's easier to write these things than to speak about them. Though he always told me he didn't want me, and to disappear from his life, I never believed him. I knew him better than he knew himself. He must have loved me, though it was hard to know.

I was sorry to leave Australia. Not as sorry as I was when we left Poland, but I was sorry nevertheless. Margarette was born there. There was plenty to eat and I was thinking that one day perhaps we might even get a house. Being born on the farm, I love gardening and I was thinking of growing vegetables. I didn't look after the flat properly. When I tried to keep it nice, Victor wouldn't even notice, so what was the point? Later I did it for Margarette because I wanted her to have a decent home, but you didn't see it then, did you?

I was frightened of Israel. I was thinking that once Victor would settle down among his own people, he would find a woman more to his liking and then I would be living in a strange land alone.

You wouldn't believe it, Irena, but we are still together. We had another child, another girl, called Ruth. Victor is good to me. He loves his children, too. Margarette is a big girl. She took part in the last war, but, thank God, nothing happened to her.

I know how to speak Hebrew, not very well though. Margarette and Ruth understand Polish very well and can say a few things if they try. Margarette is a nurse, Ruth is still at school. She has a lot of friends and I think she should marry, the sooner, the better. She has my blood in her veins.

Victor works on the kibbutz, so both of us do various jobs, as any other kibbutznik. Victor went back to his piano playing, not much, but sometimes he accompanies the children. We are happy here. We have a small place among gum trees. Good trees, and they remind me of Australia, though my memories from there are not the happiest... There is a big assembly hall where we eat, hold meetings and talk, sing, play games. I made paper cuttings which were put on the wall. They look nice. When I look at them I always think how funny it is that I am living in Israel. My own mother wouldn't have believed it, had she known. My Polish cuttings making the Jewish hall look nicer.

Now it's all right, but it was pretty bad in the beginning. The language is hard and the people in a special centre for newcomers were not very nice to me. It must have had something to do with what they went through. There was another problem: no one recognised our marriage. See, we had a civil wedding, but there are no civil weddings in Israel, so unless I convert, we are legally unmarried. Victor said I shouldn't. He was really mad at Israel. It doesn't worry me. I've lived in sin for so long it doesn't matter. It might matter to our girls. They are bastards, you know. We will see.

When did Victor change? I don't really know. It wasn't that he was bad one day, and became good the next. It was off and on for a long time. In Tel Aviv, it was bad. We lived with another family in a rented room. It was hot, even the nights were hot. The hot wind is worse here than the north wind in Australia. And then Victor met a few people he knew back in Poland and I thought it would be the end of me. They were not bad and one and then another told me how much they admired me for all I had done for Victor. And to be patient. And I thought, my good God, Victor must have told them ... Not all of them were nice. Some didn't even speak to me. Just hello and goodbye, seldom a thank-you for a cup of tea. People are people, the same the world over. Some good, some bad, some indifferent.

I have had my share of my bad days in Israel. Victor met and then invited a cousin of his first wife. It hurt me so much that I was ready to pick up Margarette and run away, but there was nowhere to go.

There was a wet mark on that spot, and I thought that most probably Mila had cried when she had written those lines. Even when her life became normal, her memories were still too vivid to be handled without emotion.

So while Victor and the woman recalled all that had been good in Victor's first wife, Mila had wished the earth would open up and bury them all. The cousin had cried while Victor talked. What had hurt Mila most was the fact that they hadn't seemed to notice her. They had carried on the conversation as if she hadn't been present, as if only the dead mattered.

And then Mila had remembered one of Victor's friends, Aaron, and he had told her that whenever she felt like seeing him, she would be welcome. So she had said to Victor: 'I'm going out'. He hadn't said a word, nor had his cousin. Mila had taken Margarette and gone out. *It's the land of the Bible, where so many miracles have happened. Jesus lived and walked here. He touched a blind man and the man regained his sight; he touched a leper and the sores disappeared. One more miracle, please God, one more,* prayed Mila. *Make my husband see, cure him of his terrible pain.*

Aaron had listened to Mila, played with Margarette. 'Only time, only time might help,' he had said. And then he had taken Mila home and on the way back Mila had asked whether Victor would change if she was dead. 'I thought you had more sense and courage,' Aaron had said.

And then the miracle had started to happen. Gradually, slowly, a good word here, a kind look, a smile, amidst silence and angry outbursts.

It's the longest letter I have ever written. I thought you would like to hear Victor is happy. I'm not even sure I will ever write another letter, not one like this, anyway. You needn't reply. The past is better left buried. I might write to you from time to time, though I can't promise. If you come to Israel, visit us, won't you?

Keep well and God bless you all.

I lived on Mila-Antosia's letter for weeks. There was so much to learn from that woman. What a pity I hadn't known Victor had settled in Israel when we had visited the land of miracles.

THIRTY ONE

Natalie was almost six weeks old. Joe and Anita were ready to go to work in London for a year. 'But who knows,' Joe said, 'if we like it there, we might even consider settling down in England.' My heart sank. No, not again. My mother had left Moscow after she'd married my father and had never seen her family again, then it had been Julian and I ... England was different, and the world had become smaller in the era of jets. It wouldn't be as if my children were driven away from their country because of the revolution, or as the result of a war. It would be a normal transition, a voluntary one, and if they didn't like it, they always had the right to return.

The days before we left Poland had been cold, the Polish December of 1947. Everything had been a problem. My mother had kept on repeating 'will I ever see you again?' and it had been difficult to obtain passports. Joe was two and trouble. It had been the time of mass migration. Such Jews as were left had wanted to leave. Except for those who had trusted the new order, believed in the brotherhood of men under the Communist regime and disregarded the outburst of new pogroms, for which they had blamed the extreme Right. 'Give us time; you can't obliterate long-lasting anti-Semitism in a matter of months. We know there is a problem, a deeply rooted one, which will be eradicated in the near future.' History had taught them nothing.

Apart from everyday difficulties, like the never-ending queues for daily necessities, there had been additional ones, like having to travel to Warsaw to submit our papers at the Ministry, a day lost. More documents had been demanded; another day in Warsaw, another loss of wages. We'd been told of people whose applications had been rejected. The severe winter weather had suited our mood. Another trip to Warsaw, and another request. We were supposed to present a full list of the books we intended to take with us: author, title, year of publication, publisher. And if we were to take any pictures, wall hangings, crystal, ceramics, anything of importance and value, they would all be photographed and presented to the appropriate authorities in triplicate, before a passport would be issued. 'Too many national treasures have been smuggled out of the country already. We can't allow this kind of practice to continue. The Polish heritage belongs to the Polish nation.'

We prepared the list of books.

We had no pictures, only a wall hanging, a kilim, my parents had bought many years before the war, which my mother insisted we take with us, as a memento from home. During the war we had been tempted many times to pull it to pieces and put the wool to a better use, like making jumpers, but in the end, we never did it and the rug survived.

I had my mother's carved wooden box, six wine glasses, a cutlery set, and a small crystal vase, that had belonged to a friend who dug it out from under the ruins of her house and gave it to us when Joe was born. She'd filled it with sweets. 'It's symbolic', she'd

274

said, 'a cradle and something sweet in it.'

Julian took photo after photo of things. 'We must have a photograph of the camera. How can I do that?' He took a photo of his camera in a mirror. The prints cost us a small fortune.

I went to the customs office. The queue was long and the official slow. I waited for a long time. I presented the list and the photographs. 'How long will it take?' I asked.

The clerk gave me a hard look. 'It depends on you, lady. It could take a month, two months, a year. You can have it within a few days ... or never. It all depends on you.'

What was he driving at, I wondered. Surely not a bribe; he wouldn't be so blunt. It must be a trap, I concluded. 'Sorry,' I said, 'I have forgotten some more photos at home. And another list of books. We've bought some more books, you know. I'll come later.'

The clerk seemed amused. 'Suit yourself, lady. Remember, it depends on you.' His voice was loud, and the message clear.

Snow was falling down and the mist was growing thicker. The street seemed all hushed, till a paperboy with a huge scarf and a red nose yelled out 'Berlin in crisis'. I shivered. It was my twenty-third Polish winter. I was used to it; surely it couldn't be because of the weather.

No one was impressed with me when I arrived home.

'Were you born yesterday?' my mother asked. 'When a man asks for a bribe, he expects one. If you don't bribe him, you'll never get your passport. Not that I care. It frightens me when I think of you going away. I know what migration means, though my experience was a picnic in comparison with what is in store for you. Your father and I were welcomed by his parents ... Unless you grow up, you're heading for disaster.'

It was all I needed to build up my quicksand morale.

Julian, though not as critical as my mother, wasn't amused either. 'It will mean another loss in wages. Can't you do anything properly? What difference will it make whether I offer a bribe, or you?'

'I can't,' I said. 'I can't do it.'

'Somehow you managed to give a pair of stockings to a delicatessen girl, which solved the problem of cheese and butter.'

'It's not the same,' I protested, though I knew that it was, and remembered when Vitek had feared that once the war would be over, people would continue to cheat, because they had become used to living in a corrupt system for so long. It had been a sharp, prophetic observation.

In the end, Julian obtained the needed documents. We received one-way exit visas and left Poland.

We took Joe and Anita, Michelle and Natalie to Tullamarine airport.

'We'll send you tapes with the children's voices.'
There had been no tape recorders when we'd left Poland.

'We'll phone from time to time.'
I had never rung my family, there still was a long waiting list for telephone connections, and Tania was still without one.

'It's a great opportunity for me, professionally I mean, and a tremendous experience for all of us. We'll be able to go to Paris over weekends and get to know the family better. They will be able to visit us in London to brush up their English.'

'I know ...' and Julian added, 'I'm really excited

for you, it's not as though we'll never see you again.'

Slurp, slurp: Michelle was finishing her airport milk shake.

'I wish you wouldn't do that,' said Anita.

'Sorry, Mummy.'

'What's the time?' asked Joe, though he was facing the clock. The announcement: 'Flight OF 1 to London, via Rome.'

'We'd better go,' said Joe. He got up, picked up a bag.

'Stay close to me, Michelle,' he said.

Anita carried Natalie.

'Let me carry her,' I asked. 'Send us a cable when you arrive.'

'Don't worry, we will.'

We kissed each other and then the doors closed behind them.

I remembered how my mother had asked me, when we were leaving Poland, whether it would be all right if she would take us to the station, and I had replied, from the pedestal of my twenty-three-year-old maturity and wisdom, that she could, on one condition: that she wouldn't cry. She had taken us to the station and she hadn't cried.

I had never thought of that till the day Joe and his family vanished down the passage way. Only then did I realise how my mother must have felt. And there was no way of telling her that I knew.

The letters from London were good. The children had taken to their new surroundings without any difficulty and Anita and Joe were thriving on what London had to offer. Joe's work was interesting and challenging and the European spring was so much more dramatic than the Australian one. 'Now I know what you mean . . .' In Australia, there is no need to protect fruit trees from the winter frost, gums stay green throughout the year and the rhododendrons, azaleas and camellias are in full bloom in July. In Europe, one is much more aware of winter. All would be dormant, the trees dark and bare. And then a bud, and in the following days the whole tree would be covered with them. The birds would become noisy and busy and then a day when the air was saturated with warmth. The buds would burst open and spring flowers appear throughout the land, adorning the fields and the parks with their freshness and vivid colours. The cattle would be taken to pasture after the long winter imprisonment, eager to try fresh food once again.

The winter has gone, to be replaced by the buzzing of insects, mooing and bleating, quacking, crowing, barking and cooing. Lilac and jasmine fill the air with an invigorating aroma. The peasants work in the fields and the city dwellers all have spring fever; they throw their windows open, air their bedding and carry flowers in their hands.

It's the time when the sun warms the earth and its creatures, and when the wind spreads the warmth around.

Dramatic European spring of 1938 and dramatic European history. Mr Ribbentrop, Mr Goering, both invited for a hunt in the Polish virgin forest of Bialowieża. 'Rare game, the European bison.' Handshakes and flags waving. A treaty signed. Everlasting friendship. Alliances cemented over the slaughter of animals. Presidential hospitality, and the Czechoslovakian tragedy. Cameras, reporters, euphoria — while the distant, underestimated voices roared *Sieg heil!*

And later, another hunt, even more rashly organised, on humans. Another bloody chapter in the history of Europe, with scarlet autumn colours to match. 'The European bison must be preserved.'

Yesterday's allies, today's enemies. Treaties signed and broken. A discarded document, resulting in wasted lives and millions of deaths.

At the end of the war, I met a Russian officer. He had saved our lives by taking us through a minefield we had been unaware of. When in the company of his comrades, he had been full of Stalin, and communism. 'We have everything we want.' 'Freedom?' 'There's plenty of freedom in Russia.' 'Food, clothes?' 'There's plenty of everything.' But one day, he had happened to see us alone. 'This blasted war', he had said. 'I started at Stalingrad. Winters. Summers. The dead. Sufferings inflicted which shouldn't be allowed. I don't see it any more. My feelings are gone.'

'You feel now.'

'Only sometimes. I wish I didn't.'

'The war will be over soon, it's not too far from Warsaw to Berlin. You believe in what you're fighting for, don't you?'

'Sure. I've seen the lot: empty villages, deserted burnt-out cities, mass graves, people. Liberated people like you ... It's more and more difficult to stomach. One of these days, I'll blow my brains out. Frozen bodies. Decomposed bodies. Bullet-ridden bodies. Filth. Exploding bombs. And loneliness. Misery. I've lost so many friends. I'm frightened to ... to come close to anyone.'

'Cheer up. You'll see. You'll go home, marry. A dashing young officer like you, you'll have plenty of children and they'll play with your medals. You'll lead a peaceful, settled life. The war will be forgotten.'

'That's what you think?' the officer had cried. 'I was drafted when I was eighteen. Just before I was due to go home, I was made an officer. I was proud at the time, but as a result, I was obliged to serve for another two years. Just before that time was up, they gave me another pip, another two years. Before they were up, the war had started. I'm due for promotion now ... They'll never let me go. Another two years, and then two years more.'

The road to Abbot Street beach goes down the hill. It was a cold day and the wind was uncertain in which direction to blow. The sky was full of rain. The clouds were full blown and never still.

Down the path I walk, alongside the scrub and bushes, weatherbeaten, trying to survive, to hold on, stretching their crooked limbs, almost bending to the ground, as if hoping to withstand the forces of nature. That is what we do, I thought.

The sea is high and the air salty. Not a soul around, only a few seagulls. Some cruising above, others standing on one leg, blinking their eyes, all puffed up. The sea is boiling, roaring, and the waves arch up, rolling over one another, till they hit the beach in a white, fizzy fury, and then swirl back in a foaming dark confusion.

The summer crowd has gone. Gone are the topless girls, children, transistors, sandcastles, young people who have eyes only for themselves, and sailing boats. Only the rusted cans remain and the fragments of broken bottles, some already blunted by the force of the sea. Gone are the umbrellas and the resonance of the spotter plane above. Gone are the bodies of all shapes and varying tans. The sonorous, the unmatched sound of the sea is overwhelming, yet comforting.

I feel alive.

I never went to the beach before I came to Australia. All this power, this perpetual restlessness, as constant and as repetitive as the human mind.

My hair is wet and plastered down, my clothes feel

damp, but my head is clear. This is my country.

I always make sure now to draw the curtains and shut the windows once the temperature soars. Our house has been repainted many times, though it takes us longer than a few hours to complete the job. We take pride in the fact that the surface is free of blisters.

The streets of Melbourne don't frighten me any more and from time to time, I meet a familiar face. We know a lot of people, and are blessed with a few friends, both old and new.

Our children are simply Australians and I am grateful to Australia for their uncomplicated lives. It's their home, and has been ours for almost a lifetime. I am still learning how to cope with certain democratic practices which were difficult to accept, like police protection offered to extreme political organisations, like the right to criticise, to state openly and loudly whatever one wants.

We have royal commissions and though they take a long time, they exist, and not even a member of parliament, not even a member of the police force, can abuse the system without it being noticed.

We have settled in a country where more money is spent on sport and gambling in a week than on all the arts put together throughout the year. We are living in a country where the fire brigade is willing to rescue a cat from a tree, or a dog from a drain. The money we spend on food for our pets in a week would support a family in less fortunate countries for months. We Walk for Want. We are progressively more conscious of the wider issues.

We do think about the future and the bomb, even though not as often as we do about our own comfort, and often without fully realising the close connection between the two.

The fact that I prefer rye bread to a sandwich loaf

doesn't keep me apart from my countrymen any more. I still can't understand how cricket or football can evoke passion, admiration, and draw huge crowds. On the other hand, my children and my grandchildren can't understand why I can't understand.

I still cling to my optimism, though we live in a constantly changing, more violent world. We have divided ourselves into 'Western Democracies', the 'Eastern Bloc' and the 'Third World'. Whatever the term, every nation consists of people with their hidden dreams, aspirations and plans. What constitutes armies are not only the weapons of destruction, but also sons and fathers, lovers and husbands and friends. I put my trust into the desperate hope that the same applies to politicians and the top brass.

Once the wind drops, it will start to rain.

We are concerned with the preservation of our wildlife, environment and quality of life: 'No dams', 'Don't rubbish Australia', 'Life be in it'. We verbally fight for human rights and consume enormous amounts of alcohol. We pour indiscriminate amounts of water on our lawns. We fight bush fires. We collect large sums of money for our hospitals and charitable organisations. We have parents' clubs and the Melbourne Club. The bulk of our population takes a bath or a shower every day. There are not many people in this land who go to sleep in fear of their lives, or hungry. And there is no excuse if there are *any*.

We seldom make world news, but lucky is the country that doesn't.

Long gone are the days of my pregnancy, when I longed for a Polish forest. The Australian gums and I have become good friends since and, for a change, I missed their rugged beauty while staying in Europe, away from home.

We enjoy barbecues, bush-walking — but, above all, that unique feeling of freedom one can enjoy only in a democracy.

The waves are rising, then falling. The first one hits the shore, the second soon follows. And if on the way some damage is done, that is to be expected. The next wave will wash the waste away. And yet another may bring some fragments back, though they will be already smoothed and weatherbeaten, hardly resembling the original.

Tomorrow, the sea will be calm again, clear, quiet water.

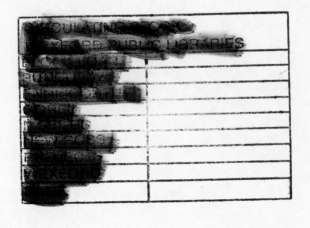